I0574548

THE
GONE
MAN

THE GONE MAN

A JACKSON GAMBLE NOVEL

GREGORY STOUT

LEVEL
BEST BOOKS

First published by Level Best Books 2022

Copyright © 2022 by Gregory Stout

All rights reserved. No part of this publication may be reproduced, stored or transmitted in any form or by any means, electronic, mechanical, photocopying, recording, scanning, or otherwise without written permission from the publisher. It is illegal to copy this book, post it to a website, or distribute it by any other means without permission.

This novel is entirely a work of fiction. The names, characters and incidents portrayed in it are the work of the author's imagination. Any resemblance to actual persons, living or dead, events or localities is entirely coincidental.

Gregory Stout asserts the moral right to be identified as the author of this work.

Author Photo Credit: Carol Stout

First edition

ISBN: 978-1-68512-230-0

Cover art by Level Best Designs

This book was professionally typeset on Reedsy.
Find out more at reedsy.com

For Carol, who has put up with all this foolishness for far too long.

Praise for the Jackson Gamble Novels

PRAISE FOR THE GONE MAN

"This is a fast-paced, exciting read. I recommend it."—Lo Monaco, author of *Lethal Relations* and *Poison Butterfly*

"In *The Gone Man*, Stout weaves an intricate whodunnit and I was guessing throughout. It ends with a shocking reveal and I found the ending to be just what I look for in a book: completely and utterly satisfying."—Wendy Sand Eckel, Author of the award-winning Rosalie Hart Mystery Series

PRAISE FOR LOST LITTLE GIRL

"When Jackson Gamble, PI and ex-cop, goes searching for the missing daughter of a strict religious couple, he assumes she's a runaway longing for a taste of freedom. But on the mean streets of Nashville, bad things can happen to a pretty teen-aged girl. Greg Stout's razor-sharp writing, complex characters, and gripping story that never lets up takes readers into the dark world of child pornography and sex trafficking. Full of twists and turns, *Little Girl Lost* will keep you guessing and turning the pages to the very end."—Skye Alexander, author of the Lizzie Crane Mystery series

"YA author Stout (Gideon's Ghost) makes his adult debut with a solid mystery, a series launch introducing Nashville PI Jackson Gamble."—*Publisher's Weekly*

"Greg Stout's writing is excellent and the story moves along quickly, taking you on an exciting ride that becomes darker as it rushes to the shocking finale."—Lo Monaco, author of *Lethal Relations*

"I am an avid suspense/thriller reader and love stumbling across a new series that looks promising. Greg Stout delivers that with his novel *Lost Little Girl*. I need a compelling story, and this novel has that. But what I look for even more are characters that I can invest in, characters I pull for as the story unfolds. Nashville P.I. Jackson Gamble is exactly that kind of character—tough, flawed but real, and at his core a decent human being you'll enjoy getting to know."—Kevin Kluesner, author of *The Killer Sermon*

"With *Lost Little Girl*, get ready to meet your newest favorite detective, Jackson Gamble...Greg Stout makes Gamble's Nashville, Tennessee as gritty and vivid—a character in its own right—as Lew Archer's Los Angeles. Can't wait for the sequel!"—Mark Levenson, author of *The Hidden Saint*

"Stout creates a realistic mix of fundamentalist religion, organized crime, profound family problems, and a surprisingly sudden love, to carry the reader through a well-paced plot that reflects some of the worst of our society and some of the best of human behavior."—Libi Siporin, author of *Bitter Maremma*

"*Lost Little Girl* is a riveting suspense story, filled with unforgettable characters and a tightly plotted narrative arc. Although the book pays homage to classic detective stories, it reaches beyond that genre with its sympathetic, if flawed hero, PI Jackson Gamble. Issues of class and privilege are threaded throughout, which adds yet another layer of complexity to this immensely satisfying read."—Lori Robbins, author of *Murder in Third Position*

Chapter One

Kady Standley had everything to live for. She died because I didn't do my job.

Kady was an up-and-coming singer who rocketed out of Altus, Oklahoma, to stand the Nashville country music establishment on its collective, conservative ear. With a voice that combined the raw power of Janis Joplin with the sweetness of Patsy Cline, her first album went gold in a little over six weeks. Albums two and three went platinum and reached the Billboard Top 10 on both the C&W and pop charts. By the age of twenty-four, she was a genuine superstar who could write a check for a million dollars and never give a thought to whether it would clear.

My first and only encounter with Kady began on an unseasonably cool Monday afternoon in late May. I'd been retained by Bob Rubin, the A&R manager at Red Dot Records, to keep Kady on a short leash while she was in town to record some overdubs for her newest release. Any time I'm asked, I jump at the chance to take on bodyguard jobs for celebrities. They're a 24-7 gig, so they pay exceptionally well, and unless the assignment includes an event that's open to the public, I don't have to do much more than stand around soaking up Diet Cokes and *hors d'oeuvres* from the studio buffet table while the client sings the song, records the track, or shoots the scene.

When he called, Rubin sounded desperate, so I made noises about how I was busy and wasn't sure I had time to take on the assignment. In fact, my bank balance was bumping along on the bottom, and I took a chance that if I played hard to get for a bit, he'd sweeten the deal. It worked, and when he finally threw me an over-the-top number, I said I'd do it. Besides, the way he described it, the job didn't sound too tough. No late-night parties, no meet-and-greets, no autograph sessions. Just keep Kady away from groupies, all-nighters, dope of all descriptions, and an occasional boyfriend and drug connection named R. J. McGraw.

Turned out, it was a more difficult job than either of us could have imagined.

I met Kady at the airport, where she arrived, unescorted, on an American Airlines flight from Tulsa. To make sure I wouldn't miss her coming off the plane, Red Dot had sent me several publicity photos, plus complimentary copies of all three of her CDs, never mind that I didn't own a CD player.

"So, you're Gamble," she said, by way of greeting. "You really a private detective?"

"Just until I finish medical school," I told her. "Then I'm starting over as a brain surgeon."

She grinned at that. "Well, least you've got a sense of humor. You're going to need it."

On the way to baggage claim to collect her luggage, I took the opportunity to look her over. She was a tiny woman, no more than five feet tall, in high-heeled suede boots. Except for her blood-red lipstick and fingernail polish, she was dressed entirely in black, including oversized Ray-Ban sunglasses and a floppy, wide-brimmed leather hat. She had a drop-dead figure, shoulder-length chestnut hair with a fire-engine red accent streak, and an I-don't-give-a-shit-what-you-think attitude that made you want to give her a high-five and a split lip all in the same motion.

She watched with barely disguised amusement as I struggled to shoehorn her three oversized suitcases and a guitar case into my geriatric Thunderbird.

"Jesus Christ," I said, slamming the trunk lid shut at last. "How long are you going to be here?"

"Couple days. Three at the most. I got a return flight on Thursday.

"And you need all this luggage?"

"A girl has to be prepared. You never know what might come up."

I didn't, but I was about to find out.

After we got on the expressway headed for downtown, she said, "How much are the assholes at Red Dot paying you to babysit me?"

"Fifteen hundred a day plus expenses, four days guaranteed," I told her.

"You work cheap," she said. "They tell you about McGraw?"

"The name came up, yeah." I was checking the rearview mirror frequently to make sure we hadn't picked up a carload of *paparazzi* leaving the airport.

"I'll bet. Did they tell you about the rest? That I was a doper and a nympho?"

"I don't recall those were the exact words, but yeah, that was pretty much the nut of it."

"Well, I guess they'd know. Every one of them silk-suited bastards has tried to stick his you-know-what into my mouth at least a half dozen times. If I let even half of 'em have their way, I'd be too worn out to hold a high note." She scrunched around in her seat and gave me a wicked grin. "McGraw's gonna find me, you know. It makes no difference where you try to hide me out. If McGraw comes looking, and I guarantee he will, he'll find me. He always does."

"Then let's hope he brings a date for me, because if he turns up, I'll be all over both of you like a fat man at a Sunday brunch."

Her grin got even wider. "No need for extra talent. There's plenty of me to go around."

I had no doubt about that. After a quick stop at the Red Dot business office to go over the next day's schedule, we drove downtown and checked into adjoining, top-floor suites at the ultra-deluxe downtown Hermitage Hotel. While I kept her company, Kady spent the rest of the afternoon fiddling around with her phone, texting, Tweeting, checking out Tik Tok and YouTube videos, and shopping for clothes at several fast-fashion websites. The country music business may be steeped in history and tradition, but Kady seemed perfectly at ease in the one-click economy.

That night, room service delivered up a dinner order that included barbecued rib tips, shrimp cocktails, crab legs, lobster claws, pink champagne, dark chocolate Dove Bars, mixed nuts, a bottle of Wild Turkey, six bottles of Stella, and a bucket of ice. When that was finished, we sat on the floor and smoked half an ounce of hash in a bong Kady said she had bought at an antique store in San Francisco. Afterward, with both of us stoned out

3

of our minds, Kady strummed her guitar and sang me a string of her hits until we both fell asleep on the sofa. Wednesday afternoon, she finished her tracks, and Bob Rubin took Kady and me out for dinner and drinks at the most expensive restaurant in the city. Back at the hotel later that night, we started smoking the rest of her hash, and when I excused myself to go to the restroom, she added a pinch of heroin to the bowl and left me conked out colder than a frozen catfish on the floor of her thousand-dollar a night hotel suite. That was the last time I saw her alive.

Friday morning, a couple of Second District Metro cops responding to an anonymous call found Kady and her guitar in a fifty-dollar tourist cabin out on Route 31. She had died from an overdose of fentanyl laced with heroin. At the inquest, the coroner ruled her death as accidental. But there was a complication. A note written in Kady's loopy hand said something idiotic about her and McGraw wanting to set their spirits free so they could be "joined together for all eternity." I found out later it was the last lyric on the last cut of her final album. All very romantic, except that McGraw didn't stick around long enough to hold up his end of the deal, and neither he nor his eternal spirit were anywhere to be found.

I never did hear the final cut of that song, or any other song on her last album, but it wasn't important. What was important was that I had let her down, and in the worst possible way. My job was to keep her safe and alive during the time she was in my care, and I had failed utterly. I made up my mind there and then that I would make it up to her in the only way I could. No matter how long it took, I would find R. J. McGraw and make sure he kept his promise to join his spirit with Kady's for all eternity.

That had been three weeks ago. I hadn't found McGraw, and I hadn't turned a lick of work since. I was beginning to think it wasn't a coincidence.

I sighed and propped my feet up on top of my desk. For the thousandth time since Kady had died, I mentally kicked myself around the office, and not just because I was convinced it was costing me work. In the short time I had known Kady, I'd gotten to like her, never mind the dope, which I was not proud of, and which I did not mention to my lady friend, Maggie. Kady was a rebel who'd made her way to the absolute pinnacle in a competitive business not known for giving many breaks, and she had accomplished it on her own terms. If I'd done my job as well as she did hers, I could have put her on the plane back to Tulsa, where at least she might have died in her own bed.

The strange thing was, nobody at Red Dot seemed particularly upset over what had happened. The vice president I spoke with, who handed me my check as well as a fat bonus, told me Kady was a disaster waiting to happen. The company considered itself ahead of the game because I had kept her alive long enough to finish her album. Good thing, too, because as it turned out, it went straight to the top of the charts the first day it hit the stores.

Chapter Two

I was staring out my office window, watching the afternoon traffic on Church Street beginning to stack up, when the telephone rang. I nearly turned over backward in my chair reaching for it. I prayed it wouldn't be somebody selling something. I didn't need a new Internet service or a walk-in bathtub. I needed a case.

"May I speak to Mr. Jackson Gamble, please?" The female voice at the other end of the line was a pleasant one, freighted with the honeyed intonations of the Old South.

"Speaking."

"Thank you very much, Mr. Gamble. Please hold for Mr. Darrow." There was a soft click, and the connection went slack.

After an interval sufficient to impress upon me that Mr. Darrow was somebody who counted his time more valuable than mine, the line returned to life with a new voice.

"Gamble, my name is Clarence Darrow. I'm an attorney."

"Right," I said, "and you have a client named Scopes, and his wife thinks he's sleeping with a monkey."

"Jesus, only in the fucking south." Darrow sighed heavily into the mouthpiece at his end, making a noise like a small windstorm in my ear. "You want to crack wise about William Jennings Bryan while you're at it, or can we get down to business here?"

"Sorry," I said, realizing that the joke was one he'd probably heard every day since law school.

"Actually, Clarence was my grandfather's name," he continued in a less

6

peevish tone of voice. "We're not related to the real Darrow, of course. Just the same, though, I feel like the guy in that Johnny Cash song about the boy named Sue."

"Maybe, but if you were a house painter, nobody'd pay any attention at all. What's on your mind, Mr. Darrow?"

"Well, as I said, I'm an attorney. I represent Mr. Richard Eberle of Springdale, Tennessee. Maybe you've heard of him?"

"Nope, sorry. Should I have?"

"It was just a thought. Anyway, Mr. Eberle has asked me to find out whether you would be available to call at his residence between seven-thirty and eight o'clock this evening. He said to apologize for giving such short notice, but to emphasize that the matter he wishes to discuss with you is of the utmost importance."

There was a pause. "In case you're wondering, those are his words, not mine."

I glanced at the clock. Quarter to five. Even if I stopped by the house to change into a clean shirt, I could still get to Springdale easily by seven forty-five.

I said, "I don't know if I can make it. Did Mr. Eberle give you any idea of the nature of his business? I'm kind of busy to be dropping everything and running out to Springdale without knowing any more about it than that."

Darrow made a noise that could have been a laugh. "I think he'd prefer to discuss that with you personally. But since your calendar is so crowded, Mr. Eberle did authorize me to tell you that he's prepared to compensate you for your time, regardless of the outcome of your meeting."

He waited, and when I didn't say anything, went on. "That means you get paid for driving out there. Is that what you were fishing for, or do I need to send a limo?"

"I can drive myself," I said, annoyed at how easily he'd cut through my hard-to-get act. "But you might ask Mr. Eberle to be patient if I'm a few minutes late. Springdale is a little off my regular patch."

"That's the first thing you've said that I can believe," he told me. "Also, Mr. Eberle is hosting a small social gathering this evening. Wear something

7

appropriate, so you don't look out of place."

"So, should I rent a tux?"

"Country club casual should do it. You'll fit right in." Then he gave me the address and hung up.

It took me a while, longer than it should have, really, to fit the Eberle name into the correct frame of reference. But a few phone calls to the right places did the trick, and by the time I finished with the last one, I had a pretty good idea what it was Richard Eberle wanted to see me about.

Chapter Three

If Nashville is the home of country music, then Springdale might as easily be regarded as The-Home-of People-Who-Have-A-Pot-Full-Of-Money. This tiny, exclusive community lies hidden in the hills just off Interstate 24, about twenty-five minutes southeast of the city. People passing by on their way from St. Louis or Atlanta rarely stop there. There is only one exit in each direction off the Interstate, and except for a single Amoco filling station, little of interest for the average tourist. People who live in Springdale prefer it that way. Visitors, unless expressly invited, are generally not enthusiastically embraced.

Something else you will not see in the Chamber of Commerce storefront window, but that is also very real, is that Springdale was once a sundown town, and, as far as anyone can remember, it had been since shortly after the end of Reconstruction. Nobody has been lynched or tarred and feathered in Springdale since FDR's second term, but even in the present day, the only faces you are likely to see around town that aren't lily-white will be found operating a lawn mower, driving a delivery truck, or busing tables in a local restaurant. For the handful of people of color whose driver's licenses show a Springdale address, they are all almost certainly live-in domestic help.

Richard Eberle's house was on Briar Hill Pike, in a part of town populated mostly by old-line Rutherford County families. Newcomers, northerners, foreigners, and *nouveau riche* country and western singers occasionally purchase homes in Springdale, but that is generally more by accident than design. And like their carpet-bagging cousins of a century and a half ago, once they arrive, they are quickly shown their place. Rarely do outsiders end up buying houses on streets like Briar Hill Pike. Quietly, subtly, efficiently, the real estate agents steer them toward one of the several newer subdivisions outside the city limits, where there are high six-figure McMansions on two-acre lots available to anyone who can qualify for a jumbo mortgage. In cities on the make, like Nashville and Atlanta, money talks. In places like Springdale, it's still the intangibles that count the most.

Before heading off for my appointment, I stopped by the house for a change of clothes. Since I wasn't altogether sure what "country club casual" was supposed to look like, I settled on a light blue button-down dress shirt, gray slacks, and a navy-blue blazer that Maggie had bought for me the previous Christmas. I debated whether to wear a tie and then decided "casual" meant just that and left the one I still owned hanging in the closet, along with my weapon. I wasn't completely sure, but I figured that, for tonight at least, a Colt .380 autoloader was probably not the right way to accessorize my rig.

Three-quarters of an hour later, I pulled past a pair of weathered limestone gateposts into the Eberle's driveway. As I drew closer to the house, I could see there were already about a dozen expensive-looking cars and SUVs, mostly European: Mercedes-Benzes, Audis, a Bentley Continental GT, and an honest-to-God Ferrari 812, parked around the front circle. A red-jacketed valet greeted me with a practiced smile and asked me to pull up to the end of the front walk. There, a second valet opened my door, took my keys, and promised to bring my car back around when I was ready to leave. So far, so good.

The Eberle home was a red brick, plantation-style two-story that stood grandly, and perhaps a bit pretentiously, like Scarlett O'Hara's Tara at the end of a quarter-mile-long driveway. It was fronted by gaily colored flower beds on either side of the flagstone walk leading to the front porch and surrounded by a clutch of old-growth oak "Witness Trees" that might have been acorns around the time of the War of Northern Aggression, as some in this part of the country still refer to it. From what I could see, the Eberle property occupied about five acres, give or take. That isn't necessarily a lot of land in this part of the country, but it's a lot of lawn anywhere outside of a golf course or a city park. If whoever had built the house had done so with the intent of making an impression, he had succeeded. I was impressed.

As the valet drove off with my car, I paused for a moment to take a look around the grounds. The muggy evening air was rich with the fragrance of mimosa and honeysuckle and the whirr of nocturnal insects singing sweet nothings to one another in the trees. In the gathering twilight, the Eberle estate seemed to take on a magical, almost storybook quality, as if time itself had been left waiting at the gate, like some Yankee snake-oil salesman. I thought that if I squinted hard enough, I might be able to spot Joel Chandler Harris out on the lawn, telling his Uncle Remus stories to a rapt group of small children. Then an automatic lawn sprinkler sputtered noisily to life from behind a hedge, and the spell was broken.

I mounted three wide steps to the front door and pressed the bell. After a moment, the door was opened by a small Black man of indeterminate age, but whom I guessed to be somewhere on the downhill side of seventy-five. He wore traditional houseman's attire, including dark pants, shoes, and bow tie, and a white shirt and jacket. His iron-gray hair was close-cropped and covered his head completely, except for a small ebony patch at the crown.

"Good evening, sir." He gave me a look of polite inquiry.

"Good evening." I handed him my card and stated my business. The Black man scrutinized the card before nodding his head.

"You can just come right in, Mr. Gamble. Mr. Eberle is expecting you."

I stepped into a parqueted foyer large enough to hold a Daughters of the Confederacy dinner dance. He closed the door softly behind me.

"Mr. Eberle is occupied just now. He asked if you'd mind waiting out on the patio with the rest of his guests. He promised he'd be just a minute."

Without waiting for an answer, the houseman turned and led me down a short hallway to a set of arched double doors at the end. The doors opened onto a wide, covered patio where fifty or so people were clustered in small groups around tall pedestal tables, conversing, sipping cocktails, and sampling finger food. Someone had figured out how to get a baby grand onto the patio, where a tuxedoed pianist was softly playing tunes from movie soundtracks. At the moment, it was "Send in the Clowns." A cut-glass martini pitcher had been placed atop the piano. It was stuffed with cash.

The guy was taking requests. Very classy.

At the end of the patio nearest the house was a bar staffed by two bartenders. There was also a buffet table with a variety of up-market appetizers, including a carving station, where a tall man wearing a white chef's apron and a revival-style *toque blanche* was slicing rare roast beef with a knife the size of a Filipino *bolo*. Richard Eberle, it seemed, knew how to throw a party.

While I was taking it all in, a medium-height, sixtyish man wearing polished loafers, no socks, canary yellow slacks, and a lime-green sport jacket over a pink polo shirt separated himself from the group he was talking with and approached me with his hand extended. I noticed his grayish hair was gathered into a small ponytail in the back, and he had a pair of Panama Jack sunglasses propped up on the top of his head. Country-club casual. I understood now.

"Welcome to our gathering," he said. "So glad you could join us."

"Thanks." I shook his hand.

"I'm Don Wetterlund," he told me. "I'm heading up the campaign. I wonder, have you had a chance to say hello to the candidate yet?"

"The candidate?"

"Why, yes. Senator Rebecca Karlson. She's right over there." He pointed to a tall, striking woman standing about ten feet away with a glass in her hand, white wine or maybe champagne. She wore a sleeveless, peach-colored dress with a cloisonné American flag pin above her heart. She was chatting animatedly with a couple of older men who seemed to be hanging on every word she said.

"Would you like to meet her? I'm sure she'd be pleased to make your acquaintance."

I started to say something, but before I could, I felt a light touch at my elbow. It was the houseman I had met earlier, come to fetch me. He said, "Mr. Eberle is ready for you now, Mr. Gamble, if you'll just come with me."

"Mister Gamble," said the man named Wetterlund, as if my name meant something to him. "Oh, of course. I understand completely. You'd prefer to make your contribution privately. A lot of our significant donors feel that way."

"Yeah," I said. "It's better that way. Then there's not so many other people snuffling around later on, looking for a handout."

As I turned to follow the houseman into the house, I heard Wetterlund say to no one in particular, "Smart fella, that Gamble. We need to stay in touch."

I followed my escort back down the same hallway through which I came in, but before we got as far as the front entrance, we turned down another hallway leading to a door at the end. The man knocked twice, then opened the door and stood to one side.

"Here we are, sir. Just go ahead on in."

The room I entered was one I would have called a den, but that in a house like this would have more properly been called a study. The furniture was tasteful, expensive, and unquestionably masculine. The lighting was subdued. The air was cool and smelled of oiled wood, cigar smoke, and expensive bourbon. At the end of the room, closest to the doors, stood a massive billiard table. It had hand-carved legs as thick as cypress trunks and looked as if it must have weighed a ton. Against the wall facing the pool table was a cue rack a plush sofa, and matching armchairs, all upholstered in leather the color of new money.

The far end of the room held a built-in wall unit with glass doors. Its shelves were crowded with leather-bound books and brass and pewter knickknacks. In front of that was an antique oak desk topped by a green blotter pad and a gold pen and pencil set in an onyx base. Behind the desk sat a seventy-something man. He had an egg-shaped head with a fringe of white hair circling the sides. He wore a dark suit jacket, a wine-colored silk tie, and a crisp white shirt with gold cufflinks and a gold collar pin. Three-quarters of an inch of monogrammed hanky poked correctly out of his breast pocket. At that, though, he did not appear well. His skin was pale and dry-looking, like someone who had lately died and was awaiting the embalmer to restore the illusion of life. His cheeks were hollow, and there were dark circles under his eyes. It made me think that whatever it was he wanted me to do, I should probably ask for my fee in advance.

With obvious effort, the old man half rose out of his seat and extended his hand. "I'm Dick Eberle. I expect you must be Jackson Gamble." He gave my hand a cool, dry squeeze and sank back into his chair. "You're right on time. I like to see that."

He made a motion for me to sit in one of the two high-backed armchairs that faced his desk. As I turned, I saw that there was another person in the room, sitting quietly in the other chair. He was an enormous man with a bull neck and hands that could have grasped a bowling ball as if it were a cantaloupe. His hair was black-going-to-gray. His skin was tanned to the point of turning leathery, giving him the look of someone who spent a great deal of his time on a golf course, or maybe the fighting chair of a Bertram fishing yacht. He had a full, fleshy face dominated by a nose that had been broken more than once. He wore navy blue slacks, a pale blue golf shirt, and a white pullover sweater that couldn't quite hide the beginnings of a paunch.

He also had a pretty good snootful of whatever was in the glass on the desk in front of him. Eberle nodded in the direction of the big man.

"Mr. Gamble, I'd be pleased to have you meet Walter Murdock. Walter is married to my daughter, and is also a partner in one or two of my business ventures."

I mouthed a greeting and offered my hand. Murdock blinked once or twice and glared blearily in my general direction. "Keep sticking that in my face, and I'll rip it off for you."

Eberle threw him a murderous look. "You'll have to excuse Walter's manners, Mr. Gamble. As you can no doubt tell, he is not in the best of humor this evening."

I raised my eyebrows, said nothing.

"I expect before we get down to business, you're probably wondering what that is that's going on out back of the house. I'm hosting a fundraiser for State Senator Rebecca Karlson. She's up for re-election in the fall, and she's facing a tough campaign. She and her husband—her late husband, I should say—have been close friends of mine for a number of years. I'm just helping her out a little. I like to do that when I can."

When I didn't say anything to that, he frowned a little. "Do I take it you don't agree with her politics?"

"I don't know much about her politics, Mr. Eberle. I don't live in this district."

"Well, that's all right, I suppose. We'll slip her a little something on your behalf just the same. You can't have too many friends in positions of influence, you know."

"Not necessary on my account, but I'm sure she'll appreciate it." When I got no response, I said, "Excuse me for being blunt, Mr. Eberle, but I have to ask. Is there something else you wanted to talk to me about, or did you just need somebody to help launder a campaign contribution?"

"No, nothing like that. But as it so happens, your question is right on the money. Walter and I were just discussing my decision to retain you to help us with a problem we've been dealing with when you arrived just now. Walter, I'm sorry to say, is not in complete agreement with me on that point."

"Excuse me." A light went on in my head. "Mr. Murdock, I'm sorry I didn't recognize your name at first. Are you the Walt Murdock who played defensive back for Alabama back a few years ago?"

"'S'me," he said, showing the smallest flicker of pleasure at the recollection.

"And then you got drafted by the Falcons, right? You had a great career, and then, what? I forget what happened."

"Was a knee," he said, patting himself on the right leg. "Got torn up against the Vikings in a preseason game. It's been about fifteen years ago, now."

"That's right, I remember now," I said. "Tough break."

"Yeah." Murdock made a rumbling noise deep in his throat. With a shaky hand he picked up his glass and threw back half the contents in a single gulp. "Look, Gambit..."

"Gamble," I corrected him.

"Gamble, then," he growled irritably. "No offense, okay? And I appreciate you remembering that I played. Hardly anybody does anymore. But I don't see where we need any help from you. What we have here is a family problem, and it oughta stay inside the family." He paused to take another swallow of his drink. "So again, no offense, but why don't you just go on back outside and enjoy the party? Have a few drinks, shake a few hands, and send us a bill for your time. I'll be happy to pay it myself if Richard doesn't want to,

Hell," he said, turning in his chair to reach for his wallet, "I probably got the cash right here."

"We've been all over this, Walter, and we're not getting anywhere," Eberle sighed wearily. "We're also wasting Mr. Gamble's time, and he has a lot of work ahead of him. So, if you're about finished?"

Murdock rapped his glass down on Eberle's desk, splashing the contents on the polished wood surface.

"Matter of fact, I'm not. I got plenty more to say." Murdock was firing on all cylinders now, and no longer addressing anybody in particular. I understood then that whatever had started the alcohol talking, there was a lot more to it than this particular disagreement.

"Maybe we should do this another time," I offered.

Eberle ignored me. "No, Walter, you got nothin' more to say. "See, what you're talking about here is family, and you're right, this here is family business. Now I don't like to get into this in front of folks we only just met, but we've been over this once or twice before, and the fact is, you ain't family. You're just some dumbass football player who sweet talked my daughter into marryin' you. That makes you not much more than hired help, about like that old colored fella fetched you in here a minute ago.."

Eberle turned to me. "See, Mr. Gamble, right there, that's the trouble with letting hired help marry into the family. First thing you know, they get to thinking they're just the same as family. Always seem to have to keep reminding 'em, they're still just another hired hand."

Somewhere in all that was the magic word. Murdock roared like a lion at feeding time and started out of his chair. I had no way of knowing how far he'd go, but I was afraid he might just be mad enough or drunk enough to try going across the old man's desk. Even in the condition he was in, it would have been impossible to keep him from doing Eberle some serious damage once he got his hands on him.

While Murdock was still getting his feet untangled from underneath him, I stuck my foot between his two and sent him sprawling, head first onto the carpet. On his way down, he banged his forehead on the edge of the desk, raising a nasty lump that began to ooze a little blood. Murdock struggled groggily to his feet and flopped back into his chair, his hands covering the wound on his head. I was hoping his playing days were far enough behind him that the combination of alcohol and pain would be sufficient to take the fight out of him. If not, I figured to be about two seconds away from needing medical attention myself.

Before anybody could do anything else stupid, I said, "Okay, gentlemen, fun's over. I drove out here tonight because I was told there was something one of you wanted to talk to me about. So far, all I've heard is two grown men squabbling like kids on a playground. Now, if somebody wants to do business, let's get to it. Otherwise, I'll just say thanks for a lovely evening and be on my way."

It wasn't the Gettysburg Address, but it got things settled down some. Eberle cowered behind his desk in open-mouthed astonishment. Murdock, still stunned into momentary docility, wiped gingerly at his forehead with the sleeve of his sweater. The bleeding had pretty much stopped, but a goose-egg sized contusion was beginning to form above his right eye.

"You'll be okay, Walter," I consoled him with a pat on the arm. "Go out in the kitchen and put some ice on it."

He pulled away and looked at me with hate-filled eyes. "You fuck," he said softly. "I could take you with one hand tied behind my back." Then he lifted himself out of his chair, did a wobbly about-face, and shuffled out of the room, dragging his tattered dignity behind him.

Chapter Four

"I apologize for that little set-to," Eberle smiled indulgently after Murdock was gone. "You need to understand about Walter. He's a pretty good fella, really, but sometimes he has trouble handling his liquor. Which reminds me," he added, "may I offer you some refreshment?"

"No, thank you. Maybe you could give me some idea what you wanted to see me about. I seem to recall your Mr. Darrow saying it was important."

The old man eyed me speculatively, like a big fish trying to decide whether to swallow a smaller one in one big bite or two little ones.

"First, tell me, Mr. Gamble. How much do you know about me?"

"Some. I didn't have a lot of time. I know you made your money in insurance and in the real estate business and that you own—or you control—a sizeable percentage of the land in this county. Word is you're a smart operator who's managed to make big money even during the last recession."

"Go on."

"Also, I have a pretty good idea of how much you're worth, although I could be off on that."

He seemed to be enjoying himself now. "What do you figure?"

"I'd say somewhere between a hundred and a hundred and ten million."

"That's pretty close. You got anything else?"

"Like I said, I didn't have much time."

"Well, I must say, you did better than I expected. Clarence Darrow was right to speak highly of you."

"Nice of him, considering we've never met."

"Not nice," he corrected, "just looking after his own skin. I paid him to find me somebody I could rely on. He did a little poking around. He tells me you're pretty good."

"I have my days, same as anybody else."

"Uh-huh, well, I expect you weren't having one the day you let that little chippy you were supposed to be bird-dogging give you the slip. You remember, don't you, that singer who turned up dead a few weeks back?"

My mouth must have dropped a little. My name never appeared in any of the police reports.

"If you'd dug a little deeper, you might have discovered I own a sizeable stake in Red Dot Records. Not that I hold what happened against you. That young woman came with her own trouble, what with liquor, and drugs, and no-account men who lived off the talent the Good Lord gave her. If she hadn't come to the end of the road here, she surely would have done it someplace else."

I said, "My understanding is that she didn't exactly end her own life. Somebody helped her with that."

"At this point, does it matter?" He made a dismissive movement with his hands. "Myself, I never cared much for her, personally or professionally. Besides, as it is, Kady Standley is worth more to Red Dot dead than alive. We held a substantial life insurance policy on her. Not only that, but her being dead and all gives her album a certain collector's value. For the last month, we've been selling CDs and downloads faster than we can count the money."

He leaned back heavily in his chair, causing the springs to creak in protest. "I'm told it might even win a Grammy. What do you think about that?"

"It's hard to know what to say," I said, honestly.

"See, Mr. Gamble, I learned a long time ago to invest cautiously and cut my losses quickly. That's how I make my money, and that's how I spend it. So, before we go any farther here, why don't you just take a minute and tell me all about yourself? It's a mite old-fashioned, I know, but I like to get to know a man some before I do business with him."

"I thought your man Darrow checked me out."

"Oh, he did, make no mistake. But I'd still like to hear it from you."

I shrugged. "There's not a whole lot to tell. I'm forty-four, and reasonably honest. I've been a private investigator for eleven years. Before that, I was with the Metro police, assigned to the district attorney's office."

"How come you left the police force?"

"I quit."

"That's not the way I heard it."

"Then you heard wrong." I took a deep breath before going on. "When I was with the D.A., I spent a year working on an unauthorized influence-peddling investigation that led to a judge who was making a little money on the side handing down some questionable rulings. Civil cases, mostly. It was an election year. My boss was an appointee himself, and didn't want the case dragged into the open. He ordered me to sit on my hands. I didn't think that was a very good use of the taxpayers' money, so I leaked part of the story to a guy I knew who worked at the morning paper. Not the whole thing, and no names. Just enough to get him started digging on his own.

"It took a few months, but eventually, the whole story came out. Some people who were counting on getting re-elected didn't, the D.A.'s office caught a lot of heat, and because I pissed off some of the wrong people, I got ticketed for a reduction in grade back to a uniform. I decided it was time to move on. The department didn't disagree."

"I expect they didn't," he said, showing me a smile that didn't quite reach his eyes. "I also understand you're a tad particular about the kind of work you do. How particular would you be, Mr. Gamble?"

"How particular can you be in this business? I don't do divorce work, I don't do strong-arm stuff, or repossessions. I also don't do murder for hire, although I've been asked more often than you might think. Other than that, if it's legal and we can agree on a price, I'll probably do it."

"Can you make any money like that?"

"Some. I get by."

"I'll bet you do. How would you feel about a missing person investigation? That is, if that kind of work doesn't run contrary to your code of ethics."

"It depends," I said. "Who's missing?"

By way of a reply, he opened his top desk drawer and took out an eight-by-ten color photograph. The picture was a portrait of a man and a woman, both in their mid-twenties. The man had a pleasant face, but a slightly vacant expression that made him look as though he had never had his picture taken before and didn't exactly know what he was supposed to do. He had fine, sandy-colored hair that touched the tops of his ears and hung across his forehead, nearly reaching his eyebrows. His eyes were blue, and his complexion was fair. A small moustache was struggling to grow beneath a nose that was neither long nor short. His lips were compressed into an awkward smile. His chin was pointed and dimpled.

The woman was another story altogether, contrasting so sharply with the man that the photo looked almost like somebody had deliberately tried to pose opposites. She had long, dark hair that cascaded in thick waves down to her shoulders. Her eyes were brown, and her skin was olive. She had a wide, professional-looking smile that showed strong, straight teeth. Looking at the two of them together gave me the impression that the picture, whatever its reason for being taken, was his idea. In the flesh, she would be a real head-turner. He would be somebody you'd walk right past and never give a second glance.

"Who am I looking at?"

"My son, Simon. That's who I want you to find."

"Who's the woman?"

He said, just a little too quickly, "Nobody special. Just somebody Simon used to be friends with. But I don't think she'd be of any help to you. Simon hasn't seen her for months."

"And does she have a name?"

"Jorie something-or-other, I think. Jorie Flowers. But I've already told you, she won't be able to help."

"Right, I remember," I said, making a mental note to check up on her first chance I got. "How long has Simon been missing?"

"Since two nights ago. That would be Saturday night. He left here right after supper, and we haven't heard from him since."

An uneasy rumble in my stomach was telling me more than just that it

21

was past my regular dinner hour. I shifted uncomfortably in my chair.

"I assume he has a phone. Have you tried calling him?"

He gave me a look like a teacher might give to a slow student struggling to grasp a simple concept. "If it was that simple, do you think we'd be here talking right now? Either he's got it turned off, or the battery has gone dead."

Or he's gotten himself dead, I thought.

"Well, Mr. Eberle, it's your money, and I'll be happy to look for him, but to be honest, forty-eight hours doesn't seem like a very long time for someone your son's age to be off someplace on his own. I mean, isn't it possible he just connected with some friends, or maybe a girlfriend," I flicked the edge of the photo he had given me, "like this one here, and decided to make a long weekend of it without letting you know?"

"My son is not in the habit of spending the night—any night—away from home. Especially without telling someone." His face was like stone. "Believe me, Mr. Gamble, I know my son. If there were no cause for alarm, you can be sure I would not have raised one."

"Okay, Mr. Eberle," I said, getting his drift at last. "And please excuse me for asking so indelicate a question, but what's the matter with your son? Does he have some kind of a mental disorder?"

He looked up, suddenly on his guard. "What makes you think there's anything the matter with him?"

"Because if there isn't, I don't understand what I'm doing here. How old is your son, twenty-five? Twenty-six? Does he have a job? You didn't say he worked with you, so what does he do all day? Whatever his situation is, he's much too old to be living at home with his father. He's also too old to have caused this much excitement just because he's gone off for a couple of days by himself, unless he's got something wrong with him."

When I got no response, I said, "Look, I heard what Mr. Murdock said. I can appreciate this is a private matter and that you may feel uncomfortable discussing it with someone you've only just met. But the only way I can help you get your son back is for you to be completely honest with me."

Eberle didn't answer right away. He spun around in his chair and opened a door in the wall unit behind him. He took out a decanter marked BOURBON and poured himself half a glass.

"You sure I can't offer you anything?"

"I'm sure, thanks."

"All right, then, and this is not to leave this room. My son suffers from a form of depression that sometimes manifests itself in some rather unpredictable ways. That's why he lives here at home. He's not usually a problem, but it's still better if somebody can keep an eye on him."

"In other words, he's suicidal."

Eberle flushed. "I must say, you do have a way of coming straight to the point."

"It seemed like time somebody did."

"I'm not sure I care for your attitude, sir."

"Well, I'm sorry about that, but if I don't get something I can work with before long, you're going to have to find a place to put me up for the night."

"All right, then, to answer your question, my son has in the past attempted suicide, so far without doing himself any serious harm."

"How many times?"

"Twice. The thing is, most of the time, he seems like a perfectly normal individual. You would never think there was anything at all the matter with him."

"What about the rest of the time?"

He swirled his whiskey around in his glass before taking another swallow. "Well, sir, it's a peculiar thing, and nobody has been able to explain it to my satisfaction. But every now and then, he just seems to come unstrung. He won't eat, won't talk, nothing. He just sits in his room and stares at the walls. That's how it starts. Then we have to watch him very closely."

"And does that happen often?"

"Not really. Oh, don't get me wrong, he's always been given to moodiness, same as a lot of other folks, I expect. The real bad spells, the ones that cause us to worry, we might not see more than two or three times a year. We don't really know what causes it, but when it happens, we can usually see it coming."

"But this time you didn't."

"No, and that's what worries me. He seemed all right the other night, maybe even a little more cheerful than usual. If something was bothering him, it went right past me."

I thought about that. "A minute ago, you said when Simon has these episodes he generally just holes up in his room. Has he ever tried running away before?"

"I wouldn't call it running away, exactly. He disappears for a day or two, and then he comes back like nothing ever happened." He took another swallow of his drink. "Why, what are you getting at?"

"Maybe nothing. You mentioned that he's tried to harm himself in the past. I was just thinking that if a person really intended to commit suicide, there would be plenty of opportunity to do it at home. Why complicate things by running away?"

"Well, that's just it, you see. He's not always affected in the same way. Sometimes he gets belligerent, violently so. Other times he just sulks. Once he got into a scuffle at one of our local taverns. It was a damn fool thing. Something to do with a woman. I forget the details. Anyway, he ended up nearly getting killed by the woman's husband. And when it was all over, he couldn't even remember what had taken place. The next day, except for a few bumps and the bruises, it was as if it had never happened at all, at least as far as he was concerned. For my part, I had quite a time gettin' everybody quieted down and keeping the whole mess out of the newspapers."

"Well, you may have kept it from being printed in the newspapers, but you didn't keep it out of police records. That husband you mentioned nearly died himself. I didn't get all the details, but the way I heard it, your son stabbed him with a nine-inch steak knife."

"So that's how it is," he said darkly. "It appears I may have underestimated you, Mr. Gamble."

"It was a while back," I said, satisfied that I had made a point of my own. "Unless he tries to kill somebody else, it isn't going to go any further than it already has. Let's get back to the present. The other evening, before Simon left the house, did he say where he was going?"

"He did not. We talked at supper, but it was nothing very important. Just the usual subjects people discuss over a meal. You know, sports, politics, things like that. After we finished, he said he had some errands to run in town and that he might be back a little late. Then he got into his car and drove off. That's the last I've seen or heard."

I said, "Town, as in Springdale or Nashville?"

"I assumed Springdale, but I could be wrong."

"And that was Saturday night, you said?"

"That's right."

"Can I ask why you waited until now to call?"

He looked sheepish. "The fact is, I didn't notice right off he was gone. I try to get to bed early, so I wouldn't have heard him come in, especially if he was late. It wasn't until last night, a full twenty-four hours later, that we missed him, and that's only because he didn't show up for supper. This is my son's home, you see. Not his prison."

"That still leaves almost a full day between last night and this afternoon, when Darrow called me. What did you do during that time?"

"Well, naturally, we checked around a little. Springdale is a small community, and most people know all the members of the family. But nobody remembers seeing Simon the other night or yesterday, so we had to conclude that wherever he got off to, it wasn't around here. That's when I decided we needed professional help."

"Have you contacted the police?"

He brushed at a spot of lint on the sleeve of his jacket. "It was my understanding I could depend upon your discretion, if you take my meaning."

"Right. So that's a no." I thought about how to frame my next question. "Mr. Eberle, apart from his occasional emotional difficulties, has anyone ever suggested to you that Simon might have a drug problem?"

"Certainly not! Whatever would give you a notion like that?"

"I'm just trying to consider all the possibilities. From what you've told me, your son has a history of unstable behavior for which there is no obvious explanation. I'm no doctor, so I can't evaluate the situation from that perspective. But at the risk of rubbing salt into an old wound, I've had experience with similar cases, and in quite a few of them there was evidence of substance abuse. In your son's case, the fact that he only has occasional episodes of irrational behavior suggests that there may be an external cause."

"So right away, you accuse my son of being an addict?"

"No, sir. I'm not accusing anybody of anything. I'm only asking about what seems to be a possibility."

"I appreciate your concern," he said icily, "but you're barking up the wrong tree. My son is not some red-dirt rock-and-roller like Kady Standley. I'll grant you Simon has his problems, but being a coke-sniffer or a pothead is not one of them."

"All right, forget I asked."

"Look here," he went on, in a more reasonable tone of voice, "I've already explained that this is not the first time Simon has run off like this. Why read anything more into it? I think it's far more likely that, for some reason, he's had one of his episodes come on and that he's gone off to the city looking for trouble. He's done that before, and believe me, that's bad enough all by itself. That's why I asked you to come out this evening. I want you to find my son. Find him and bring him home before he gets hurt, or hurts somebody else."

He sighed, and a look of sadness crept into his eyes. "Do that for me, Mr. Gamble, and I'll pay you anything you ask."

Chapter Five

Pleasant dreams about how I might go about spending Richard Eberle's money were interrupted by the sound of the study doors opening and closing again. Without getting up, I turned in my chair to see who had come in. I was afraid it might be Walter, back for round two with the old man, or maybe with me. It wasn't Walter, though. It was someone much more interesting.

She was about forty, give or take a year. She was tall and slender, with, so help me, violet eyes and honey-colored hair that no stylist would ever be able to duplicate. She wore a cream and tan linen dress, a gold wristwatch, and a wedding ring set with a diamond the size of a hazelnut. Eberle popped out of his chair as if he'd been launched by a powerful spring. For the first time since I'd met him, his face showed genuine warmth.

"Mr. Gamble, this is my daughter, Elaine. Elaine, this is Mr. Gamble. He's the private investigator I asked our friend Clarence to contact for us."

She took a seat in the chair recently vacated by Walter, momentarily exposing an immodest expanse of thigh. She caught me looking and quickly shifted her position. "I hope I'm not interrupting anything."

"Not at all. I was just bringing Mr. Gamble into the picture on our, well, what shall we call it? Our situation here, when you came in."

She gave me a brief smile. "My husband says you'll be able to find Simon for us, Mr. Gamble. Is that right?"

I very much doubted that was what Walter had really said to her. I said, "I'm going to try my best, Mrs. Murdock. Guaranteeing results is a luxury I'm afraid I don't have."

27

"Just try?" She pressed her lips together into a small frown. "That's not the expression of confidence I was hoping to hear."

"Well, I can see where it might not be what you wanted to hear, and under the circumstances, I really can't blame you. But I'm only just now hearing about this for the first time, and until I have a little more to go on, there isn't much else I can tell you."

"Besides," I went on, "in all likelihood, Simon will turn up on his own tomorrow or the next day. That's usually what happens in cases like this."

"And if he doesn't? Then what?"

"Then I'll go and find him."

Elaine Murdock knotted her hands together in her lap. "Mr. Gamble, do you think anything serious might have happened to my brother? I mean, you read so many terrible stories these days."

Before I could answer, Eberle cut me off. "Elaine, I don't see any reason for you to upset yourself over this. Why don't you take Walter and run along home? Mister Gamble and I can finish up here just fine. The sooner he can get started, the sooner he can find Simon and fetch him on back."

She looked as if she wanted to argue, and then thought better of it. "I suppose you're right, Daddy. You always are."

She turned to me. "Mr. Gamble, my father may not have told you that Simon and I have always been very close. When he goes off on his own like this, I worry. Very likely too much, but I can't help it."

"I understand."

"You will find him, won't you?"

"I'm very good at what I do, Mrs. Murdock. I'm sorry if I disappointed you earlier."

"Well then, good night, Mr. Gamble. Please let me know if I can be of any help." She leaned across the old man's desk and gave him a daughterly peck on the cheek. "Good night, Daddy."

Eberle waited until she was out of the room. Then he was all business again. "Alright, let's get to the nut cuttin' here. What are you going to need to get started?"

"I'll need that photo for one thing."

He handed it across the desk. "What else?"

"I think you ought to notify the police. I'll do my best, but the problem is, I'm only one man, and there are only so many hours in a day. In a situation like this, we can use all the help we can get."

He did a bad job of pretending to consider the idea. "I'll keep it in mind. For the present, I'll rely on you to act in our interests. Alone."

"If that's the way you want it."

"It is. Now, what other questions do you have?"

"Well, if Simon's been missing for two days, it seems reasonable to assume he must be staying someplace. Could you give me a list of friends, acquaintances, anybody who might put him up for a night or two?"

Eberle leaned back in his chair and stared thoughtfully at the ceiling. "I'm not rightly sure who that would be. Simon has friends, of course, same as anybody else. I can't say I know who all of 'em are, but he's got a few. Problem is, I can't think of anybody that's close enough to be willing to take him in, no questions asked. Springdale is a pretty small town, and most everybody around here knows us. If Simon showed up on one of their doorsteps looking for a place to spend the night, word would be sure to get back here pretty quick."

"Is there anybody in the city he could be staying with?"

"Maybe. But if he is, your guess is as good as mine who it is. Simon generally likes to keep pretty close to home."

"What about old girlfriends? This woman here?" I picked up the photo of Simon and Jorie Flowers. "How about her?"

He shrugged. "I couldn't say. As I told you, Simon broke off with her several months ago. As far as I know, he hasn't seen her since."

"Any others? Is he seeing anybody now?"

"Not that I know of."

I sighed. "Look, Mr. Eberle, I know this is difficult for you, but I'm having a very tough time believing that anyone, your son included, could get to be twenty-odd years old without knowing a single soul he could call on in a pinch. Surely there must be somebody."

"Well, I don't know what good it will do, but I guess you could try Dave

29

Kelso."

I took out my notebook and wrote down the name. "Where do I find him?"

"You mean right now?"

"Any time of the day or night," I said with exasperation. "Midnight at Mount Olivet Cemetery would be just fine."

"I don't know for sure where Dave lives. Hendersonville sounds right for some reason, but I could be thinking about somebody else. I know he runs an auto repair place over on Melrose Avenue. I'm not sure of the name of it, though."

"I'll find it. Anybody else you can think of?"

"Not right off."

"Okay. When Simon goes out by himself, where does he go? What kinds of things does he like to do?"

"He likes to listen to music. I can tell you that. I know there are a couple of places downtown he goes sometimes. Here in Springdale, I couldn't say. We're not exactly a hotbed of nightlife, especially for a young person. Besides, we've already looked into things at this end on our own."

I didn't like the sound of that. "Looking into things how? And who's been doing the looking?"

"Aw, it's nothing to worry about. Walter, he wanted to see if he could help out a little, so he started checking around with some of our local tavern owners. He hadn't been at it more than a couple of hours when somebody from the sheriff's office called up to find out what was going on. Right about then, I figured I better whistle him off before he got a lot of folks stirred up over nothing."

"You're not treating this situation like it's nothing, Mr. Eberle."

"That's not what I'm talking about. See, Walter, he likes to feel important. Now don't take this wrong, because he's a fella that tries awfully hard to please, and he does mean well. But ever since he got hurt and had to quit playing ball, he hasn't been able to figure out quite what else to do with himself. I've tried to keep him involved in some of my business ventures, but I guess insurance and real estate just don't have the same excitement as professional football. More often than it should, it just seems like he goes to fart and ends up messin' in his pants instead."

"How about your house man, what's his name?"

"Odell."

"Is it possible Odell might have talked to Simon before he left?"

"I asked him about that. He says not."

"I'd like to ask him again, if you don't mind."

"You do whatever you think is best, Mr. Gamble. My only interest is that you find my son and bring him home before he gets into trouble."

"Well, that raises another point. I can find Simon, and I can try to convince him he should come back home. But he is an adult, and unless he's been declared legally incompetent, or there's an outstanding warrant for his arrest, I can't make him do anything he doesn't want to do."

"Your job is to find him. I'm counting on you to be resourceful enough to know what to do next."

"I appreciate your confidence," I said. "Would you mind if I took a look around his room before I leave?"

"Whatever you think will help. Will you need anything else? If not, I should go and see to my guests. I've kept them waiting too long as it is."

"Just one or two more questions. What kind of a car does Simon drive?"

"A BMW. A new one, red."

"I don't imagine that's turned up either?"

"Not hardly."

"How was he dressed when he left the house the other night?"

"About like you are now. Blue sport coat, tan slacks, white shirt."

"How much money would he have been carrying?"

"Maybe a couple hundred dollars, no more."

"Okay. You didn't ask, but my fee is three hundred a day, plus expenses. If I have to co-op anybody else, it's liable to get expensive, but I'll check with you before I do that."

He didn't say anything. He looked a little glassy-eyed, as if the Jack Black he had been sipping had suddenly hit him square on. I said, a little louder, "Is that satisfactory?"

It seemed to startle him. "You'll have to excuse me, Mr. Gamble. I'm not as young as I once was, and sometimes I get a little tired. You were talking about your fee. Of course, it's entirely satisfactory. I'll mail you a retainer in the morning."

Without getting up, he offered me his hand. His grip felt weaker than when I had come in, as if something very precious had already slipped through his fingers.

Chapter Six

U nder the watchful eye of Odell, I gave Simon Eberle's room a thorough going-over. For all that I found, I could have saved the effort. The room told me as much about Simon Eberle as the average Holiday Inn room might reveal about the man or woman who stayed there the night before. Except for an expensive audio system and an Apple computer sitting on a small desk, I could have made myself believe I had wandered into a minimalist display grouping in an IKEA store.

The bathroom proved equally uninformative. The tub sparkled, the shower doors gleamed, and there wasn't as much as a molecule of dried soap or toothpaste in the sink. There was a new bar of soap in the dish and two nearly new toothbrushes hanging in a rack. I checked the medicine cabinet. There was a tube of toothpaste, a box of band-aids, some floss, a can of aerosol deodorant, and a bottle of contact lens washing solution. In the cabinet under the sink, I found several rolls of toilet paper, a can of air freshener, several bars of Irish Spring soap still in their wrappers, and a package of disposable razors. All that made me stop and think. Unless Simon kept a travel kit packed and ready to go, there was a good chance that wherever he had gone last Saturday, he hadn't expected to stay overnight. Otherwise, he would have taken at least some of his necessities with him.

I looked in the vanity. One drawer held an electric shaver, a hairbrush and a hair dryer. The other contained a tube of Chap Stik, a can of athlete's foot powder and a brown prescription bottle with no label.

I opened the bottle and emptied the contents into my hand. Two dozen green and white gelatin capsules, about the size of a common antibiotic caplet. I put all but one of the pills back into the bottle. I dropped the old maid into my jacket pocket. Odell, who was standing in the doorway, saw me take it and clucked disapprovingly.

I held the bottle up for him to see. "Any idea what these are?"

"No, sir."

"Or where they might have come from?"

"I wouldn't know. Young Mr. Eberle gets to sneezin' with hay fever in the springtime. Guess they could be for that."

"That's probably what they are," I said, not believing it for an instant. "These rooms are very nicely kept. Who does the house cleaning, you?"

"No, sir. We have a service that comes in twice a week."

"What days?"

"Mondays and Thursdays."

"So that means they were here today?"

"This here is Monday, so yes, they were. Plus, with Mr. Eberle's get-together comin' up, they did a little extra today."

I went back into the bedroom and started pawing through the dresser. Underwear, socks, some expensive pullover sweaters, not my size. On top was a jewelry box with a few pairs of cufflinks, a gold collar pin and some foreign coins, none of them valuable. I pulled the drawers all the way out and felt underneath. Nothing was taped or pasted there except the manufacturer's label. I was wasting my time. I cursed softly. I cursed out loud.

Odell moved out of the doorway. "If you can say for sure what you're lookin' for, maybe I could help you with findin' it."

"If I knew what I was looking for, I wouldn't need any help." It was a foolish thing to say, and I regretted it instantly. I stopped what I was doing and smiled apologetically.

"Excuse me for that, Odell. I'm sorry. I'm not thinking very clearly. I'm looking for something—anything, really—that might give me an idea where Simon might have gone, or at least what makes him tick. From the look of things here, it's almost as if he didn't even exist."

"Well, he surely do exist, I can tell you that. Any rate, he did when he left

34

here on Saturday night."

"Did you talk to him before he went out?"

"No, sir."

"But you did see him?"

"I seen him walk out the door. Don't know where he went after that. He just got into his car and left."

"Did he take anything with him? A suitcase, or an overnight bag, maybe?"

"Just what he had on. I figured he had a date."

"You mean with a woman?"

"Ain't that generally how it do?"

I showed him the photo Richard Eberle had given me. "Any chance his date was with this woman here?"

"Maybe. Coulda been anybody, though, since he left here by himself."

"But you have seen her before."

"Once or twice, I expect. Been quite a while, though."

"But just to be clear, you think he had a date. Can I ask why?"

There was a note of irritation in his voice. "'Cause of how he was dressed. He had on a coat and a tie. Only time he ever does that is if he's seein' a lady."

"Well now, that's odd. Mr. Eberle led me to believe that Simon isn't dating anyone. Also, when I talked to him earlier, he didn't mention Simon wearing a tie."

"Then I expect I must've seein' things what ain't there."

"Not necessarily. It's possible, isn't it, that Simon could have a date or even a steady woman friend without his father knowing about it?"

"Lots of things are possible." He gave a small shrug. "All I know is what I seen. Far as the rest goes, I try to make it my business not to get involved in things that ain't none of my concern."

"You mean, not like some people we know?"

Another shrug. "If you don't take offense to my sayin', you don't talk like no cracker I ever heard."

"Missouri," I said, "and no offense. After I got out of school, I traveled around for a while. Nashville seemed like as good a spot as any to settle, so this is where I wound up."

He nodded. "Myself, I ain't ever been more'n a hundred miles from the place I was born, down to Tullahoma. Don't know how it is in Missouri or anyplace else, either. Round here, though, things don't change so much. Go back two hundred years. Just like now, come sundown, I'm just one more old black man, workin' for one more old white man."

"I understand," I said. "I'm sorry."

"No need. It's just the way things are." He reached through the doorway and flipped off the bathroom light. "Will you be wantin' me for anything else?"

"Not right now, thanks. You don't have to stick around here if you don't want to. I'll let myself out when I'm finished."

"Then I'll say good night. I expect by now Mr. Eberle's wondering what become of me."

After he was gone, I sat down on the bed and took another look around the room. Odell, or maybe it was Mister Odell, had a point. I didn't have the first idea what I was looking for, except that I knew I should be seeing something. Unless Simon had an entirely separate life someplace else, he should have had all kinds of personal belongings here in his bedroom. As it was, there was no address book, no letters from friends, no photo albums, no nudie magazine in the bottom drawer of the nightstand. It was almost as if he had deliberately tried to eliminate any trace of himself from his surroundings.

I thought about booting up the computer, to see if he was hooked into any Internet connections that might provide some information. Then I realized that, without a password, all I'd end up doing would be playing electronic solitaire games. I began to feel sorry for the guy. Even if he hadn't started out depressed, it wouldn't have taken him long to get that way living in a fishbowl like this.

I took one more look around, this time checking underneath the furniture, without finding a thing. I didn't bother turning off the lights on my way out. I figured Richard Eberle was a man who could afford it.

Chapter Seven

Standing on the front porch of the Eberle place waiting for the valet to return my car, I could hear that the tempo of the gathering around back had picked up considerably. The piano player, who had been playing softly when I arrived, was now noisily banging out Tammy Wynette's signature, "Stand by Your Man," accompanied by what sounded like two dozen intoxicated voices singing along at the top of their lungs. It actually sounded like fun, and I wondered if maybe I should go back and have a couple of beers.

Maybe Richard Eberle really did know how to throw a party.

When the valet brought my car back around, I saw that he had scooped up a passenger along the way, and that the passenger was sitting in the front seat smoking a cigarette. After the valet got out, he handed me my keys and gave me an exaggerated wink. I nodded as if I knew just what he meant, and after he walked away, stuck my head in the open window on the driver's side.

I said, "Good evening again, Mrs. Murdock. Did you forget where you left your car, or would you like me to give you a lift somewhere?"

She exhaled a lungful of smoke. "Neither one, Mr. Gamble. I was just waiting. I didn't think you'd mind if I waited here."

"Don't mind at all." I opened the door and slid in behind the wheel. "It's getting a little chilly out here, though. I hope you haven't been sitting too long."

"No. I enjoy the night air." She took a final drag on her cigarette and tossed it out on the lawn. It glowed for a few seconds like an oversized firefly before dying in the damp grass.

After what seemed like a suitable interval, I said, "Are you going to tell me what it is you're waiting for, or am I supposed to guess?"

She gave me a nervous laugh. "Forgive me, Mr. Gamble. I was waiting for you, of course. I wanted to apologize for the way Walter behaved tonight. You were right to deal with him the way you did."

"I didn't deal with him, Mrs. Murdock. I tripped him when he was drunk and didn't have his balance. I'm not proud of what I did. In a fair fight, your husband would send me and a half a dozen more just like me out the door in body bags. Besides, how do you know how he acted? You weren't in the room at the time, as I recall."

"I didn't have to be. He's always the same when we come to Father's. Walter and Father don't get along very well, and when the two of them get to drinking, well, sometimes they say things they don't really mean. When that happens, they're not very careful about who's in the room to hear them."

I said, "Where's your husband now?"

"Sleeping on the couch in the living room. He's had a very bad day and a lot to drink, and he just dropped off. I'll go in and wake him in a moment, but I did want you to know I'm sorry."

"Nothing to apologize for, Mrs. Murdock. In my business, I meet all kinds of people. Most of the time, they're not glad to see me."

She turned in her seat until she was facing me directly. I felt her hand crawl into my lap. "There's no need to keep up all this formality. Elaine will do just fine."

I removed her hand and placed it back in her own lap. "I think I should stick with Mrs. Murdock. That way, we'll both be able to remember it."

It stung her. She groped in the darkness for the door handle and found it. Then the anger seemed to melt out of her, and she sat back in the seat again.

"We don't seem to be getting off to a very good start, do we?"

"A good start at what? If you'll pardon my saying so, for all the apologies you and your father keep making for your husband, he's the only one of you I've met so far who's able to say what's on his mind. If there's something you want to talk about, why don't you just say what it is?"

"Are you always this rude to your clients, Mr. Gamble?"

"I try not to be. Sometimes it just slips out. And anyway, with apologies, you're not my client. Your father is, so like I said—"

"All right!" she cut me off sharply. "I've got the message, damn it. I just wanted to know—I want to know what's going on here. I want to know what happened to my brother, and what my father told you."

I shifted in my seat to face her directly. "You already know as much as I do. Simon left the house the other night without telling anyone where he was going. That was two nights ago, and apparently, no one has heard from him since. Your father is worried and wants me to find him."

"What else?"

"So far, that's pretty much everything. The rest of it, if there is a rest of it, is what I'm being paid to find out."

She was quiet for a moment, thinking. "Mr. Gamble, no doubt you noticed my father is a bit of a throwback in certain regards. He believes, for example, that women are delicate creatures who are totally incapable of dealing with even the most routine unpleasantness. Hence, his suggestion that I don't need to bother myself with any discussion of Simon's disappearance. He thinks that if it isn't talked about in my presence, I won't think about it or worry about it. I'll just put on my sun bonnet and my white gloves and trot off to the garden club, or wherever women go to occupy their time in that antebellum world he inhabits." She took a deep breath and kept right on going.

"Well, all right, maybe I'm partly responsible for that. God knows how many times I should have stood on my hind legs and demanded to be treated like an intelligent adult woman instead of a bubble-headed southern belle. I didn't, though, and I suppose that's because he's my father, and I'm his daughter, and that's the way we've been behaving toward one another for as long as I can remember.

"But that doesn't mean I have to put up with that same shit from you, excuse my language. We're talking about my brother here, not some two-timing husband you're trying to catch in a motel room with his shorts down around his ankles. And I don't imagine my father mentioned it to you, but I

39

practically raised that boy after our mother died, so I have more than just a casual interest in all this. I have a right to know, and I want to know right now. And since Father won't, I expect you to tell me."

She stopped, out of breath. I said, "Anything else?"

"No."

"All right, then, what would you like me to tell you?"

"I want to know why my brother ran away. I want to know when he left and why it was necessary to hire a private detective to find him. And I want to know why in God's name nobody told me anything about this. How long has Simon been gone, anyway?"

"Since Saturday. You already know that. When did you find out about it?"

"This afternoon. Walter and I came over as soon as we got the call. That means Simon had already been gone for a day and a half before my father decided to tell me about it. I'll bet if Simon had turned up before lunchtime today, nobody would have said anything about it at all."

"I guess that's possible."

"And you agree with that?" she challenged.

"I didn't say that. I said it was possible, and that's only because you suggested it first."

"You're infuriating. All right then, what happened to make him run off? No doubt he and my father had another of their famous rows?"

"It sounds like your father can't get along with any of the men in the family."

"So then, it was that."

"I didn't say that either. I honestly can't tell you why your brother ran off, Mrs. Murdock."

"Can't, or won't?"

"In this case, it's pretty much the same, but the simple answer is, I don't know."

She started to say something else, but I stopped her. My experience was admittedly limited, but I was beginning to get tired of the Eberle's and the Murdock's and their displays of bad temper.

I said, "Look, Mrs. Murdock, maybe I'd better explain something to you before we get into a fight neither of us is looking for. In the first place, I've

40

told you the truth. Your father didn't tell me any more than what you already know, which is that your brother left home two nights ago and hasn't been heard from since. As far as why he did it, I don't have an answer. From what I've been told, it isn't the first time he's done something like this. If he had a fight with your father, nobody said anything about it to me." She opened her mouth to argue, but I kept plowing ahead.

"I think maybe you should consider that your father doesn't really treat you any different from the way he treats anybody else, except that he's a little more courteous to you. Maybe he's just the kind of man who doesn't like anybody else knowing what he's thinking. Now, as far as I know, there isn't anything more to the story than what I told you. But even if there were, no matter what it was, I couldn't tell you."

"Because you don't think I could deal with it?"

"No, because it's my business not to. Your father is my client. He's paying for my services, and he's entitled to have me respect his confidence."

"So, it's the money," she said slowly. "I should have guessed. Well, then, how would it be if I hired you myself? Say, for double your regular fee? That would make it all right, wouldn't it?"

"Make what all right?"

"For you to keep an eye on Father for me. Keep me posted on what he tells you." She lowered her voice conspiratorially. "I think he's been working too hard. You saw yourself how worried he looks. You'd be doing this for his own good. What would you say to a check for a thousand dollars? Just as a retainer, of course, until I could get you some more."

I sighed. "Mrs. Murdock, I'm not looking for any more money. I was just trying to explain to you in a nice way that I can't tell you anything, and I wouldn't if I could. I'm sorry. I really am."

She sat quietly for a moment, looking out the window. "I must look like a damned idiot."

"Not at all. You look like somebody who wants answers and isn't getting them. You're worried about your brother and your husband and your father and probably a lot of other things we haven't even talked about. You're angry, and you're frustrated, and I can't say I blame you. But until I have a chance to dig into this, I don't know anything more about what's going on with your brother than you do. In the meantime, the best thing I can tell you is to go home and let me worry about Simon for a while. I know that's probably not much comfort, but it's all I can offer you right now. If you want to talk later on, here's my card. I can't promise I'll be able to tell you anything more, but I'll be glad to listen."

She clutched my card in her hand. "I suppose I should be grateful. Maybe I am. I don't know what else I could have expected from you. After all, you're just doing your job, aren't you?"

"Yes, I am," I said.

She sat for a moment, thinking, I supposed. Then the door opened and closed, and she was gone. The crowd in the back was singing along with "Crazy." I drove away, shaking my head.

Chapter Eight

In any missing persons investigation, there are certain steps that have to be taken as a matter of course. Ordinarily, my first move would have been to talk to the police, to see if they had anything that could help get me pointed in the right direction. But since they knew nothing of Simon's disappearance, and since I was also under strict orders not to get them involved, I had to let that slide—for the time being at least. Later on, I'd check with the county morgue, to see if there had been any new arrivals over the weekend. I'd also check with the local hospitals, to see if any unidentified white males had turned up in their emergency rooms. I frankly didn't think either of these would yield any results. Unless Simon had been the victim of an assault that left him both beaten senseless and robbed of his identification, his family, as well as the police, would have been notified immediately upon his arrival at either location.

So, with no prospect of getting any help from the cops, my first stop was a CVS pharmacy, around the corner from my office. For an exorbitant upcharge, I got them to do a rush job making two dozen eight-by-ten prints of the photo of Simon Eberle and Jorie Flowers. Then I drove out to the airport, where I distributed them to the ticket agents at Delta, American, United and Southwest Airlines.

Nobody I talked to could recall seeing either Jorie or Simon in the last several days, although I had a hard time convincing one ticket agent at the airport that the people in the picture weren't really Brad Pitt and Angelina Jolie.

"I thought they done busted up," he said.

"They did. It was very sad. They couldn't work things out," I told him. "A damn shame, too. But I think they still get together with the kids around the holidays."

"Oh, well," he said, "that's a good thing, then."

I left behind a few extra copies, along with my telephone number and the promise of a $500 reward for anybody who could produce a record locator for either of them.

After that, I made the rounds of hospital trauma centers in Nashville and in Murfreesboro. As expected, none had treated or admitted anyone named Eberle, or any John Doe who looked like Simon Eberle, in the past seventy-two hours. A woman named Flowers had showed up at the Baptist Hospital ER on Sunday night. She was promptly taken to the maternity floor, where she gave birth to a seven-pound baby girl.

The last stops were the Rutherford and Davidson County morgues. There, at least, no news was good news. No toe tags with the name Eberle or Flowers, and no John or Jane Doe matching the photo.

That took care of the basics.

The thing I had been counting on from the outset was that Simon would be like most runaways, in that what he really wanted was not to be lost, but to be found. In my experience, the majority of people who disappear do not really want to leave behind their lives and families for all time. They are simply looking for a little breathing space, whether it's marital or job troubles, or just plain emotional exhaustion. After a few days, they either come home on their own, or else leave a trail of plane tickets, credit card receipts and telephone records so obvious that only someone not looking could fail to follow. At least for the time being, however, Simon was keeping his head low. That meant either he meant to stay gone, or something a lot worse had happened.

I got back to the office about two o'clock, and found a pair of customers in the waiting room. The woman was tall, wearing an expensively-cut, maroon pantsuit, matching high-heeled shoes and an ivory blouse, with the top two buttons strategically unbuttoned. A small cloisonne American flag was pinned to her right lapel. From ten feet away she appeared to be about thirty-five, but on closer inspection she quickly aged another fifteen years. Just the same, it was a good fifteen years. Her hair was dark blond, her makeup was understated and expertly applied, and her eyes were indistinguishable behind an oversized pair of sunglasses, as if she had just come from a visit to an ophthalmologist.

Her companion was the younger of the two by half. He had a muscular build and was wearing a dark suit that was stretched tight across his shoulders and chest. He had close-cropped brown hair, ice-blue eyes and a carefully cultivated two-day stubble on his cheeks and neck. He was also strapped with a Smith & Wesson .40 caliber in a shoulder rig that hung inside his jacket on his left side. To my thinking, that made him a bodyguard. My first thought was that this was going to be trouble, and then I remembered that I had seen the woman before, as recently as the previous evening. That meant there was something else going on.

I opened the door to the inner office and motioned for them to come inside and take a seat in the visitor's chairs. Then I took out a pad of paper and a pencil.

"Okay," I said. "Ready when you are."

The woman looked at her companion. He looked back at her, and then they both looked at me, as if they weren't sure what was supposed to happen next. I said, "Senator, why don't you start?"

She removed the sunglasses, folded them, and put them into her purse. "Then you know who I am." It wasn't a question.

"Sure. You're State Senator Rebecca Karlson. I saw you at Richard Eberle's get-together last evening. You represent that district south of here where all the conservatives live. I should say, all the rich conservatives, anyway."

"Then I take it from your tone you don't agree with some of my positions."

"What I know, I don't agree with any of them, but it doesn't mean we can't do business," I said. "I don't reside in your district, and even if I did, I only vote the top of the ticket. So how about if you tell me why you're here, and then we can figure out if there's something I can do for you."

She shifted in her chair. "I was hoping you might be willing to do a favor for me. Of course, I'll pay you for your time."

"Then it isn't a favor, Senator. It's a job. Question is, why me?"

"We have a mutual friend, or since his political views are the same as mine, maybe I should say a mutual acquaintance. The job I'm asking you to do will involve the delivery of a rather large sum of money. Our friend says I can trust you."

"You can, although I think you already know I'm busy with another assignment. I don't have a lot of time to take on another case right now."

"I'm aware of that. What I need you to do will only require a couple of hours tomorrow evening. I'm sure you can manage that, and I'm willing to make it more than worth your while."

I was pretty sure the acquaintance she was talking about was Richard Eberle. And since I don't believe in coincidences, I was just as sure that at least some of the money I would be delivering was the same money she had raised the previous evening at Eberle's backyard sing-along.

I said, "How much are we talking about, Mrs. Karlson? And what are we buying back?"

"The individual we're dealing with wants one hundred thousand dollars, in cash. As to what we're getting in return—well, what difference does it make?"

"If I don't know what I'm buying, how will I know whether I got it?"

The bodyguard spoke up in a tone that I guessed was supposed to intimidate me.

"If the Senator says it doesn't make any difference, that's all the answer you're going to get." He gave me a hard stare, just in case I missed his point.

I said, "Why don't you go and wait in the other office and let your mother and me finish our conversation? I think if you look around out there, you might find a coloring book and some crayons."

He started to get out of his chair, but the senator put her hand on his shoulder. "It's all right, Scott. Maybe it would be better if Mr. Gamble and I discussed this privately."

"But," he started to say.

She shook her head. "It's okay. Go ahead, I'll explain later." We waited until he went out and closed the door behind him.

"How did you guess he was my son?"

"I didn't know until you took off your sunglasses. Then I got a look at your eyes."

"Yes," she said, with just a hint of maternal pride in her voice, "there is a similarity."

She drummed her nails on the arm of her chair. She crossed her legs, then uncrossed them, and crossed them again. I waited for her to get comfortable. It took a while. I waited. She seemed to be having trouble getting to the point. Finally, I said, "What are we talking about here, letters, photos, or videos?"

"Photographs, actually. Digital prints.

"Of you?"

"Yes. They show—well, they're very intimate."

"So," I said. "Revenge porn?"

"I don't know that I would call it that. I mean, the person who has the photos has no reason to be angry with me, and no reason to want to damage my senatorial campaign. This is not a political thing. This is a money grab, pure and simple." She paused, as if to gather her thoughts. "Do you need to know more than that?"

"No, I don't think so. But I am going to need to know who contacted you. And I need to know how you're so sure this person actually has the photos. I understand from our mutual acquaintance that your husband died some time ago, so I'm guessing this is someone else you were close with after that."

"Actually, it was before that." She paused again.. "My husband passed away about five years ago. We had been married twenty-three years at the time. I'd forgotten all about the pictures until…until I got a scan of one of them attached to an email that I received the other day."

"Did the email come through your office?"

"No. My personal account. I use that for friends and family."

"So, as far as you know, they haven't been made public."

"Not yet."

"And do you know who sent the email?"

"Yes. It came from a man I was seeing—how do I say this? There was a time a few years before my husband died—well, we hit a rough patch."

"Got it." I nodded. "You had an affair."

"More like a fling," she said. "Anyway, there was a weekend getaway. My husband was invited on a fishing trip to some lake in Minnesota, and he took Scotty along, so I was at home by myself. At that time, my husband ran an insurance agency, and I wasn't involved in politics yet. There was a man who worked in my husband's office. He was good-looking, He was attracted to me, and I thought I might be attracted to him. So, when my husband went fishing, we took a long weekend together at a resort hotel in Gatlinburg. As it turned out, we didn't really hit it off. But on that particular weekend, we did a lot of drinking, and…well, he took some pictures. Afterward, I felt ashamed, and told him I didn't think we should see each other again. I guess he got the same bad vibe I did, and he agreed we should stop. He promised he would delete the photos. I thought that was the end of it."

"And then you got one of the photos in your email. And you got scared."

"That's right. I never told anyone about what happened. For certain, Scotty doesn't know, and as far as I know, neither do any of my constituents, I'd like to keep it that way."

"Except for Richard Eberle, you mean. I suppose it would be fair to say that if word of this got out, those good Christian conservatives down your way might decide it would be time to start looking for a new state senator. Someone who might better reflect their, what shall we say, their values."

"Yes," she said. "I'm sure they would. But I've become a different person since then, Mr. Gamble. I never once cheated on my husband after that, right up until the day he died. I've prayed for forgiveness. I've accepted Jesus Christ as my savior. I've done everything I can to make amends."

I leaned forward in my chair. "I'm not your confessor, Mrs. Karlson. It doesn't make any difference to me one way or the other what you did before, or what you're doing now with your life. If it's absolution you're looking for, talk to your pastor. If it's the photos you want, I can get them back for you."

When she didn't say anything, I said, "Which is it, Mrs. Karlson?"

"I want the photos."

"Okay, then, let's get to it. This guy who has them, does he have a name?"

She nodded. "It's Willingham. Peter Willingham."

I wrote that down on my pad. "How do you want to play this?"

"I'm to meet him tomorrow night with the cash. He'll hand over the photos, I hand over the cash, and that will be that. Or at least that's what he says. If I don't, he says he'll post the photos on social media. You already know what that would mean to my reelection campaign."

"Well, it doesn't appear you need any more protection than you've already got, so what is it you want me to do?"

"I don't want to see him. I want you to go in my place. Give him the money and get the photos."

I thought about that. "If he's expecting you, what makes you think he'll be willing to deal with me? Also, how will I know who to look for?"

She took out her phone and fiddled with it for a moment before holding it up for me to see. "Here's a picture of Peter. I took this the same weekend we were together. I doubt he's changed much." The photo showed a reasonably handsome, middle-aged guy with thick brown hair, graying at the temples.

"We're to meet at the coffee shop at the bus station at eight-thirty. There are several arrivals and departures just about then, so the waiting area will be crowded. Nobody will pay any attention to either one of you. The coffee shop has three booths. He'll be in the middle one."

"So, then what? He takes the money, hops on a bus, and heads for tall timber? Do you need me to follow him, find out where he's going and try to get your money back?"

"No. He can have the money. I don't care about that. But I need you to make clear to him this is the end of it. If he tries to come back for more, there will be repercussions."

"Okay," I said. But it sounded too easy. I didn't like it.

"Look, Mr. Gamble, I'd do this myself, but there are people who might recognize me. I don't want my photo turning up in the newspaper or on television, especially sitting in a booth at the bus station with a man I used to see socially."

"Socially," I said.

"All right, for one weekend at least, he was damn good in bed. Is that what you were wondering about? I'll bring the money by your office tomorrow afternoon about four o'clock. We can go over any questions you have, or if there's a change of plans, I can let you know. Otherwise, I'll see you tomorrow. Meantime," she reached into her purse and took out a plain envelope, "How about if I just go ahead and pay you now? That way if something goes wrong, I won't have taken up your time for nothing."

I said that would be fine. She laid a thick envelope on my desk and promised to be back the next afternoon. We shook hands, and then she left.

Just in case things went sideways, I didn't touch the envelope with my bare hands. I used a Kleenex to pick it up and drop it into the bottom drawer of my desk. Then I locked the drawer and went down the hall to the vending machine where I bought a can of Diet Coke.

* * *

When I got back to my desk, the phone was ringing.

"Good afternoon," Elaine Murdock greeted me. "I hope this isn't a bad time."

"Not at all. What can I do for you, Mrs. Murdock?"

"Well, obviously, I was hoping you'd have something to tell me about my brother. And please, if I promise to behave myself, won't you call me Elaine? All this 'Mrs. Murdock' business is starting to make me feel like somebody's grandmother."

"All right, then, Elaine. Far be it from me to want to age a beautiful woman beyond her years."

"Hmm, now who's being ingratiating?"

"Point taken."

"Thank you. Now, what about Simon. Any luck so far?"

"I haven't had much time," I said, briefly summarizing the day's efforts. "You've answered one of my questions, though. I take it you haven't heard anything either."

"No, and neither has Father, unless he's holding something out on me

50

again. I talked to him earlier this morning, and I can tell, he's really worried. I think frightened even, though he won't admit it, of course."

"Something tells me he'll pull through okay." I had meant it as a sarcastic remark, but as soon as I said it, I realized it could be taken another way. Another way was how she took it.

"I hope you're right. He puts up a brave front, but he's nowhere near as strong as he looks. If anything happened to Simon, I'm afraid it would kill him. "

"I wonder." That reminded me of something I had noticed the night before. "Elaine, I want to ask you something. You don't have to answer if you'd rather not."

"What is it?"

"Last night, when I was talking with your father, he did not look at all well. He said he was just tired, but I've seen that look before, and more often than not, it led to a bad outcome. I'm just wondering if whatever is wrong with him is something I should know about."

"My father has pancreatic cancer," she said after a moment. "It was diagnosed fairly early, but even so, he has about six months to live. His doctors don't give him any more than that, and that's if he's lucky."

I said, "I'm sorry, Elaine. I won't bring it up again."

"Don't be sorry. Father says if we all lived forever, there wouldn't be any reason to live at all."

"He has a good outlook."

"You say that as though he has a choice."

"I guess he doesn't at that," I said, regretting having brought it up. "In the meantime, if I'm ever going to find anybody, I'd better get started. I was about to call your father anyway. There are a couple of things I need to ask him."

"I wish you wouldn't do that just now. Last night's fundraiser ran quite late, and he's absolutely worn out. I think it would be better if he had a chance to get a little rest."

"Fine, I'll call him tonight. Maybe by then, I'll have some information for him."

The nuance did not escape her. "Still playing it close to the vest, are we?"

"I'm not being cagey, Elaine. It's just that I've learned on more than one occasion not to go around speculating out loud when I've got nothing to go on. Which is why I've got to get to work."

"Then I don't want to keep you, do I? Except that there was one other thing I wanted to ask you. And besides, you did say I could call you if I wanted to borrow a sympathetic ear."

"You want sympathy now?"

"No. I was hoping you'd let me treat you to lunch tomorrow, that is, if you can spare me the time. You do seem to be a mighty busy man, Mr. Private Detective, sir."

I laughed. "Okay, Elaine, you win. Maybe I am overdoing the Sam Spade routine. Tomorrow's no good, but I can do Thursday if that works for you. Do you want me to meet you someplace, or what?"

"Why don't you just come by the house? I'm told I make a pretty good shrimp salad, and we can mix up something with a little rum and sit by the pool. Say, about twelve-thirty?

"I'll be there," I promised, and regretted it almost immediately.

Chapter Nine

H anging up the phone reminded me that I had a call of my own to make, to a former associate named Wanda Beaudry.

Wanda was a woman I had worked with for a year or so, back when we were both with the cops, assigned to the district attorney's investigative detail. She was a couple years older than me, and had come to Nashville from Baton Rouge, Louisiana, right out of LSU, with a degree in criminal justice. We were never an item, but we got to be pretty good friends during the time we worked together. She was funny, smart, and a solid investigator. Unfortunately, she had a bad habit of taking up with men that she would have been better off avoiding.

One night late in the winter, I got a call from Wanda. She was having trouble speaking, and I could barely understand what she was trying to tell me. I was able to make out a few words that sounded like "hurt" and "help." Without waiting for her to finish, I hung up the phone and took off for her apartment in my Crown Vic copmobile, Code Three, lights and siren. When I got there, I found her on the floor, unconscious. She had been severely beaten all over her body, but especially around her eyes and mouth. I'd radioed for backup on the way over, and when I saw what her condition was when I got there, I made sure she was breathing, and then called for EMTs. By the time help arrived, I had cleaned up her face with a damp towel and covered her with my overcoat.

It took some time and a lot of persuasion to get the story of what had happened. Turned out, the laid-off construction worker she had been living with off and on came home drunk. After words were exchanged, things went off the rails, and he worked her over pretty thoroughly. A considerable amount of time passed, but eventually, she recovered, although she needed some dental implants and her eye socket had been shattered, so that her vision was partially impaired. That got her permanently off field work, and she was reassigned to a desk job in human resources. She was able to keep her badge and pay grade, as well as her service weapon. And when she declined to press charges, or even to name her assailant, I had no trouble figuring out how the story was going to end. There was nothing I could do to prevent it, even if I had wanted to, which I didn't. And so, all there was left to do was sit back and wait.

Nothing else happened until spring, after the weather had gotten warm again. And then, one Sunday morning the former boyfriend turned up dead, stuffed inside the firebox of a retired steam locomotive that had been donated to the city back in the 1950s, and placed beneath a canopy in Centennial Park. He had been shot in both kneecaps, both elbows, and then once in the back of the head. Some kids playing around the engine noticed a smell coming from inside the firebox. They opened the butterfly doors expecting to find a dead varmint and instead got the surprise of their lives.

From the amount of blood on his pant legs and shirt sleeves, it was apparent that there had been a considerable amount of time between the fourth shot and the fifth one that finished him. The gun was never found, but ballistics had no problem matching the weapon to a Walther .22 caliber autoloader that had somehow gone missing from the police evidence locker. Without the weapon, what little evidence the detectives assigned to the case had been able to come up with was circumstantial, but the brass up and down the line had an easy time figuring out what happened. Under the circumstances, there was no choice except to file charges. At the arraignment, Wanda pleaded not guilty and was released ROR.

After learning the details, the female A.D.A. assigned didn't seem particularly motivated to prosecute, and more or less tanked the case. Wanda was never convicted of anything. However, her career with the police was finished. With her disability payments plus an off-the-books settlement to avoid a wrongful termination suit, she enrolled at Vanderbilt and got a master's degree in sociology, then opened a shelter for battered and abused women. She's still running that shelter today, and occasionally, when she needs help with a special problem, like the one she herself had faced, she gets in touch with me. And she always has the same reason. There is a score to be settled. Sometimes she lets the bad actors off easily, with a broken bone or a critical part of their bodies missing. Other times, she goes the distance, and nobody ever sees them again.

This time, it was me who needed her help.

I called the shelter and asked to speak to Wanda. As was their standard procedure to head off crank calls, the receptionist took my name and asked for a callback number rather than putting me directly through. I gave her my office number, and then hung up and waited. Ten minutes later she called me back.

"It's been a while," she said when I picked up. "What have you been doing with yourself?"

"Just trying to make sure the world is the blissful place we all know it should be."

She laughed. "Blessed are the peacemakers, for they shall inherit. Something I can do for you?"

"I hope so. Do you still have your password for NCIC?"

NCIC is the National Crime Information Center, a database maintained by the FBI in cooperation with state and local police departments. NCIC keeps track of all kinds of records of missing persons, sex offenders, violent felons, stolen property, parole violators, and other bits of useful information regarding questionable characters. It is very comprehensive and is updated daily. However, it's not a public site. To access the actual records, you have to be in law enforcement. Wanda, I hoped, still had her password to get in.

She hesitated for just a moment. "Somebody special you're looking for?"

"Very special."

She hesitated for just a moment. "This is a little outside your lane, isn't it?"

"This one's personal, Wanda. Do you remember hearing about a singer named Kady Standley? She died a month or so back?"

"I saw it on TV. They said it was an accidental overdose."

"Right, that's what the medical examiner ruled, but I don't think that's what happened. I'm pretty sure that a guy named R. J. McGraw was with her at the time of her death. I think he and Kady had some kind of a goofy suicide pact, only I don't think she was serious about it. I think it was just part of a song she had been working on. Whatever happened, though, he left her to die alone in a shitty motel room."

"So?"

"So, I was supposed to be bodyguarding her."

"Ah," she said. "Got it. And now you're wanting him to hold up his end of the deal, is that it?"

"No flies on you," I said.

"Are you planning to punch his ticket?"

"I want to hear what he has to say. Then I'll decide."

"So, that's a yes."

"That's a hard maybe."

"Okay. I'll see what I can find. Do you have an LKA?"

"I'd start in Altus, Oklahoma, but he could be damn near anyplace."

"Give me a few days," she said. "I'll let you know what I come up with. And Gamble . . . I liked Kady's music. When you go to settle up with this fucker, I want to be there with you."

I had no problem with that, and said so. Wanda told me she'd see what she could turn up and get back to me.

* * *

After I finished talking with Wanda, I put in a call to Clarence Darrow, the attorney who had recruited me for Richard Eberle. My hope was that he could provide me with something more solid in the way of information on Simon. My thought was that if Simon had been in any real trouble before, as he would have been after the stabbing incident, he certainly would have needed a lawyer. Darrow seemed the logical choice to start asking. I figured that if Darrow was as worried about looking out for his own skin as Richard Eberle had suggested, then he ought to be willing to give me whatever help he could to find Simon and bring him back home safe and sound. After all, we were in this together now, were we not?

It was good reasoning, but poor timing. Darrow's secretary informed me in her sugary voice that the attorney had just left the office to take a deposition, and that she didn't expect him back until the following morning. She wasn't sure what time. I got her to pencil me in for a nine-thirty appointment, with the understanding that if we misfired, it wouldn't be her fault. I said that would be fine and thanked her for her trouble.

That left me with the rest of the afternoon free, and a choice between Dave Kelso and Jorie Flowers as places to spend it. However, there was no Jorie Flowers listed in the online directory, and since it was the middle of the afternoon and I had no idea where she worked, I decided to start with Dave Kelso.

I found Kelso's Auto Service on Melrose Avenue, not far from the old state fairgrounds. It occupied what used to be a Union 76 service station. I remembered the station and the guy who leased it last. In exchange for a badly needed valve job, I'd once spent a day and a half helping him figure out how one of his employees was skimming the till without him seeing it. It wasn't difficult. A customer comes in and buys a few gallons of gas for his lawn mower, or a roller dog and a Mountain Dew, and pays with cash. The pump jockey doesn't ring up the sale, he just pockets the cash. It's only a few dollars at a time, but over the course of a day, it could be fifty or a hundred dollars. The gas isn't enough to be missed when the owner checks the tanks, and the other stuff gets chalked up to normal shrinkage. The problem was solved without the help of the police when the owner and his brother took the employee out back of the station and beat the living hell out of him. That had been seven years ago. Since then, he'd had bigger financial problems, the kind that raised the interest of the IRS, and that would take more than a private detective to square. The last I'd heard, he'd managed to plea-bargain his way down to eighteen months at Tallahassee, plus back taxes, accrued interest and a fine, and the loss of his business license.

When I walked into the service bay, I found Dave Kelso, or at least his legs, sticking out from underneath a rusty Ford F-150 pickup truck. He was wearing what had once been a pair of blue cotton Oshkosh coveralls. They were greasy enough that I had to look closely to be sure of the color.

I squatted down next to him and braced myself against the pickup's battered front fender. I said to the legs, "You know where I can find Dave Kelso?"

"You found him," a voice drawled from ground level. "Something I can do for you?"

"I'd like to talk to you if you've got a couple minutes."

"You selling anything?"

"Not me. You buying?"

"Nope." A greasy hand extended itself, palm up. "Hand me that three-eighths socket over there, would you, pardner? It's right here by my foot." He wiggled his left foot by way of direction. I found the tool and dropped it into his hand.

"I need some information about a friend of yours. I was told you might be able to help."

"I got no friends, buddy, just people that owe me money."

"I don't think this guy falls into that category. I need to find Simon Eberle."

Kelso stopped what he was doing and pushed his creeper out from under the Ford. "Maybe I better get a look at you, buddy, while you tell me who the hell you are."

"Name's Gamble," I said, giving him a look at my license. "I've been hired by the Eberle family to locate Simon. He left home two and a half days ago. Nobody seems to know where he went. They think he might be in some kind of trouble."

Kelso got up off the floor and wiped his hands on a dirty shop towel. He was a stocky man with thick forearms highlighted by intricate, colorful tattoos. His square face was sunburned, and his longish red hair was pulled back into a ponytail held in place with a rubber band.

"This locating you're doing supposed to have something to do with me?"

"I don't think so. His father—that's who I'm working for—his father says you and Simon are friends. I figured if Simon was in trouble, he might have come to you for help."

"Help with what?" He squinted at me from beneath a pair of eyebrows bushy enough to trim with a Toro. "Did his old man send you down here to stir up shit for me?"

"Why would he do that?"

"Because me and him don't get along too good. He doesn't figure I'm good enough to be associating with the likes of his boy because I ain't no college graduate. So, if he sent you down here to lean on me...." He left the back half of his threat unfinished for me to fill in with whatever terrified me most.

I said, "Let's start over. The reason I'm here is because Simon Eberle has gone missing. He left his house Saturday night and hasn't been heard from since. That's now coming up on seventy-two hours ago.

"As far as Richard Eberle is concerned, he didn't send me anywhere to do anything. As it was, I practically had to drag your name out of him just so I'd have a place to start looking. The only thing I was able to get was that you and Simon were friends in high school, and that you still keep in touch. Even finding out that much was like pulling teeth.

"Now, if you are friends, you know the problems Simon has had. His father is worried he might get himself into some kind of trouble, and from the little I know about him, I'd say that's a strong possibility. So, unless you've got some reason for wanting to see your friend take a fall, it seems to me you'd want to do whatever you could to help."

He thought about that for a moment before reaching into a Styrofoam ice chest and pulling out a can of Dr. Pepper. "Want one?"

"Sure." He tossed me a can. I popped the tab and waited.

"Well, I don't know what I could tell you that'd do any good."

"Why don't we find out? Have you talked to Simon since Saturday?"

"No."

"When did you talk to him last?"

He thought for a moment. "I guess it's been more'n a month ago."

"Where was that?"

"Here. He stopped by with a six-pack about the time I was closing up. We drank the beer and shot the shit for a while, and then he took off. I ain't heard from him since."

"When he was here, did he seem all right to you?"

"What do you mean?"

"Well, for instance, did he act like anything was bothering him? Was he nervous, spaced out, anything like that?" Like a traffic signal changing from green to yellow to red, Kelso's expression switched in quick succession from puzzlement to comprehension, and finally to anger.

"I get it now. You want to know if he was acting crazy. I expect that's what his daddy must have told you, isn't it? That he's crazy?"

"He never used those words, no," I said, without directly contradicting him.

"His sister, what's-her-name? Did she tell you that too, or ain't you run into her yet?"

"You mean Elaine Murdock?"

"Elaine, yeah, that's her. Did she tell you Simon was nuts?"

"No. She said she was worried, that's all. She said she and Simon are very close."

He snorted. "Close isn't the word I'd use."

I took a drink of Dr. Pepper. It was much too sweet. I said, "What word would you use, Dave?"

"I don't know for sure. I'm a lot better workin' with my hands than I am with words. But I'd say she treats him more like he's her little kid than her brother. It ain't quite natural. It's been that way as long as I've known him."

"How long is that?"

"Like you said, since high school."

"In all that time, would you say he was given to violent behavior?"

"Simon? Naw, not hardly. I mean, he can get pretty excited now and then, but he ain't ever been much of a fighter."

"He very nearly killed a man out in Springdale last winter," I reminded him.

"See, now, right there's what I'm talkin' about." I noticed him clenching and unclenching a fist with his free hand.

"Simon stepped in between some old boy and his wife. The guy was beatin' the hell out of her, and Simon tried to get him to quit. A real fighter would've known how to go up against a man what's bigger'n him, or else he would've had enough sense not to. Simon was just tryin' to take up for that woman, and the next thing he knows, he's in a battle for his life. A man in that situation is apt to do whatever he needs to just to keep from gettin' killed."

I showed Kelso the photograph Richard Eberle had given me. "Is this how Simon looked the last time you saw him?"

"Pretty much, except his moustache is bigger now. Say, there's old Jorie, too." A sly look crept across his face. "Does Simon's old man know about this picture?"

"He gave it to me. Why, is there something wrong?"

"Only that Richard Eberle hates Jorie with a passion."

"Why would you say that?"

"Aw, well, hell, maybe that ain't quite being fair, but Richard never liked the idea of Simon spending time with Jorie. She runs a little to the wild side sometimes, and he sorta worked it out she'd be a bad influence." He extracted a pouch of Red Man from his hip pocket and stuffed a wad into his mouth.

"Chaw?" he offered.

I shook my head. "Trying to quit."

He folded the pouch and stuffed it back inside his overalls. "I remember one night after I closed up, me and Simon and Jorie went down to the Million Seller—that's a bluegrass bar here in town—and had a few drinks. We met up with some gal Jorie knew while we were there. A real good looker, too, although I think she might have been a pro, if you take my meaning."

I took it. "Does Simon still hang at the Million Seller, do you know?"

"Only place he ever goes, 'cept on Sundays and Mondays, 'cause they're closed them two nights. I can tell you I don't go there no more, though, and that's for damn sure."

"Why is that?"

"Two reasons." He spat a mouthful of tobacco juice on the floor. "One is, I'm a married man, and the women down there are way too free and easy to be any good for me. Two is, there's a lot of drugs gets bought and sold. Hell, you can watch that shit changin' hands easy as orderin' a beer. Now, I ain't sayin' I'm a saint or nothin', but these days I'm a businessman, and I can't afford to get my ass busted in a place like that when I got customers go to church Sundays. Plus, I got a business license to think about."

"That would be a problem," I agreed. I tried something else. "The last time Simon was here—I think you said about a month ago—was Jorie with him then?"

Kelso wrinkled his brow in thought. "No. But when he left, he said he was heading over to her place. I expect you can guess what for."

"Are you sure about that?"

"Pretty sure, yessir. Is it important?"

"It's interesting, anyway. His father said Simon and Jorie had stopped seeing one another several months ago."

"That's what he knows," he laughed. "I don't know what good it'll do you, but if you want my opinion, you can have it." He spat again, this time in the direction of a steel trash barrel filled with oily, discarded parts.

"What I think is that Simon finally got tired of having every damn person in his life tellin' him how he should live his. I got no idea where he is now, but my hunch is he don't mean to have anybody find him any time soon. And if you do find him, and you've got some idea about tryin' to make him go home again, you might just have to knock him on the head first, 'cause otherwise, he's not going back."

And with that, I decided to call it a day. I had a dinner date that evening with Maggie, and Simon Eberle could wait another night before it was time for me to find him and knock him on the head.

Chapter Ten

When I got to Maggie's condo—on time, for once—to keep our dinner date, she wasn't ready—as usual. Instead, she was trying, so far without success, given her petite size, to lure her cat, Stanley, down from the valance over the top of her front windows.

"You're taller than me," she said, by way of greeting. "See if you can reach him. He's starting to climb the drapes, and I don't want him to get in the habit."

"Throw a little water on him," I said. "He'll get down quick enough."

"If you do that, you'll scare him. Just grab him," she said, as if that was final, and went upstairs to finish getting dressed.

Stanley was a fifteen-pound tabby with emerald eyes, gray fur with black mackerel stripes, and the general disposition of a honey badger in a trap. He had previously belonged to a fourteen-year-old girl named Gabrielle Hawkins. I first encountered Stanley, and later Gabrielle, after she had run away from home with a man twice her age. Her mother had hired me to find her and bring her back, which I did. But as it turned out, retrieving Gabrielle was only the first act in what turned out to be a tragedy of staggering proportions. Before the investigation was finally concluded, Gabrielle, her mother and father, the man she ran off with, as well as his former girlfriend, all wound up dead. With nobody left to care for him, Stanley was carted off to the city animal shelter where, because of his age and general orneriness, he almost certainly would have been euthanized after a few days. When I mentioned that to Maggie, she went straight to the shelter and brought him home with her. That had been just short of a year earlier. During that time,

Stanley had more or less bonded with Maggie, but he had no use whatsoever for me. His usual greeting was a menacing hiss before he bounded up the stairs to hide under Maggie's bed.

I met Maggie Totten the same day I met Stanley. Maggie was working as a guidance counselor at the high school where Gabrielle Hawkins was a student. I spoke with Maggie a couple of times, trying to get a lead on Gabrielle's possible whereabouts after she disappeared from home. That led to a dinner date, and eventually, to the committed relationship that we have today, but not before Maggie herself came perilously close to being killed by the same man Gabrielle had planned to run away with. She survived the encounter, but only because I showed up at her home unexpectedly and shot him in the head. The police called it justifiable homicide, so I wasn't charged with anything. But for Maggie, the outcome wasn't quite as simple.

After an overnight hospital stay following her ordeal, Maggie was discharged, with a prescription for painkillers and tranquilizers. Victim services provided a referral for a psychologist, whom she visited off and on for a few months. Eventually, the burn scars on her belly and breasts, where her would-be killer had tortured her with a lighted cigarette, had mostly faded. The memory of all that had happened that night, however, did not, and even now, when we are in bed together, she still insists on wearing a T-shirt or a camisole top.

Over the months since *the occurrence*, as we'd come to call it, her moods had by gradual degrees become darker and more unpredictable. Sometimes, maybe most of the time, she was fine. Other days, she would get angry over small things, or refuse to leave her home, because, she said, she was afraid of what might be out there. By some miracle, she didn't blame me for allowing her to become involved in the investigation that nearly got her killed. But she wasn't the same Maggie as before, and it had me worried. She owned two 9mm handguns, one that she kept by her bedside, and one in her purse, and with practice, she had become a dead shot with both of them. But neither the nines, nor the citalopram anti-anxiety pills, nor the Thorazine tranquilizers that she had come to depend upon, had done much to alleviate the problem.

Most weeks, instead of going home after work on Fridays, Maggie stays with me at my house. I cook supper, or we go to a restaurant, or to a movie, and then hop into bed and sleep late on Saturday morning. Those are the good nights, and we look forward to them together. But there are other times as well.

The bad nights, when she's at home alone, the memories of her ordeal come cascading back in the small hours, and she wakes up screaming. When that happens, she calls me and I come over and stay with her, lying next to her in her bed and providing what comfort I can.

Sometimes, it gets even scarier.

Not long after *the occurrence*, Maggie and I were having supper at a roadhouse located on Highway 31, several miles south of the city. It wasn't the kind of place we would ordinarily go as a couple, since her tastes are far more up-market than mine, but the menu had gotten good reviews from some of her friends at work, and she said she wanted to give it a try. So, after a forty-five-minute drive, we found the place, which was situated at the far end of a poorly lit, unpaved, gravel parking lot. As I expected, the place, including the décor, the menu, the house band, and the overall ambiance, was pure country. On the other hand, she'd heard the fried chicken, the catfish, and the country-fried steak were the best this side of Alabama, and you'd have to go all the way to New Orleans to find better shrimp. That was enough, at least for this night, to seal the deal.

It took maybe half an hour before we were able to get seated, so we passed the time having drinks at the bar, which was faced with white pine logs that had been split lengthwise and varnished to a high gloss. There was a television attached to the wall above the bar, tuned to the local Fox news station, where some red-faced clown was gesticulating wildly, rabble-rousing about whatever was his issue of the moment. We couldn't tell what had gotten him upset, because the sound had been turned down. So instead, we listened to the four-piece band playing country standards, and watched a few folks dancing in the area in front of the bandstand that had been cleared of tables and chairs.

Eventually, we were seated at a table-for-two next to a larger table where four large men with prominent facial hair were talking loudly and knocking back bottles of beer almost as fast as the waitress could bring fresh ones. At some point, while the band was playing an ear-splitting version of a Kenny Rogers tune called "You Decorated my Life," Maggie leaned across the table and said something to me. Over the noise, the only thing I could make out was "dance." I pointed to my ear and shook my head, no, trying to indicate that I hadn't really gotten whatever it was she'd said. But one of the very big men sitting at the next table evidently heard what he thought was Maggie asking me to dance. At the same moment, he saw me give her a head shake, so he leaned over and said something in her ear. Probably he asked her to dance, since he guessed I'd turned her down. She gave him a look and said "No, thank you," loud enough this time that I could hear it. But I suppose between the beer and the fact that, compared to me, he was a semi-truck, and I was a Honda Civic, he was emboldened by the mismatch and grabbed her by her arm. In a move so quick that would have made Stanley on the attack look like he was stuffed and mounted, she was out of her chair with her 9mm Ruger pointed squarely at the man's head. I saw, more than I heard, her say something, and then she grabbed her purse and headed for the door. I threw a couple of twenties on the table and followed, with my Colt in my hand, and walking backward, never taking my eyes off the big man. Between the noise and the crowd, I doubt whether more than a handful of customers realized what had happened, and, in any event, nobody came after us.

When we were both in the car and down the road, I said to her, "What did you say to that guy?"

"I told him if he touched me again, I'd blow his fucking head into that bowl of chili he had in front of him.

"Nicely played, if a bit heavy-handed. Meantime," I said, noticing that she still had the Ruger in her hand, which was shaking from the sudden rush of adrenalin, "how about slipping that roscoe back in your purse? I'd hate to end up as collateral damage here."

That had been several months ago. Tonight, I wasn't expecting anything quite so theatrical. She sounded okay on the phone when I called to confirm our date, and I had no reason to expect anything was amiss. It was just an evening when we had planned to go to dinner and then come back to her place to watch a late movie and crawl under the covers. But first I had to deal with Stanley.

I didn't throw any water on him, but I did try to coax him down. Once or twice, when I thought he was looking elsewhere, I tried to grab him, but when I did, he arched his back and hissed at me. Finally, I decided to let Stanley be Maggie's problem. And so, when she came back downstairs after getting dressed for our date, he was still right where she had left him.

Despite my earlier impression, Maggie seemed subdued during our drive to the restaurant. I knew when she got like that, something was bothering her. But I also knew better than to ask what it was, and that she'd tell me when she got ready. Most times, the best way to start her talking was for me to say something to get the conversational ball rolling on some other topic. And so, after we were seated at our table, I began telling her about the day I was having, including looking for a rich man's son who had gone missing, and then, later, being handed a fat envelope filled with cash to buy back some compromising photos of a marginally influential female politician. I thought the comically sexual nature of that story might distract her from whatever was on her mind, or that she might become interested enough to try to tease the name of the involved party out of me. But instead, she finished her second appletini—her favorite cocktail—in one long swallow and banged the glass down on the table, hard.

"I lost my job today, Gamble."

"Wait a minute, what?" She had caught me completely off-guard. "How could you get fired? Don't you have tenure?"

Like public school staff everywhere, degreed professionals are granted tenure after a certain number of years. In Tennessee, it's five years. Maggie, I knew, had been working in the district far longer than that, as both a teacher and a counselor.

She said, with some irritation, "This morning, while you were out doing whatever it was you were doing with the *hoi polloi*, I got called to a meeting at school. The district superintendent was there, along with about half the school board and the union president. So were the counselors from all the other schools. We didn't get fired, exactly. They were careful to explain that.

Tenured staff can't be terminated without cause. But we're all out of our jobs just the same."

"You lost me, Maggie."

"They eliminated our positions. Completely. The district is on a noble quest to save money, no doubt to keep their precious football program going. God knows, they're not going to touch that. So, to cut costs, they've chosen to hire a third-party provider for counseling services. Beginning in the fall, an outside counselor will come in a couple days a week, no benefits, no insurance from the district, to work with the kids. Under the terms of our contract, we have the choice of staying on as teachers, or hiring on with the new company as gig workers."

I tried to think of something I could say that would be helpful, but nothing came to me. The best I could manage was, "When do you have to let them know?"

"You mean whether I stay or go? August first. If we decide to remain in the district, we can use our seniority to select an available teaching position, which means some non-tenured teachers will get bumped and lose their jobs. After that, it gets complicated."

I wanted to ask more questions, but our meal arrived, and Maggie ordered another cocktail. In the year or so we had been together, I learned that, in stressful situations, Maggie and alcohol mixed together could produce some interesting results, not all of them good. Most of the time, she was strictly a consumer of diet soda/unsweetened tea/cranberry juice, but when she was upset, she would reach for something stronger, as she had said to me on another occasion, for courage. That meant that, whatever was on her mind tonight, she was having a hard time getting around to it. And I probably wasn't going to like it.

She didn't tell me what it was until after we had finished our dinner and returned to her condo. She unlocked the door. We went inside, and she kicked off her shoes and flopped down on the couch. Stanley was nowhere in sight.

"I've decided to go away for a while, Gamble. I'm leaving the day after tomorrow."

"I understand," I said. My head was spinning. I didn't understand at all.

"No, I don't think you do." She must have detected something in my voice. "This doesn't have anything to do with you. I'm not leaving you, or dumping you, or whatever it's called these days. I love you. You know that. I just need to—Gamble, it's just this place, this apartment. I can't shake the memories. I need to be somewhere else for a while. Hopefully to clear my head."

I sat down next to her. "Okay. How long is a while?"

"I don't know yet. A couple weeks. Maybe a month. No more."

"Where will you go? Have you decided about that?"

"Back to Ohio, I think. I want to spend some time with my family. After that, I don't know, except that I'll be back before the end of the summer. But I want us to say our goodbyes tonight. Tomorrow, I'll finish getting packed, and take Stanley to the kennel. Thursday morning, I'll be heading out early, but I don't want you to be here when I drive away. I think that would be too hard for both of us. So tonight, I want you to stay here with me, and hold me close, and then we can say 'so long for a while' in the morning."

And that was exactly what we did.

* * *

The next morning, Maggie was up early. She made us a big breakfast, and then we went back upstairs and said our goodbyes, for real this time, in bed. After that, I grabbed a quick shower, kissed her one last time, and let myself out. Maggie told me I should keep the key, she said, because I'd be needing it again after she got back.

Chapter Eleven

It was just past zero-eight-thirty when I left Maggie and drove downtown to the office. My head was still spinning from the events of the previous evening. I understood Maggie's wish to spend time with her family, and to get away from Nashville for a while, especially considering all that had happened to her during the time we had been together. I also understood that losing her job was like cutting a major connection to the community. And although I hoped otherwise, it was more than possible that, even though she said she loved me—and I believed her—that might not be a strong enough reason for her to return at the end of her self-imposed exile. For the moment, all I could do was hope that it was, and even though I had only just left her a short time earlier, I was missing her already.

Feelings aside, however, I still had a couple of jobs to take care of, including handing off a bagful of cash to buy back, some sexually-charged photos of a Tennessee state senator whose constituents would be horrified beyond words if the photos were made public. More importantly, I had to get seriously busy finding Simon Eberle.

Not having any useful leads that might help me with either assignment and since tapping into my usual sources at police headquarters was out of the question for the moment, I started making telephone calls. Straight out of the gate, however, I drew a blank trying to find numbers for both Jorie Flowers, Simon's girlfriend, and Peter Willingham, Rebecca Karlson's blackmailer. No surprise, neither one was in the book, and I couldn't find any information for either of them online. A call to directory assistance confirmed that there was no number for either one in their system. In

Jorie's case, at least, that probably meant her only phone was a cell, and there would be no listing for that. In Willingham's case, who knew? His actual residence could be anywhere on the planet and he was just coming to town long enough to hoover up the money he was planning to extort from Rebecca Karlson. So, with nothing to lose, I made a second call, this time to a woman I used to be friendly with who worked at the telephone company.

A little sweet talk whispered into her ear got me a number for a landline for Jorie Flowers that had been disconnected a few years back, and a three-year-old address on the west side of the city. There was nothing at all for Peter Willingham. I thanked my friend and promised to send her a fifty-dollar spiff to compensate her for her trouble. Then I made a note of Jorie's address and hung up.

My next call was to a guy named Drew Logan, who worked at the Department of Motor Vehicles. I had given Drew some no-charge help a few years back with a particularly nasty divorce, and in return, he fed me a little information from time to time.

"I need a favor," I said when I got him on the line.

"Now tell me something I don't know," he chuckled into the mouthpiece. I heard a noise like paper rattling at his end of the connection. Then he said, "Okay, shoot."

"I need a DMV on Willingham, Peter, no address and no other available information, Eberle, Simon, address Springdale, and Flowers, Jorie M." I read him the address I had gotten from my lady friend at the phone company. "I don't know if it's current, and I don't have a DOB or a social security number."

"I don't think I like this. Are these people in some kind of trouble?"

"Not as far as I know."

"Uh-huh." There was a pause. "Just out of curiosity, how close is this to landing a criminal charge as an accomplice to some damn thing on my resume?"

"Don't even dream of it," I said, trying to sound hurt. "This is just background on a routine investigation."

"Yeah, right." Another pause. "Look, I have a meeting in a few minutes, so it'll be this afternoon before I can get back to you. Okay if I just email it to your office?"

I said that would be fine. "By the way, how's the wife?"

"One, two, or three?" We both laughed at that, and then he hung up.

I thought about calling Richard Eberle to see whether he had heard from Simon since we spoke last, or whether he had somehow remembered the names of any of Simon's other friends, then decided that if he had something else to tell me, he would have already gotten in touch. So, with nothing better to do and still an hour before my nine-thirty appointment with Clarence Darrow, I decided to check out Walter Murdock's career statistics as a member of the Atlanta Falcons.

According to NFL.com, Walter played with the Falcons from 2004 through 2007. During that time, he compiled 408 tackles, or slightly more than 100 per season. By comparison, Dick Butkus rang up 1,020 tackles between playing for the Chicago Bears between 1965 and 1974, while Lawrence Taylor made 1,080 tackles for the New York Giants in 12 active seasons. That meant, on an annualized basis, like Butkus and LT, Walter Murdock was a monster in the defensive backfield, and if he had been able to keep on playing, he might well have been elected to the NFL Hall of Fame. It made me feel worse to realize that I had taken advantage of him when he was intoxicated, and not at the top of even his diminished game.

With my curiosity satisfied, I shut down my computer and headed out to keep my appointment with Clarence Darrow.

The attorney's office was in the J. C. Bradford Building, about a five-minute walk from my own office. I showed up promptly at nine-thirty, which was just in time to catch his secretary heading out for coffee. I introduced myself and asked whether her boss was in.

"No, but I'm glad you got here before I left. Mister Darrow telephoned just a few minutes ago. He said he was tied up in a meeting and wouldn't be free for another hour or so."

"Did you tell him I wanted to see him?"

"Yes, I did, and he said if you could wait, he'd be happy to talk to you when he got back."

That left me with an hour of downtime, which I burned by walking around the corner to a drug store on Charlotte. I bought a Diet Coke and a copy of the morning paper. Nothing much seemed to be going on in the world, though, and I got through it quickly. On the plus side, there were no obituaries and no headlines with Simon Eberle's name in them.

When I got back to Darrow's office, the attorney was there, waiting. He was a tall, angular man of about fifty years, who looked as if he'd been assembled from a box of spare parts. He wore rimless glasses and a brown suit that fit him the way my father's suit fit me when I first got it as a hand-me-down. We shook hands and he ushered me into the inner office. He sat on the edge of his desk. I parked in the customer's chair.

As lawyers' offices go, I'd been in a lot fancier. In fact, except for his filing cabinets being green instead of gray, it wasn't much different from mine. And that's no compliment to either one of us.

He saw me taking inventory. "I'm moving the end of the month, soon as the lease runs out."

I looked at him. "What are you, a mind reader?"

"Just a good guesser. Sooner or later, everybody asks." He spoke in a jerky, rapid-fire manner. "I imagine you want to know how come I recommended you to the Eberle's."

"Right again," I told him.

"I had my secretary pick you out of the phone book."

There wasn't an answer for that, so I didn't offer one.

"A joke," he said after a moment. "Actually, it was Eberle who suggested you to me. After that cluster fuck with the record company a while ago, he wanted me to check you out. I think he might have had an idea about suing you. Apart from the fact that you don't have any money, I thought it could have happened to anybody, and that he would have been wasting his time going after you. That's what I told him, and on that basis, and my gut feeling that you were somebody who could be trusted to keep his mouth shut, he said to give you a call."

"Then I guess I should say thanks."

"You're welcome. And I guess the reason you wanted to see me was to ask about Simon Eberle?"

"You're three for three."

"Okay. Before we get started here, you should know I checked with Mr. Eberle after you called earlier. He said I should answer any questions you might have about his kid. Anything other than that, meaning his business activities, for example, I can't help you. Understood?"

"Got it."

"Okay, shoot. What do you want to know?"

"I'd like to know where I can find him. I don't suppose you're a good enough guesser to work that out for me, are you?"

"I thought that's what we were paying you to do."

"You are, but so far all I seem to be doing is spinning my wheels. What I need is a hook. Anything, really, that might give me an idea where to start looking."

"And you figure I must be an expert on the Eberle family." He took off his glasses and wiped the lenses with the back of his tie.

"Let me tell you where I'm coming from on this, okay? Up until two years ago, the Eberle family's affairs were handled by a guy named Henry Morris. I don't know, maybe you ran across him sometime?"

I shook my head.

"Well, no big deal. Henry died and I got the business. Eberle never told me why. For all I know, he picked me out of the phone book. Anyway, you'd think a client like Eberle would keep a whole army of lawyers busy, what with all his business interests and so on. And you'd be right, he does. But those are corporate attorneys, employed directly by the various enterprises he controls. I handle his personal business, period. To date that's consisted of updating his will and paying off some hillbilly his kid stuck a knife into a while back."

"I heard about that. How much did he settle for, if you don't mind my asking?"

"Too much. A quarter mil. If it had been any other client, I'd have recommended telling the guy to go fuck himself, but Eberle wanted it settled out of court." He shrugged. "So, we settled. What the hell, it's his money."

"Yes, well, I did a little nosing around on my own, and from what I was able to find out, I think Simon could have made a pretty strong case for self-defense."

"Oh, without a doubt. Any first-year law student could have beaten that one without half trying. But like I said, that wasn't what he wanted."

"How were you able to get the criminal charges dropped?"

"Simon consented to get psychiatric help. Or maybe I should say resume getting psychiatric help."

"Resume?"

"I guess nobody told you about that. Simon Eberle has been in and out of various psychiatric outpatient programs for the better part of his life."

"I did know. Has he ever been declared legally incompetent?"

"Negative. As far as the law is concerned, he's a solid citizen. He can drive a car, run for mayor, if nobody looks too hard, buy a gun, whatever he wants to do. The only reason we had to have him agree to therapy this time was to give the sheriff something to put in his report so the judge could dismiss the criminal charges."

"So then, Simon never actually got help?"

"He did, at least when he was younger. I couldn't say for sure how long."

"Was a doctor ever mentioned by name?"

"Matter of fact, he was. It's Tabor. Frank Tabor. He runs a clinic, named after himself, out in Franklin." He screwed his face into a look that said he didn't think much of doctors who name clinics after themselves. "He and Simon go back quite some time, I understand."

I noodled that around for a minute. "Any Eberle money tied up in the Tabor Clinic, if that's what it's called?"

"First answer, that's what it's called. Second answer, if Eberle bankrolled any part of it, it's news to me."

"Okay, this sheriff you talked to out there. Did he ever say anything about Simon Eberle having a record of previous problems with the law?"

"Like I said, his record is absolutely clean. Why, what are you looking for?"

"Anything at all, although I'd be especially interested in anything drug related."

"No drugs as far as I know, why? You know something that says otherwise?"

"I don't know what I know. I'm just trying to find an explanation I can understand for some of the ways this kid has been behaving."

His interest picked up a little. "So, you're guessing narcotics?"

"Could be, but a guess is all it is. Funny thing is, when I suggested it to his old man, he had an answer all ready for me. I got the impression it wasn't the first time somebody had asked the question."

"And what was the answer?"

"The answer was a hard no. But then, later on, when I was looking around Simon's room, I found this." I showed him the green and white gelatin capsule I found in the bathroom. "He's got a whole bottle just like this one."

"What is it?"

"It's supposed to be for hay fever, but the bottle it was in didn't have a label."

"Is that so?" He picked up the capsule and held it up to light between his thumb and index finger. "Maybe the doctor gave it to him directly. Doctors do that sometimes, especially with new drugs that have just come on the market."

"Yeah, I thought of that, too, but usually they're in a package with instructions on the label. I was going to check it out when I got time." I took the capsule back from him and put it in my pocket.

"Let me know if you find out anything interesting," Darrow said. "I'd be curious."

"Maybe we can help one another," I offered. "I'd like to know about the will you mentioned before. What kinds of changes did Eberle ask you to make?"

The bony lawyer gave me a cool stare. "Come on, Gamble, you know better than that. We're talking about a missing person investigation here, not murder one."

"Are you sure that's all it is?"

"Are you?" He let his eyes roll up toward the ceiling. "Don't go getting all 'Law and Order' on me now. When you get something that says foul play for sure, come back and see me. Otherwise, I can't divulge anything about Eberle's will without his permission."

"Okay, but answer me one thing, if you can. Does his will make any provision for what happens to Elaine Murdock's share of the estate in the event anything happens to Simon?"

"Both shares go into trust, to be paid out at a fixed amount annually. Neither Simon nor Elaine gets any more or less, no matter whether one or both are alive to collect. Eberle set it up that way so Elaine's husband couldn't get his hands on any of the money. If both Simon and Elaine are no longer living, the remainder of the estate goes to a variety of charities."

He gave me a look of exasperation. "Jesus, what were you figuring, that Elaine knocked off Simon to collect his share of the inheritance?"

"It was just a question that needed to be asked."

"Well, for God's sake, don't ask it anywhere Eberle can hear you. He dotes on those two kids like they hatched from golden eggs." He looked at his watch. "Anything else you need right now? Otherwise, I got a client coming in."

"Thanks. I think I'm set for now."

"Okay. Keep in touch, you hear? Oh, and Gamble, just so you don't walk out of here with the wrong idea. I may seem a little unconventional to you, and maybe I am, I don't know. But I'm also damn good at what I do, and I make a pretty fair living at it. If you don't believe me, you can check it out."

"So?"

"So, before I called you, I checked you out with everything but a proctoscope. You seem to be okay. A little unconventional yourself, maybe, but who am I to criticize?"

"And your point is?"

"Just this: You come through this for me, I can return the favor in a big way. You think about that."

"I'll treasure the thought always," I said.

"I'm sure you will. One other thing: This Eberle kid—Christ, I don't know why everybody keeps calling him a kid. He's twenty-five years old, for God's sake. Anyway, he's not a bad guy, not at all. And I'd hate like hell if he didn't manage to make it home in one piece, okay? I'd hate it like hell."

"So would I," I told him.

Chapter Twelve

At four o'clock, as promised, Rebecca Karlson was back in my office, seated in the same chair she had occupied the day before. The kid was absent today, perhaps parked at the curb with the engine running, in case she needed to make a quick getaway. Today she was dressed down considerably, wearing stylishly faded jeans, suede calf-length boots and a plaid, short-sleeved top. If she had accessorized her outfit with a straw hat and a stalk of wheat sticking out of the corner of her mouth, she could have stepped right onto the stage at the Grand Ole Opry.

"I brought the money." She placed a leather briefcase on my desk. I looked inside. It was stuffed with cash, tens, twenties and fifties, all used bills. I supposed that was the way Peter Willingham, whoever he was, had specified the payoff.

"Any point in my asking, how you raised this much cash so fast?"

"Don't be so middle class. My constituents love me," she said. "Do you want to count it?"

"No reason to. If you're short-sheeting this guy, that's between you and him."

She gave me a look. "So, is it me you don't like, or is it politicians in general?"

"I like you fine. You're a good-looking woman, but there's a reason I don't vote local." That got me a small smile that, under other circumstances, might have held an invitation.

I said, "Just to be clear, is there any possibility this ex-boyfriend of yours is likely to come up shooting? I mean, after all, he's expecting to be meeting with you. What's he going to think when you turn up looking just like me?"

"He's going to think I was afraid to come by myself, which is exactly what I want him to think. You just have to convince him. Tell him a good story, then give him the case. He'll give you the photos, and that will be that."

"What will I be I getting, a flash drive, a SIM card, prints, what?"

"You'll be getting prints and a SIM card. As I explained yesterday, Peter took them when we were on…what? When we were on vacation in Gatlinburg. There should be about a dozen of them."

"And after we make the switch, then what?"

"Then I'll meet you back here at your office after. If everything goes as planned, and I have no reason to think it won't, you give me the photos, and I'll be on my way. Simple as that."

But things didn't go as planned, and it wasn't one bit simple.

I got to the bus station at eight o'clock. I wanted to be early so I could make sure the booth where I was supposed to meet with Peter Willingham would be available. I needn't have worried. When I walked in, the station was nearly deserted except for the agents at the ticket windows, three women behind the lunch counter, and an old guy dressed in dirty clothes sitting in the back near the rental lockers. The old-timer's name, as far as anyone knew, was Hamburger. I met him once, when I was working another case with a missing persons detective named Carl Sutton. Hamburger was Sutton's eyes and ears at the bus station. Sutton kept him happy, and more or less focused on the job, with regular handouts of Big Macs and twenty-dollar bills, and since he didn't cause any problems, the bus station let him more or less live there. I caught Hamburger's eye and gave him a wave. He responded with a nod of his head before looking away. With a few minutes to kill, I ordered a Diet Coke and slid into the middle booth to wait for Peter Willingham.

I didn't have to sit for long. At quarter after eight, a bus from Atlanta arrived, followed a few minutes later by an arrival from Birmingham. All at once, the terminal was bustling with travelers meeting friends or family, heading toward the outside cab stand, or checking connections for wherever their eventual destination might be. Out of the crowd came a dark-haired, middle-aged man I recognized from his photo as Peter Willingham. He was wearing tan slacks, a black t-shirt, and a light gray summer-weight sport coat. It didn't look as if he was carrying a gun, which made me feel optimistic the exchange might come off without a hitch.

He walked over to where I was sitting and smiled. "I wonder, since you're here by yourself, if I could ask you to take a seat at the counter. I'm expecting to meet someone here to transact some business, and it would be more convenient if we could use this booth."

I said, "As it happens, you're meeting with me this evening. Why don't you take a seat, and we can get this over with? I assume you have the merchandise?"

The smile left his face. "I think there's been some kind of a mistake here. Perhaps I should be moving along."

"Up to you, Mr. Willingham, but I can give you a hundred thousand reasons why you might want to stick around for a minute."

He hesitated for a second or two and then slid into the booth across from me.

"Who are you, and where is Rebecca Karlson? She was supposed to be here tonight."

Before I could answer, an announcement came over the loudspeaker that the bus that had arrived from Atlanta would be leaving for Louisville in fifteen minutes. People began moving toward the designated departure area. It was starting to get noisy.

I said, "It doesn't matter who I am. I'm here on behalf of Senator Karlson because she didn't want to be seen with you. If you have the pictures, I have your money."

"How do I know you're not the police?"

"If I were the police, you'd already be in handcuffs. Look," I lied, "I've got a bus of my own to catch. Do you want the money, or should I keep and spend it myself at the casino in French Lick? Makes no difference to me, but you've got thirty seconds to make up your mind."

It was twenty more than he needed. "How do you want to make the trade?"

"I'm going to move over and sit next to you, on the outside. I'll hand you the briefcase with the money. You're going to put the pictures and the SIM card on the table in front of me. That way we've each got what we came for. You can take your time and make sure the money is all there. I'll look over the pictures. If they look like what I'm expecting to see, I'll get up and leave, and you'll be free to go. If they're not, you and I will have a very big problem. Does that sound okay to you?"

"All right," he said, after a moment, "let's do it."

I crossed over to his side of the booth and passed him the briefcase. He handed me a brown manila envelope with what looked like a dozen images printed on copier paper. What I found were pictures of Rebecca Karlson, amateurishly posed in various suggestive ways, and in various stages of undress, ending up with four pictures of her completely naked, both sitting and lying on a bed, cupping her breasts with her hands, and her legs spread apart. She appeared much younger in the photos, and her hair was longer, but there was no mistaking who I was looking at. By contemporary standards, I didn't think they were terribly vulgar, but then, I wasn't a state senator representing a district that believed Billy Graham was a liberal.

I glanced over at Willingham. He was thumbing through the bundles of cash, satisfying himself that it was all there, and the bills didn't appear to be marked. When he finally finished and closed the case, I said, "Are we done here?"

"We're done."

"Okay." I slid out of the booth and stood up. "I'll be running along now, and I expect you're wanting to get going too. But just a word before we leave."

"Yes?"

"I don't know how many pictures are supposed to be here. I'm taking your word that this is all of them. But either way, if you try this again, it will not go well for you. You need to take your money and do with it whatever you want, but you are not to contact Senator Karlson again for any reason. Because if you do, you will see me again, and if that happens, I will be the last person you will see this side of an intensive care unit. Do you understand?" And without waiting for him to answer, I turned and walked toward the boarding gate for the Louisville bus. I figured I could mingle with the passengers at the boarding gate until I was sure he was gone.

I walked out onto the platform and waited there, like I was seeing somebody off. About five minutes later, the bus pulled away. As the noise of the diesel engine faded in the distance, I heard the unmistakable sound of gunfire, three shots—pop-pop-pop—in rapid succession, coming from the parking lot adjacent to the bus station. That was followed by the sound of a car driving off in a hurry. I folded the envelope with the photos and stuck it in my jacket pocket. Then I ran toward where the shots had come from. There was no reason to hurry, though. I already knew what I was going to find.

A small crowd had begun to gather, other people from the bus station who had heard the same thing I had, and a few passers-by from the street. Some were taking pictures with their phones, and one person was talking on his, calling, I supposed, 911. I got close enough to see what they were looking at.

Peter Willingham was on his back, his eyes open, staring up at the darkening sky, seeing nothing. There were three bullet holes in his chest. The briefcase I had given him just a few minutes earlier was nowhere in sight. I glanced over my shoulder and saw a uniformed security officer from the bus station approaching on foot. In another minute or two, the place would be crawling with cops.

There was nothing to be gained by sticking around, so I got in my car and drove back to the office, where I was sure Senator Karlson would be waiting. And I was equally sure that the hundred thousand was already on its way back to her favorite constituent.

* * *

As I expected, when I walked through the door to the outer office, she was there, waiting. This time, she had the kid with her.

After we all got settled in our seats, I tossed the envelope with the photos and the SIM card across the desk. "I guess you'll be wanting these."

She picked them up and riffed quickly through the stack. "Did you look at them?"

"I did."

"And should I ask, what did you think?"

"I'd say you haven't lost a step. A lot of the women I know would be jealous."

"It's nice of you to say so. I heard what happened to Peter, though. It's too bad. I guess he won't get to spend the money after all."

I looked at them both. "How did you happen to hear about that?"

"It's a terrible thing," the kid said. "Word gets around fast."

"I'll bet it does. And I'll also bet the money he was carrying is moving just as fast."

Senator Karlson raised her eyebrows. "And what is that supposed to mean?"

"I think we all know what it means. And frankly, I don't care one way or the other about Peter Willingham. He was a grifter, and he took his chances. It didn't work out, and he paid the price. Too high a price if you ask me, but that's the way it goes sometimes."

"But," she said.

"I signed on to deliver a package, which I did. Now, it's possible somebody at the bus station might have recognized me, and I'll be named a person of interest in a shooting. If that happens, and the cops come around asking what I was doing there, I won't lie for you. Protecting a client goes with the job, but withholding evidence in a homicide investigation most definitely does not."

"I understand. I'll rely on you to use your best judgment."

"Okay, good." I leaned back in my chair. "Also, if I were you, I'd make sure Junior, here, gets rid of that Smith. When the cops run the ballistics, and they connect Willingham to you, as they're almost sure to do, they're going to come nosing around looking for a gun." I shrugged. "Of course, I could be wrong. I often am."

Rebecca Karlson looked at me for a long moment. "I think we're finished here, Mr. Gamble. Thank you for taking care of this for us. I'll send you a little something extra for the trouble you went through this evening."

And with that, she and her son were gone. It was the last time I ever saw or spoke to either one of them.

That night, Maggie called to let me know she'd be leaving first thing the next morning. Also, she had decided to take Stanley with her. She said she missed me already and that she'd call again when she got to Mansfield to let me know she was okay. Then she told me again that she loved me and not to worry. Everything was going to be just fine.

Chapter Thirteen

I was back in the office the next morning, trying to figure out whether there was anything I could do about Senator Rebecca Karlson and her son, Scott, who seemed to have nailed down gainful employment as her mop-up man, and who had, in all likelihood, shot and killed Peter Willingham. I wondered whether it was even worth the effort to try. By now, Scott Karlson almost certainly would have gotten rid of the murder weapon, and he and his mother would have cooked up a watertight alibi to make sure they were both in the clear.

I could have gone to the cops and told them what I knew, or at least what I thought I knew. But that would have dragged me into an investigation that would not have resulted in a good outcome for me, if for no other reason than I hadn't actually seen anything. Plus, it would have been my word against Senator Karlson's, and I had no illusions about how that would end up.

What I had done in acting as her bagman was not strictly illegal, but if my role in the story ever came out, the publicity wasn't something that was likely to do my future relationship with the police any good. Also, I had a pretty good idea where Senator Karlson had gotten the money to buy back the photos so quickly, and I didn't think Richard Eberle would appreciate being named a person of interest in a homicide investigation. I decided that since I couldn't come up with a better plan, I'd let the police conduct their own investigation. Maybe a witness saw something: the car, perhaps, or the shooter himself, that would lead them to the Karlson's without my having to get involved.

* * *

The rain that had been falling steadily since early morning began coming down harder. Lightning, followed by thunder, followed by a drenching downpour, arrived about the time I locked up my office and headed down to the parking lot where I had left my car. I wasn't in a hurry, so I stood in the entryway of my building and waited for it to let up. In the humid air, the doorway smelled of sour urine and stale screw-top wine. The signature of some after-hours occupant, marking his territory. I wondered whether it could ever rain hard enough to wash away that smell.

Ten minutes later, a final thunderclap pushed out the rain. A minute after that, the clouds split, and the sun came out. By the time I got to the car, sweat was running down my back from the ninety-degree heat. I remembered reading somewhere that the invention of air conditioning had made the modern south possible. Maybe so. Too bad nobody had figured out a way to make it work outside.

Before leaving the office, I had checked my voicemail for messages. There had only been one, from Richard Eberle, letting me know he was flying over to Kansas City on business, and wouldn't be back until the next afternoon. He would get in touch with me then. There was nothing from Drew Logan on a current address for Jorie Flowers, the only one of the three I had requested that I still cared anything about. I already knew where Simon Eberle's residence was located, and I was past needing anything more on Peter Willingham.

Forty-five minutes later, I found the address Elaine had given me and pulled into the Murdock's driveway. The house was a rambling white brick ranch with a three-car garage, a pair of magnolia trees in the front yard, and a nice view of the Stones River in the back. I could only guess what it might have cost, but between what he would have earned in the National Football League and his various partnerships with Richard Eberle, I imagined Walter Murdock had done very well for himself.

Elaine met me at the door wearing a red silk blouse, white slacks, and white sandals. Her hair was unpinned and brushed out, so that it fell softly across her shoulders. A gold pendant with a single diamond hung from her neck. The eye-popping wedding ring she had been wearing the night we met was missing from her left hand.

"I hope you brought your appetite," she said in greeting. "I'm afraid I made way too much food for just two people."

My stomach gave a little warning kick. "Walter won't be joining us?"

"Walter isn't here. He left this morning to keep a golf date, and to have lunch with some friends." She made a clucking noise with her tongue. "What's the matter, Gamble? You aren't afraid to be alone with me, are you?"

"I can't help thinking I should be."

"I won't bite you." She took me by the arm and led me into the house. "Come on, I promised you food."

Still clutching my arm, she steered me through the house to the family room. It was decorated with early American furniture and rough-cut wooden beams running across the ceiling. One wall had been turned into a gallery of Walter Murdock's football memorabilia. There was the obligatory oil portrait of the late Alabama football coach Bear Bryant, wearing his trademark houndstooth hat. In fact, Walter never actually played for Bryant, who died in 1983, but for Alabama alums and football fans, there will never be a greater hero. There were framed photos of Walter wearing his team jerseys and newspaper clippings with Crimson Tide and Falcons headlines and game stories.

The centerpiece was a glass display case with his Number 57 Alabama helmet and the red and black headgear he wore during his playing days in Atlanta. In the corner of the room were an oversized flat-screen TV set and a large bookcase filled with videotapes and DVDs. Elaine caught me checking them out.

"Go ahead and say it. In the world Walter lives in, all the clocks stopped the day he blew out his knee. Time hasn't moved a single tick since." She half-smiled, but her tone made it clear that the subject of Walter's athletic heroics was one she had long since grown tired of talking about. For some reason, that annoyed me.

I said, "You know, Elaine, Walter is the first professional athlete I've met, but I have known a few people who got to the top in the music business."

"Is that so? And do they sit around all day listening to their old records?"

"Some of them do, yes, but that's not what I'm getting at. The point is, for a lot of people who have achieved something really special in their lives, the transition from being a star to being just another face in the crowd isn't easy. Most of them eventually find a new groove, but either way, when the crowd stops cheering, the adjustment can be difficult."

"And the ones that can't adjust, what happens to them?"

"About what you might think. They sink to the bottom of a bottle, they wind up broke, or on the wrong side of the law. Either that or they hang around too long and become an object of ridicule."

"Like Walter, you mean."

"Not at all," I said. "Your husband had a great career. I saw him play. He was good, Elaine, really good. If he's having trouble letting go of the past, all I'm saying is that he's not the first one."

"Does that make him some kind of tragic hero?"

"No. Heroes ride fire trucks and pull people out of burning buildings in the middle of the night. Tragic heroes save the baby and die in the fire. Walter is a good man having a hard time finding another rainbow, that's all."

She didn't say anything to that, but the look on her face told me I was getting close to pushing the point too far.

"Look, Elaine, I'm sorry if I said too much. I'm just saying how it looks to me. I know it isn't any of my business."

"No," she said coldly, "it isn't."

"Well, then before I say something else that I'll end up apologizing for, how about if we just have lunch?"

She looked at me, deciding. Then she let her face relax into a small smile. "As you wish, sir."

She crossed to the other side of the room and pulled back the drapes. The wall behind was glass, with a sliding door in the middle. Beyond the glass was a screened-in swimming pool surrounded by a wide concrete apron. A table for two was set poolside. Next to the table was a server that doubled as a portable bar. I took the seat facing back into the house. An idiosyncrasy acquired during my time with the cops, but ever since the night a couple of coked-up gangbangers walked into a bar where I was having a beer and started blasting away at a couple other guys wearing the wrong colors, I'd made it a point not to sit with my back to the door.

"Something to drink before we start?" Elaine asked.

"Whatever you're having is fine."

"I'm afraid it's just rum and lemonade. It's really more of a sand-and-sun drink, but I guess there's nothing that says we can't pretend, is there?"

"Nothing at all," I agreed. I watched her start to pour. "Easy on the rum for me. It's still early."

She handed me a tall glass and held hers out. We touched the rims together and sipped the contents. Despite my request to go easy, it was very strong, not the sort of thing I should be drinking in the middle of the day.

"Beautiful place you've got here," I said, trying to find a topic that wouldn't send us off on another unhappy tangent. "It must be great being out in the country like this."

"Yes. Walter and I designed the house ourselves. My father gave us the land about a year after we were married. He called it a belated wedding gift."

"That was generous of him."

She shook her head. "My father is not a generous man."

"No?" And just like that, we were off into the weeds again, but I didn't have the faintest idea how to get back onto the pavement. I decided I might as well go along for the ride, to see where it might take us.

"No." She lifted her glass again and began turning it slowly around, as if she were searching for something floating around inside. "It's a long story."

I took another swallow of my drink. "Try me. I told you, I'm a good listener."

She looked doubtful. "I'm not sure where to start."

"Maybe I can help you, then. I'm curious about Walter and your father. What happened to set them at one another's throats the way they are?"

"It goes back a long time. I imagine you already know Father is in the real estate business. You may not know that he also owns, or has a financial stake in a large part of the undeveloped land in this county."

I nodded. "I didn't think it was a secret."

"It's not, but that's how he came to own this particular piece of land. It's actually three parcels, about thirty-four acres altogether. He bought it because it was relatively cheap, and because he wanted to build a subdivision on it. The problem was, except for right where this house is, the composition of the soil is all wrong for the size houses he had planned. There's too much sand and not enough clay, so it's too unstable for construction purposes. Also, we're very close to the river, as you saw when you drove up. Because of that, the houses all needed to be set far enough back, so there's no damage when the river floods."

"Okay, so he gave you the land and took a tax write-off. Maybe it doesn't come straight from the heart, but it's not the worst thing I've ever heard."

"Not when you put it that way. But there's more to it than just a tax loss. See, nobody knew it at the time, but my father had made a deal with some men at the county board to approve a variance in the building codes so he could put up his development."

I said, "By 'deal,' are we talking payoffs?"

"If that's what you call cash changing hands in plain envelopes. Anyway, everything was all set. All my father had to do was deliver the money, and the variance would be approved. No one would ever be the wiser."

"What happened?"

"Walter happened." She took another swallow of her drink and set the glass down on the table, hard enough that a little of it sloshed over the rim. I realized this wasn't her first drink of the day.

"Walter had just retired from football. We had moved back from Atlanta to Springdale, and we were looking for a place to build a home. My father invited Walter into the project as a minority partner, to give him something to do, and to help get him started in the real estate business. Plus, he was counting on Walter's star power as a celebrity football player to help promote the project to the public and among real estate agents. I guess you could say it was his way of welcoming him to the family."

"Go on." I took another swallow of my drink. *Damn, it was strong.*

"He wasn't supposed to, but somehow Walter got hold of the soil analysis. He didn't really know what he was looking at, but he had taken some engineering courses while he was at Alabama. For no particular reason, he started fooling around with the numbers and figured out that the houses couldn't be built. They were too large for the ground to support without a lot of settling. He determined that within a few years, there would be problems with walls and foundations cracking. Also, there was no city sewer system at the time, and because of where the septic fields were to be located, sewage would leach into the river."

"So, he blew the whistle?"

"Not right away. He went to my father and told him what he'd discovered. Father said not to worry about it, that he must have made a mistake. But he hadn't made a mistake, and he knew it.

"Walter had just been released by the Falcons, and his style was still more attuned to cracking heads than negotiating. So, not surprisingly, they got into a fight, and Walter threatened to take his findings to the full board of supervisors."

"Did he?"

"Yes. My father offered him money to keep quiet, but Walter didn't want any part of it. In the end, two of the men on the zoning commission, the ones Father was working with, had to resign, and the project was abandoned. My father lost a lot of money in the process."

"Couldn't he have built smaller houses?"

She shook her head. "My father doesn't do small. Plus, it would have involved re-zoning the land, and the county wasn't about to go for that. Not after what had just happened. Anyway, smaller homes would have been more attractive to the wrong kind of people, if you take my meaning."

I did, loud and clear. "That explains the hard feelings, then."

"Yes. And in all this time, he hasn't gotten over it. Now, there's nothing left on the tract except this house and some construction buildings they put up by the river when it looked like the project would go through."

I waited while she drained her glass and poured herself another drink. Well, what the hell, I thought. I finished my own drink, and she immediately refilled my glass.

"When we finalized the plans for the house, Father made us a gift of the land. He has a particularly acute sense of irony that way. It was an embarrassment to him, not to mention a reminder of a lot of money down the drain. But the worst thing was that it represented failure, and that was something he couldn't bear. That's why he gave it to us, you see. It was Walter's punishment."

She shook her head sadly. "Poor Walter. His life has been like a nightmare, almost from the day he married me. All because he tried to do what he thought was the right thing."

I said, "Where do you fit into this, Elaine? Why is your father punishing you?"

"For marrying Walter, of course. As far as my father is concerned, Walter is a failure, never mind his football heroics. Marrying him made me one, too. So now Father keeps Walter on his payroll to sit around and do nothing. It's how he keeps him under his thumb."

"Why not just walk away? You and Walter could go someplace else and start over. You surely don't need the money."

She stirred uneasily, as if I had touched a nerve. "We used to talk about it all the time. Go to California, to Florida, to Mexico, anywhere, as long as it was far away. Walter thought he might like to try his hand at coaching, and I could get a job as a teacher. We never did, though, and now it's too late. Besides, there's always been Simon. I couldn't leave him with just Father to take care of him."

"Yes, well, maybe Simon decided he didn't want anybody taking care of him."

She looked at me. "What are you talking about?"

"I talked to a friend of Simon's yesterday afternoon. A man named Dave Kelso. I assume you know who he is?"

She nodded. "Simon and Dave went to high school together. He works repairing cars or something now, I think."

"That's him. He thinks there's nothing wrong with your brother that a strong dose of independence wouldn't cure. He says Simon ran away to escape from you and your father."

"That's ridiculous," she said angrily. "Father and I both love Simon, and he loves us. What is there to get away from?"

"He could just feel smothered from all that love. Maybe all he wants is a little time to himself."

"You're being a psychologist again, Gamble. You couldn't begin to understand why...." She let the thought trail off.

"Couldn't begin to understand what?"

"Nothing. I mean—I don't know what I was going to say. I just wish I could do something, that's all." She lifted her hands and let them fall helplessly into her lap. "I feel completely useless just sitting here like this."

"Then help me find him. I need you to tell me, as simply as you can, what's the matter with your brother."

"You already know. Clinical depression."

"Yeah, I got that, but why? He didn't just roll out of bed one morning depressed. You're more up on this than I am, but we both know a condition like Simon's is one that's either developed over a long period of time or else is the result of serious trauma. Now straight out, what's eating that boy?"

She sat quietly for a minute before answering.

"When Simon was a child, his stepmother—our stepmother—committed suicide. She took a gun and blew her brains all over her bedroom. Simon was in the room when it happened. He saw her do it. He's never gotten over it."

Chapter Fourteen

Elaine mixed us each another drink. I tossed half of mine back in a single swallow. This one was a lot stronger.

She said, "Our mother—her name was Clara—she and my father married late. Clara was thirty, and Father had just turned forty at the time of the wedding. I was born a year later, but it was another fourteen years before Simon came along. However, there were serious complications with the delivery, and Clara died a few days later. Actually, her doctors more or less expected it. Mother never was very strong as it was. She was in her early forties, and the fact that Simon was born at all was something of a miracle. Mother was strongly advised against a second pregnancy. But she went ahead anyway, and it cost her life."

"Why did she do it?" I asked. "Did she want another child that badly?"

Elaine shook her head. "My father did. He wanted a son. It took him thirteen years, but he finally got his wish."

"So then, after your mother died, he got married again?"

"Yes, but not right away. When Simon and I were small, our father traveled almost constantly, getting his business off the ground. There were times when we hardly ever saw him, except on the weekends. He barely had time for me and Simon, let alone another wife."

"Nobody ever got on the cover of *Fortune* by putting his family first."

"And what does it get them, I wonder. A few days after Mother's funeral, we brought Simon home from the hospital. That same day Father called me into the study. He held me on his lap and told me I'd have to be the mother of the house for a while. I'd have to take care of the new baby."

"How old were you then?"

"I'm fourteen years older than Simon. Can you imagine? Fourteen years old, and my father is telling me I've got to take care of a baby. I was barely more than a baby myself. As it turned out, it was four more years before he found a new wife, and even then, he wouldn't have except that I was leaving to go to college. For once in his life, he was left without a choice."

"Surely you had help, didn't you?"

"Oh, yes, of course. There was a nurse, then a nanny, then a housekeeper, then another housekeeper, and so on. But the thing was, there was never any doubt that I was responsible. Any time Simon was sick, or hurt, or sad, it was up to me to do something about it."

"Is that what your father told you?"

"No, but he made me feel it. Or maybe I made myself feel it, I don't remember anymore. Either way, it was a heavy burden. It's not as though I wanted him. I just ended up with him."

"When your father remarried, how did Simon feel about that?"

"He was excited. He had been without a real mother since day one, so he was happy he would finally have a mom like the other kids he knew. He was crazy about Alicia—that was her name—and she took to Simon right away. I was happy for both of them."

"How about you? Were you happy?"

"Yes, but not the same way." She removed a cigarette from her pack and lit it. "I was just glad I could finally have a normal life. I didn't need a mother. I just needed to get out of the house. Going off to Tuscaloosa was like being let out of jail."

I said, "Not to keep bringing it up, but when Simon was small, what kind of a kid was he?"

"Nervous. Shy. I don't know. What are you looking for?"

"Well, for instance, was he ever told what happened to his birth mother?"

"Yes, of course, he was told. What would have been the purpose of hiding it?"

"I don't know," I said. "I'm just trying to get a sense of what's going on inside his head. When his stepmother took her life, what was he told about that?"

"That she was sick, and that sick people sometimes do things that nobody can completely understand. Why, where are we going with this?"

"I think Simon is running away from something. If we can figure out what that is, it might tell us what he's running toward, or at least how to keep him from running again, once we've got him back."

"And you believe there's a connection between the death of his mother and his stepmother and his own disappearance last Saturday night?" She took a deep drag on her cigarette and blew the smoke toward the skylights.

"Don't you think that's a little bit of a stretch?"

"Put yourself in his place. Suppose he's found a woman he loves. Or, to put it into the right context, a woman he thinks loves him. Maybe this Flowers woman he was dating, maybe somebody else. What happened to the last woman who loved him? It could be he subconsciously believes that he needs to get away from here to keep this new woman safe."

"You're forgetting about me, aren't you?" she said. "I love him, and nothing has happened to me."

"Then maybe it's you he thinks he's protecting now." I sighed. "What the hell, I don't know. I didn't say it was an airtight theory."

"Well, it makes as much sense as anything else I've heard." She stubbed out her cigarette and took another swallow of her drink. "How about if we change the subject, Gamble? I've practically told you my entire life story. Why don't you tell me a little bit about you?"

I shrugged. "What do you want to know?"

"Okay," she said, "how about this? Is there somebody in your life right now?"

"There is. Or at least there was. She left a couple days ago."

"Is she coming back?"

"Don't know," I said, but it came out more like "dunno." My tongue was feeling thick, and I was beginning to slur my words a little. The drinks were even stronger than I thought.

"That doesn't sound good. Did you have a fight? Did you say something?"

"No. Nothing like that." And so, I told her the whole story about Gabrielle

Hawkins and Maggie Totten, and what had happened to her on a cold night in December. I also explained that just this week, Maggie was told she would no longer have a job at the beginning of the new school year, at least not the one she thought she'd have. And for some reason, I felt myself getting angry as I recounted the story. If Elaine noticed, she didn't let on. She just listened without interruption until I was finished.

"It sounds like she loves you. I don't think you have to worry. She's just got some issues she has to sort out for herself." She pushed her chair back from the table. "I'll go and get lunch. Fix yourself another drink if you want one." I did just that and finished it quickly. Then I poured another one.

While Elaine busied herself in the kitchen, I wandered back into the house. I looked over the video collection in the bookcase. She had been right about Walter having a lot of them. There were dozens, arranged in chronological order from his junior year at Alabama until the end of his final NFL season. I couldn't imagine wanting to watch them over and over again, but then, it wasn't me performing on the field. I would never know what it was like to have adoring fans cheering my every move.

I walked back outside and sat down. A moment later, Elaine returned, carrying a serving tray. "Sorry to be so long," she said. "I had to make a phone call to the doctor."

"Is somebody sick?"

"Not somebody. One of the horses. He split a hoof."

"You keep horses here?"

"We have three. Here, give me a hand, will you? This is getting heavy." She held out the tray so I could take the food. "The wind's out of the south, or you would have smelled them when you drove up."

She sat down at the table and passed me a plate. "Do you ride?"

"When I was a kid," I said. "I had a girlfriend who loved horses. I haven't been on one in years. Where do you ride them?"

"All around." She gestured expansively with her fork. "This property isn't good for much else. In fact, except for the jeep, horseback is about the only way to get out to where the houses were to be built. What road we had washed out years ago. If we hadn't had all that rain this morning, we could take a ride out there."

"That's okay," I said honestly. "Another time will do just as well."

"I want you to know I'm going to hold you to that, Gamble." She gave me a look whose meaning was unmistakable. "You can call me any time."

We finished eating lunch in silence. Without the distraction of conversation, and loaded to the eyeballs with Captain Morgan rum, I found myself being drawn more and more deeply into Elaine's presence across the table from me. I inhaled the scent of her perfume. I studied the contours of her face as she nibbled at her food. I became fascinated by the rhythmic rise and fall of her breasts in time with her breathing. And I realized that, without meaning to, my interest in her had ceased to be professional and was drifting in a direction it had no business going.

Elaine looked up and caught the look in my eyes. Without saying anything, she stood and leaned across the table. She kissed me, tentatively at first, and then deeply, her mouth crushing hungrily against mine. Maybe it was the alcohol. Maybe it was the frustration I was feeling toward Maggie for leaving me so abruptly and with so little explanation. Or maybe it was the prospect, even if only for a short time, to be with a woman as beautiful as Elaine Murdock. Whichever it was, I realized in the tiny part of my lizard brain that was still functioning that whatever it was that was on the verge of taking place was no good. I placed my hands gently on her shoulders and pushed her back into her chair.

"This isn't right, Elaine," I said. "I can't do it. It's like you said, there's somebody in my life right now. And there's somebody in yours. Promises have to mean something."

She looked at me. I couldn't read the look in her eyes. Was it anger? Frustration, or maybe sadness? I said, "Don't they?"

Without saying anything, she got up from the table and disappeared back into the house. She was gone for a few minutes, during which time I used my napkin to wipe the lipstick from my face and to try my best to get my head clear. Elaine evidently had the same idea, because when she came back, her appearance gave no indication that anything at all had happened besides a shared lunch with a new acquaintance around the pool on a hot summer afternoon. Her lipstick was fresh, and her hair looked as if she had just stepped out of a stylist's salon.

She came over to me and put her arms around my neck. "I meant what I said," she whispered softly. "You can have me any time you want. Just call, and I'll come to you. I know how that sounds, and I don't care. I'm not promising anything, but right now, I need you, for more reasons than I can begin to tell you."

In another lifetime and under different circumstances, it might have been interesting to try to find out what they were, but I was beginning to think more clearly now, and I knew it was time to get out of there. But before I could make my excuses, I heard a car pull into the driveway and park in front of the house. Elaine heard it at the same moment, and her eyes grew wide with fear bordering on panic.

She quickly stacked plates and leftovers onto the serving tray and disappeared back into the house. Guiltily, I put my jacket back on and tried to smooth my hair into place. I heard the front door open and close, followed a moment later by the sound of angry voices coming from the living room. I couldn't make out exactly what was being said, but then, I really didn't need to. Even without the sound rack, I knew where the scene was heading.

The argument was cut short by the sound of a hard slap. I heard Elaine cry out in pain and surprise, then nothing. A moment later, Walter Murdock appeared in the doorway. He had a butterfly bandage on his forehead where he'd cracked it on the desk two nights earlier. Barely controlled fury radiated off him like heat from a cast-iron stove. His jaw was screwed down tight, and his huge hands were clenched into ham-like fists.

"My wife has developed a headache," he said evenly, savoring his heavy-handed irony. "She's asked me to see you out."

As a rule, I don't go around armed when I'm invited socially into someone's home, so if Walter decided to have a go at me, there was nothing within my reach I could use to defend myself. I tried not to be too obvious as I let my eyes drift around the room, looking for something that might serve as a weapon. The only real choice seemed to be the fireplace poker. The problem was that I'd have to get past Walter to get to it.

"It must have come over her unexpectedly," I said, meeting his look. "She seemed okay a few minutes ago. But I guess you already know what a bump on the head can do."

"You're getting very damn close to finding out for yourself. Or maybe you think you can take me." He took a step toward me. "Come on, you piece of shit, why don't you make your move?"

And good fucking luck with that, I thought. He had me by four inches and an easy fifty pounds. Without the poker, the only way I could have stayed in a fight with him was if somebody nailed his shoes to the floor before we started.

I said, "I might be able to make you wish I hadn't tried, but you know what? I owe you one from the other night, so if you want, you can take the first shot."

He shifted his weight just slightly, as if to take me up on my offer, and I thought I might have just handed him a death certificate with my name already filled in. But then his hands relaxed a little, and something that looked like sadness crept into his eyes.

"What's the point? You're not the first, and you won't be the last. But just the same, I want you out of my house, now."

He walked ahead of me to the front door and pulled it open, nearly yanking the knob out of the wood in the process. Then he stood to the side to let me pass.

"One more thing, Gamble, just so you can't say I didn't give you fair warning. The other night, you fucked me and got away with it. Today, for all I know, you fucked my wife and got away again. That's all you're going to get. No more. If you come back here again, no matter what the reason, I will kill you."

He stepped back from the door and closed it in my face. As he did, I saw Elaine standing in the hallway. At first, her face showed no emotion, and except for the beginnings of a deep red handprint on her left cheek, no color. And then, for the briefest instant, she turned her head slightly toward me, and her face took on a look of deep satisfaction.

I drove away, feeling embarrassed and ashamed. In the space of a little more than two hours, I had gotten snot-flying drunk, nearly broken faith with Maggie, and in his own home, come inexcusably close to cuckolding a decent man who had done me no harm whatsoever. I decided that tomorrow, I would call Richard Eberle and tell him I was dropping the case. And then, a mile or two down the road, I thought some more about the look on Elaine's face and realized with jaw-dropping clarity that I had been played. And if anything, I felt even worse.

Chapter Fifteen

Next day, I didn't get to the office until late. I'd spent the previous evening, and well into the small hours of the morning, nursing a rum hangover and revisiting, with regret, some of my life's choices, including most recently, my lunch meeting with Elaine Murdock. In the clear light of day, I realized that my behavior on the previous afternoon was due in large part to my being upset with Maggie over her leaving town the way she did. But I also knew that was a reason and not an excuse.

I remembered Richard Eberle had said he would be in Kansas City until later in the day, so I decided that I'd wait until he called me to tell him I was dropping the case. In the meantime, I thought I'd take one last shot at making a little progress on the job he had hired me to do. That way I could at least walk off the job with a clear conscience.

Checking my email, I found the DMV reports for Jorie Flowers and Simon Eberle that Drew Logan had sent over. Not surprisingly, there was nothing for the late Peter Willingham, which meant that either he didn't have a driver's license, or he didn't live anywhere in the state of Tennessee. Either way, it didn't much matter anymore.

The record for Simon Eberle included a DOB of 4/12/96, two moving violations dating back two years, currently driving a 2019 BMW 3-series, two-door coupe. For Jorie, full name Marjorie Michelle Flowers, DOB 5/11/94, address Nashville, the record indicated no moving violations and not so much as a parking ticket in the past three years. A blue late-model Buick Regal four-door was registered in her name. I made a note of the address and her plate number and headed out to pay her a call. I thought if I could make contact with her and come up with at least some information on Simon's most recent movements, I'd feel better about telling Richard Eberle I was giving up the case.

The address Drew gave me for Jorie turned out to be a middling apartment complex off Donelson Road, not far from the airport. It consisted of half a dozen uninspired-looking two-story frame buildings arranged in a semicircle around a gently rolling hillside. I remembered the place from when I was a uniform with the Metro cops. The complex was newer then, and because of its proximity to BNA, a lot of the people who lived there were airline flight attendants, usually two or three to an apartment, sharing space to save money.

One night, my partner and I got a domestic disturbance call from a couple of the tenants living in the complex. Two young women in a ground-floor unit said someone in the apartment directly above them was screaming to the rafters. When we went up and knocked on the door, the guy who answered was holding a meat cleaver and was covered nearly head to toe in fresh blood. The woman, his girlfriend, as it turned out, was sitting on the couch, crying hysterically. From the amount of blood on the walls, on the floor, on the furniture, we figured we were looking at a multiple homicide, only there didn't seem to be a body. When we got the girlfriend calmed down enough to talk, she told us the guy had gotten fed up listening to her three small dogs barking constantly, so he hacked them to pieces with the cleaver and threw what was left of them over the back balcony railing. We contacted animal control, then cuffed the guy and pulled him in on charges of drunk and disorderly, disturbing the peace, and three counts of animal cruelty. I never found out what happened after that.

* * *

I cruised through the parking lot from one end to the other on the off chance that I might spot Simon Eberle's red Beemer. I didn't seriously expect to find it, and, sure enough, I didn't. Simon might be playing with a deck that had a couple of extra jokers, but if he were seriously on the run, he would have had more sense than to leave his car parked in front of one of the first places anybody would think to look for him.

I located Jorie's building and found her name next to the mail slot for apartment 106, a ground-floor unit. I wondered about the chances of somebody buzzing me in if I pressed all the doorbell buttons at once, and then decided it would be simpler to just flip the outer lock with a strip of stiff celluloid that I carry for just such occasions. It only took a few seconds, which pretty much said all there was to say for the security system.

The downstairs hallway was newly carpeted and dimly illuminated with forty-watt bulbs that glowed sullenly in amber glass globes. The air smelled of new latex paint and weapons-grade cleaning solution. I found 106 and rapped on the door with the tiny brass knocker screwed to the center. No answer. I rapped again. Nobody home.

I stood in the empty corridor, trying to decide what to do next. A reprise of the celluloid trick was out of the question. Unlike the outside lock, the deadbolt on Jorie's door wasn't about to be defeated by anything smaller than a two-pound sledgehammer. I was about to write it off as a dead end when I heard a door open behind me. I turned and saw six inches of a young woman's face looking at me through the opening. It was a good face. It had deep brown eyes, a freckled nose, and a small, dimpled chin.

The face asked, "Are you looking for Jorie?"

I admitted that I was and tried to project a look of boyish innocence. "She doesn't seem to be home, though."

"No, I don't think she is. At least I haven't seen her for a couple of days."

"I don't suppose you'd have any idea where I could locate her, would you?"

"Sorry, no." There was a pause. "Is she in trouble?"

I shook my head. "As far as I know, she's not. Why would you think that?"

"Because you look like a policeman."

I smiled. She didn't. She said, "Well, are you?"

"I was. I'm private now." I handed her my card. "Are you a friend of hers? I'd like to get a little information if you've got a couple of minutes."

She passed my card back through the narrow opening. "Do you have any other identification?"

I showed her my photo ID and license. She looked them over dubiously. "Got anything else, Mr. Gamble?"

"That's pretty much everything, unless you want to see my Costco ID." When that got no response, I said, "Look, if we're going to keep on talking like this, how about at least letting me see who I'm talking to? I feel like a Jehovah's Witness out here."

The eyes flickered, revealing rays of gold within the brown. "Of course, just hang on a moment." She closed the door and unhooked the chain, then opened it again.

"Please come in, Mr. Gamble. I didn't mean to be rude. I just try to be careful about who I let in."

"Perfectly understandable," I said. "And no need to apologize."

When I finally got a good look at her, I saw that the woman attached to the face in the doorway was in her early twenties, maybe half my age, attractive but not beautiful. She was medium height with shoulder-length brown hair, parted on the side. She was dressed in faded denims and a maroon and gold University of Minnesota sweatshirt. She was barefoot and wore no makeup and no jewelry.

"Just sit anywhere," she said, sweeping aside a pile of newspapers scattered across the couch. "Can I get you a cup of coffee? I just made some fresh."

"No thanks."

"Do you mind if I pour one? I'll just be a minute."

"No, go ahead."

While she was gone, I took a look around the apartment. It reminded me of the first place I'd called home after I finished school. The room I was in was a combination living room and dining area. Behind that were the kitchen and a blue-tiled bathroom I could partly see, and a bedroom that I couldn't. The furniture was well-worn, but comfortable looking. Against the outside wall was a battered upright piano. I walked over to it and tried picking out the melody of a tune I used to know. When I hit the same wrong note twice, I gave up.

She returned from the kitchen and took a seat on the couch. "Do you play, Mr. Gamble?"

"Obviously not." I sat down on the piano bench. "I'm surprised you can get away with a piano in an apartment building. I'd think the neighbors would complain."

"This is an end unit, and for now, the apartment upstairs is vacant. Anyway, most of the people who live here work during the day, so it's really not a problem."

"Well, that's lucky for you, then, Miss..."

"Robbins, with two b's. Serena Robbins."

"And is it Miss, Mrs., Ms., or none of my business?"

"I'm not seeing anybody right now, if that's what you're asking."

"All right, then, let's call it Miss Robbins. I'm trying to get in touch with Jorie Flowers. There's no trouble as far as she's concerned. I just need to ask her a couple of questions about a matter I've been hired to look into. I would have called first, but she's either got an unlisted number or just a cell phone, so I haven't been able to actually speak with her."

She took a sip of her coffee. "Well, I don't know whether I can be of much help. I mean, I don't really know her any better than any of the other people in the building. We say hello if we see each other in the hallway or the laundry room, but that's about it. We're not what you'd call close friends."

"Do you know whether she has any other friends here I could talk to?"

"She might, but I wouldn't know who to tell you. I don't know whether it would do any good, but I guess you could try knocking on doors."

"How about men friends? Is there anybody she sees regularly?"

She shifted in her chair. "There's a guy I see who comes around every now and then, but I mean, it's not like I'm keeping track. Anyway, I never heard his name."

"Simon?" I prompted.

"I don't know, could be. Are you looking for him, too?"

"I'd like to talk to him," I said. "When was the last time you saw him?"

"Well, now that you mention it, it was just last week. I want to say Saturday night."

"Are you sure about that?"

"Pretty sure, yes. I was just going out, and he was coming in. We walked right past each another. I was in a hurry. I was running late for work."

"You work nights?"

"I'm a musician, what can I tell you? I work odd hours. Weekends I play piano in the lounge at the G-Spot downtown, eight 'til closing."

"I know the place," I said. "It can get pretty crazy sometimes."

"That's the one," she said. "Other times, I get a little session work over on the Row, but it's nowhere near steady. They call when they need me. I do commercials, background vocals, keyboards, whatever they need."

"Anything I might have heard?"

"I don't know. Do you listen to country music?"

"I knew a singer once," I said, thinking of Kady Standley. "One time, she played some of her songs for me. That's about it."

"Then you probably haven't heard me, unless you've heard the radio commercial that they're running for that mall up in Madison. That's me singing, 'Thirty great stores, all exciting and new. Each and every one has something special for you.'"

"I'll have to listen for it."

"Okay. And thanks for not laughing."

"Did I miss something funny?"

"Well, you know. You probably run into a million people a year who come to Nashville hoping to make it in the music business."

"Once in a while, somebody does. No reason why you can't." I shifted back to business again. "Serena, does Jorie have any other men friends you know about?"

That put her on her guard. Her eyes narrowed, and her voice got colder. "I couldn't tell you. And before I answer any more questions, I think maybe you should tell me why you're so interested in Jorie's men friends. Has this got something to do with a divorce, or a custody dispute?"

"No, I don't do that kind of work. I'll tell you what I can, but I'll have to ask you to keep it to yourself."

When that got no answer, I continued, "This man we've been talking about, the one you might have seen in the hallway. His name is Simon Eberle. He's not dangerous or violent, but he does have emotional issues, and sometimes he gets himself into trouble. He's been missing from home for a few days, and his family wants me to find him and make sure he's all right. Because he's friendly with Jorie, I thought she might have some idea where I should start looking. That's really all there is to it."

"Do you think he would do something to hurt Jorie?"

"Absolutely not. There's nothing in Simon's background to suggest anything like that. I think it's more likely he would have come to Jorie looking for a place to lay low until he can figure out what to do next. My guess is he's confused, and maybe a little bit frightened. I just want to make sure he's okay. What happens after that is between him and his family."

I handed her another card and got up to leave. "I wonder if I could ask you to do one other thing. If you happen to see Jorie, I'd appreciate it if you'd ask her to give me a call. Could you do that?"

She looked at the card, then at me. "You said Jorie isn't in any trouble. Suppose I believe you. I hope that's not a mistake."

"Why would you think that?"

"I mean, I didn't tell you anything that would get her into trouble, did I? I was honest with you. I'd feel a lot better if I thought you were being honest with me."

Her expression said she wanted to believe me, but didn't, completely. I couldn't blame her. What I had told her was somewhere between wishful thinking and the truth. On a scale of one to ten, it was probably no higher than a six.

"It's like this," I said. "This guy comes from a family with money, and he's still living at home. I've checked him out pretty thoroughly, and I can't find anything to suggest he would hurt a woman. Least of all, one that he likes, or who he may even be in love with. For all I know, Jorie and Simon are honeymooning on a beach somewhere in the Caribbean, knocking back yellow birds and having the time of their lives. I hope that's how this turns out. But I still have to find out where he is, and that he's okay. That's the best I can tell you until I find out more."

I paused to let that sink in. "Do you believe me?"

"Yes," she said. "I think I do. Thank you for being honest." She hesitated, as if trying to make up her mind about something. "And Mr. Gamble? Please don't take this wrong, because I don't mean it wrong. But if you're not doing anything some night soon, you might drop by the G-Spot. It'd be nice to see a friendly face in the crowd, and I'll even play you a song or two that I wrote myself."

"If I get the chance," I said, but the memory of my date with Elaine Murdock was still fresh in my mind.

Chapter Sixteen

After I left Serena Robbins, my plan was to go back to the office and wait for Richard Eberle to call. When he did, I would tell him I had made no progress locating Simon, and that he should consider either going to the police, or else retaining another agency, one with better resources than what I could offer. But he didn't call, and instead, I found in the mail a retainer in the form of a check for five thousand dollars. So, I decided, the hell with it, I'd stay with the case for another day or two and see if something turned up.

For a weekday night, the Million Seller Lounge was doing a land-office business. I had to cruise the block between Twenty-Second and Twenty-Third Streets three times before I could find a place to park, and even then, I had to wait for somebody else to pull out first. Then I had to walk another block and a half.

The Million Seller was a throwback to the days when Elliston Place was still just a city neighborhood, and when Nashville was still legally dry. Back then, all they served was three-two beer and overpriced setups to those who snuck in with their own bottles. The city stopped being dry longer ago than I can remember, and Elliston Place has grown up to become a trendy, millennial hangout. Meantime, the Million Seller just rolls along, serving low-octane suds, pricey mineral water, and ear-splitting, string-band country music. On the weekends, there are headline acts and ten-dollar cover charges. During the week, most weeks, you get Earl Owens and his Poor Relations Revue. That's because Earl owns the Million Seller.

A dozen years ago, Earl was on the verge of breaking his act into the big time. But then, for reasons that were never made entirely clear, he got himself crossways with the Nashville country music Establishment. The story that made the rounds at the time said something about bilking unknown songwriters out of royalties for non-copyrighted material. That was strictly for the rubes. Those who knew better said that Earl simply picked the wrong man's wife to take to Lake of the Ozarks for a long weekend. Whatever was the real story, after that, he was professionally dead in the water. In the music business, like any other business, success depends as much upon having talent as it does to making sure to stay on the right side of the right people. Earl stepped over the line and paid the price. Since then, he's had to content himself with being a club owner without a liquor by the drink license, and a minor cult hero to a small legion of devoted fans.

And from the look of tonight's crowd, he was doing just fine, thank you very much.

I walked in the door about ten forty-five, which was just in time for the last set. A red-haired, freckle-faced country boy who looked strong enough to single-handedly lift the engine out of a GMC pickup collected my five-dollar cover and marked the back of my hand with a rubber stamp that read PAID in red ink. The big kid told me there might be a few empty places at the bar if I wanted to try sitting there.

"Otherwise, just pull yourself up a chair anyplace you can find one. Nobody's gonna mind if you just go ahead and set down with 'em." I nodded thanks and moved inside.

The Million Seller hadn't changed much in the three years since I'd last been there. It was a long, low-ceilinged building with a stage at one end and a bar at the other. In between were tables and chairs, and a small dance floor. Near the door was a souvenir counter with CDs by Earl Owens and his Poor Relations, and T-shirts, hats, beer mugs and bobbleheads imprinted with the name of the Million Seller. Between sets, the stuff was for sale at outrageously marked-up prices.

Tonight, the place was just short of full. The crowd was noisy and mostly young. Here and there were a few older, overdressed types who figured either to be tourists looking for a little local color or traveling salesmen out for a night of high jinks on the company's nickel.

I squeezed over to the bar, weaving among the tables to see if I could pick out Simon Eberle somewhere in the crowd. It was fairly obvious what I was doing if anybody was paying attention, but I doubted anyone was. Either way, it didn't accomplish anything except to finally land me at the bar. I found an empty stool in the corner where I could lean back against the wall and get a good view of the house, just in case. Just in case what? Just in case Simon walked in wearing a fruit salad hat on his head, that's what. It was about the only way I'd ever pick him out of this constantly moving sea of humanity.

One of the bartenders, a pretty young woman, caught sight of me and moved over to where I was sitting. "What'll it be?"

"What have you got on tap?"

"We got Bud."

"What about in a bottle?"

"Bud."

"Then I'll have a Bud. In a bottle."

She smiled. "Good choice."

In a moment, she was back with the bottle and set in front of me on a cardboard coaster. "Be four dollars. You need a glass?" I shook my head no and laid a five on the bar.

"I noticed you come in a minute ago," she said. "You look like you're looking for somebody."

I decided to lay my cards on the table. "Have you been working here all night?"

She looked at me with a mixture of suspicion and amusement. "Yeah, but I probably ought to warn you, this sounds like the beginning of something that's going to get you thrown out of here."

"It's nothing like that." I couldn't see any point in jerking her around with a made-up story, so I showed her the photo of Simon I had folded in my jacket pocket.

"I'm looking for this guy here. I was told he comes in here fairly often and that this might be a good place to look for him. I just thought you might have seen him earlier."

She looked at the photo. "Is he in some kind of trouble? Are you the police?"

"No trouble and no police, either." I took out my ID and license and laid them on the bar. "My name is Gamble. I'm a private investigator. The person I'm looking for is named Simon Eberle. He lit out from home a couple of days ago, and his family is getting nervous. They asked me to put eyes on him, just to make sure he's okay."

"That's it?"

"That's it. Just see he isn't in any trouble and report back."

I couldn't tell if she was doubtful or disappointed. "I don't know. It's kinda hard to say. He looks like half the guys here right now. If he came in earlier, I didn't notice. You want me to ask the other guys? Maybe Ray or Artie might have seen him."

"Thanks. I'd appreciate it."

The lady bartender nodded and moved away. I took another swallow of my beer and turned to watch the band tune up before starting the last set.

There were five musicians in all. Earl Owens played fiddle and did most of the singing. Backing him up as the Poor Relations was a cadaverous-looking girl wrestling with a bull fiddle twice her size, and an equally gaunt older woman who cradled a battered guitar. Behind them were two guys in Rhinestone Cowboy outfits. One played the banjo and the other a mandolin that looked as strange in his big hands as the bull fiddle did in the embrace of the tiny girl.

A few more twangs, and they were set to go. There was a moment of expectant silence, and then the band broke into a breakneck rendition of "Fox on the Run." With the first chords, the crowd jumped to its feet and began whistling and clapping in riotous approval. I had to blink twice to be sure it was really Earl up there on the stage and not Jimmie Rodgers back from the grave for one last encore.

They played a Jimmie song, "Mule Skinner Blues," and the Carter Family's "Wildwood Flower," and then Earl went into his storytelling routine. I'd heard it before. It hadn't changed much since the last time. This one was about growing up in the hills back in West Virginia. The band seemed bored, or maybe just embarrassed, but the crowd was eating it up. They especially liked the part about how Earl's family had been so poor they had nothing to keep them warm on a cold winter night except the love they had for one another, and the music they shared. I got a kick out of that part myself. I knew for a fact that Earl hailed from Little Rock, Arkansas, where his daddy earned a good living as a division superintendent for the Missouri Pacific Railroad. I doubted Earl could have located the West Virginia burg he claimed to be from on a map if you spotted him the name of the county and the number of the main highway through town.

"Something I can do for you, mister?" I looked up to see who was asking. It was one of the other bartenders, a smallish guy with an eighties-era, shoulder-length mullet and a drooping handlebar moustache. An unlit cigarette hung from the corner of his mouth, and he appeared to have a congenital squint, as if he had been staring at the world too long through a thick cloud of smoke.

"Maybe," I said, showing him the photo of Simon. "I'm looking for this guy. His name is Simon Eberle. Do you know him?"

"I know who he is. He ain't been in here tonight. What do you want with him?"

"Just to talk. He's been missing for a couple of days. His family is worried. They want to make sure he's all right."

"Well, he ain't been in here tonight so far as I know. Maybe just stick around for a while and see if he shows up. Sometimes he comes in late."

Something in the tone of his voice told me what needed to happen next. "You sound like you might know something about him." I took a twenty-dollar bill out of my wallet and placed it on the bar with two fingers over it. "What'd you say your name was?"

He stared at the twenty with interest. "Ray."

"Well, Ray, here's a double sawbuck for you if you can help me find Simon. Now, I hear he's got a girlfriend someplace he could be staying with. You know where I can find her this time of night?"

He gave me a quizzical look. "You sure he isn't in any kind of trouble?"

"If he were in trouble, you'd be talking to the cops. All I want to know is

115

where I can find him so I can tell his family he's okay."

He licked his lips nervously and glanced over his shoulder. Earl was about finished with his shtick, which meant the band would be starting up again. Then it would be too noisy to talk.

"I go on break in a couple minutes. Meet me out back over where the trash bins are, and I'll tell you what I can. I don't know how much help it'll be, though."

"I appreciate it just the same." I took my hand off the twenty and watched it disappear into his fist the way a dragonfly disappears into a hungry bullfrog. Ray walked back to the other end of the bar. Earl went back to playing music. I finished my beer, made a visit to the necessary room, and went outside.

Ray had picked a good spot if privacy was what he wanted. It was as dark as the inside of a black hat and hidden from the street by a high wooden fence with a gate that opened onto the alley behind. Next to the gate were two dumpsters which, at the moment, provided cover for a couple of howling and hissing cats that were either fighting over turf, or trying to consummate a romantic tryst. I stood there for what seemed like a lifetime as the band sawed its way through "California Zephyr," "Rocky Top" and Don Gibson's "Sweet Dreams." I was beginning to get nervous about Ray. I had just about made up my mind to go back and see what had become of him when somebody rounded the corner and started walking toward me.

It wasn't Ray. It was the big country boy who had taken my cover charge at the door. I went over to meet him.

I didn't like it. Something was wrong. I said, "What's up?"

"Not much." His eyes darted around as if he were looking for somebody else. "Customer come in just now and said there was somebody around back looked like he might be sick. Are you okay, mister?"

"I'm fine, thanks. I just wanted to get a little air."

He began to swivel his head around, as if he were looking for something he couldn't quite see. "Are you waitin' on Ray?"

"Yeah, he said he might have some information for me."

His eyes seemed to settle on something behind me. "That's him right over there."

I started to turn around and look. It was a beginner's mistake, but it was late, and I wasn't expecting trouble. The big guy reached out with his left hand and spun me around. With his right he hit me square in the middle of the stomach, hard enough to lift me completely off my feet. I staggered back toward the wall and slumped against it.

"Again," said Ray, stepping out of the shadows. "We don't want him gettin' away so easy as that." The big kid must have been having second thoughts, because nothing happened right away.

"I told you to hit him again," said Ray, and this time the big guy struck a sledgehammer blow to my chest, right above the heart. I sagged to my knees and doubled over, my forehead touching the ground. Between gasps for air, I heard Ray's reedy voice drifting down from above.

"He ain't lookin' so fine now, is he?" He giggled excitedly. "I told you he was gonna be sick. You feel sick now, don't you mister?"

I tried to say something, but all that came out was a ragged wheeze. I managed to get my arms under me and lifted myself up on all fours. That was another mistake, but then, this seemed to be my night to be making them. Ray, apparently having no qualms about kicking a man when he was down, did exactly that, booting me hard in the ribs and knocking me over again. For a little shit, he could kick like a mule.

"What's that? I couldn't quite hear you. Could you talk a little louder?"

Nausea washed over me like angry surf. A large foot stepped on my neck while a pair of hands patted me down, lifting my wallet and turning out my pockets. Seconds dragged by like hours, and then I heard Ray's voice again. It sounded like the hiss of a leaky radiator.

"Listen, mister asshole private detective, I knew your story was bullshit the minute you opened your mouth. And I know who that bitch is you're working for. Now I'm gonna tell you something, and I want you to hear me good. You come around here asking any more questions, you better bring a lotta help, 'cause you're gonna need it. You got that, asshole?"

He grabbed a handful of my hair and lifted my forehead off the ground. "I asked you if you got that."

I made another wheezing sound.

He slammed my head against the pavement and stood up. "Okay. Here's a little something just in case you get any ideas about changing your mind." He booted me again, one time in the ribs, and then stomped down hard between my shoulder blades.

"No extra charge," he laughed as two pairs of footsteps moved away.

I lay there on the damp ground for I don't know how long, drifting at the edge of consciousness. In the distance, somewhere above the clouds, it seemed, I heard voices singing about something called the Orange Blossom Special. Then merciful blackness overtook me, and I didn't hear anything more.

Chapter Seventeen

"You're free to go, Mr. Gamble," said the uniformed officer who unlocked my cell and handed me my watch, wallet, pocket change, and car keys. "Mr. Owens has declined to press charges."

I moved my head slightly to one side, causing a tremor of pain to rumble through my brain. "That was good of him," I said. "What was the beef, or have we already been over that?"

He consulted the clipboard he was carrying. "Drunk and disorderly. Assaulting a patron in a public establishment. Trespassing. Quite an evening you had yourself. You should be grateful those two bartenders stepped in before you got yourself into any real trouble."

"Words fail me," I said, and meant it.

"Funny." He handed me a pen. "Sign here. Says you've got all your possessions and that you have declined medical attention."

I signed. "Somebody want to tell me where my car is?"

"Impound lot, on Jefferson Street. You want me to call you a cab?"

Twelve dollars for the cab and seventy-five dollars towing and storage charges later, I was back in possession of the 'Bird, now missing both front hubcaps. I drove home accompanied by a splitting headache and a pain in my midsection that felt like my intestines had been removed and replaced by a coil of razor wire.

The cops had found me face down in the alley behind the Million Seller sometime around one in the morning. According to the arrest report, I had gotten into an argument with another customer at the bar, at which time I was politely asked to leave. Instead, I took a swing at one of the bartenders,

119

who then forcibly removed me from the premises. Nobody took the trouble to explain how I got from the front door to the alley, and nobody had any idea how I could have been drunk enough to pick a fight when my BAT indicated a blood-alcohol content of .0005.

Back at home, I showered and toweled off slowly, examining myself carefully as I went along. Despite the lick I'd taken to the midsection, I wasn't passing any blood, and except for bruises and plain old soreness, I didn't think I had suffered any serious damage.

I made a quick inventory of my coat and pants pockets. The contents of my wallet were all still there: credit cards, P. I. license, insurance card, carry permit, even the twenty-dollar bill I had used to try to bribe Ray. My jacket was in less salvageable condition. Only part of me wound up on dry pavement. The rest of me had come to rest in a puddle of evil-smelling water, which not only ruined my coat, but also dissolved into nothingness the gelatin capsule I had lifted from Simon Eberle's bathroom. That was the bad news.

The good news was that I had touched a nerve. Somebody had flinched and bumped the Eberle investigation off dead center.

I checked my watch: eight-fifteen. Too early to do anything about finding Simon, particularly in the shape I was in. I fell back down on the bed, intending to rest for another hour or so. When I woke up again, it was after noon, and the telephone was ringing. I checked the caller ID. It was Maggie.

"Miss me yet?" She sounded cheerful and excited when I picked up. It was the first time we'd spoken since she had taken off for Ohio.

"If you only knew," I said. She must have caught something in my voice, because she said, "You don't sound so good. Are you okay?"

"I'm fine," I lied. "I thought I'd take a shot at cleaning the gutters and slipped on the ladder."

"You're cleaning gutters in the middle of the summer?"

"What can I say? I'm OCD."

"Okay. Have you found, what's his name? Has he turned up yet?"

"Simon Eberle is his name, and no, I'm not even close. I don't think I've ever looked for anyone who seems to be as nowhere as this man. There's a term for it that I read once. *Spurlos verschwinden*, I think it is. It's German. Means lost without a trace. It's as if he just went into the ozone. I don't even know if he's alive or dead."

We talked for a few more minutes after that. Yes, she was enjoying her visit with her family. No, she hadn't decided whether to resume teaching, take the job with the counseling firm, or quit altogether. And, yes, she missed me. But we never quite got around to the only question I wanted to ask, which was, when are you coming back?

Three-quarters of an hour later, after we had hung up, I was dressed and out the door, on my way back to Jorie Flowers's apartment. I was determined to get a look inside, even if I couldn't speak to Jorie herself. I leaned long and hard on her door buzzer and got the same response as yesterday. At that, I should have counted myself fortunate. At least nobody came out into the hall to beat me up.

I walked back to the car and retrieved a pair of surgical gloves and a twelve-inch screwdriver from under the front seat. I put on the gloves and slipped the screwdriver into my belt. There were other, more elegant ways of breaking and entering, I knew, but most of them take time, and you have to know what you're doing. That routine you see on television with a lock pick seems pretty slick until you try it on a good lock. I'd gotten a look at the inside hardware yesterday. It was good enough to keep me picking for a week.

As I'd hoped, the back of the building was a different story. Each ground-floor unit had its own outside entrance and a small patio that could just about accommodate a couple of lawn chairs and a portable grill without any of them spilling over the edge. To provide a measure of privacy, or maybe just to make sure that nothing actually did fall off, each patio had been enclosed on two sides with a five-foot wooden privacy fence. It was a second-story man's dream. Short of an open door, or maybe no door at all, you couldn't ask for an easier setup for breaking in.

You could get it, though.

Somebody had already paid a visit to Jorie Flowers's apartment. Somebody who was even less fastidious about how he got in than I was planning to be, and who wasn't in the least worried about who knew it. The aluminum frame around the sliding door was bent and torn, as if the intruder had gnawed his way through to the lock. The latch mechanism was broken and scattered across both sides of the doorway. The door had been left open about eight inches. I slid it back and eased through the opening. Then I closed up behind me.

The first thing I noticed was that the apartment was almost unbearably cold. Somebody had turned the air conditioner on high, and with no lights on, and the drapes across the sliding door drawn, it couldn't have been more than fifty-eight or sixty degrees in the living room.

I got another surprise when I flipped on the overhead light. Jorie Flowers's apartment was a scene straight out of a disaster movie. It had been torn completely apart, trashed from top to bottom. Books, pictures, and knickknacks had been dumped off shelves and left in a pile where they fell. Vases and flowerpots were smashed. Furniture had been pulled away from the walls, the cushions and linings slit open. Even the cover plates had been unscrewed from the electrical outlets in the walls.

The kitchen was more of the same. Cabinets had been emptied of pots, pans and dishes, the refrigerator stood open, and the flour and sugar canisters had been dumped into the sink, where some overachieving ants were busily working on the leavings. Whoever had taken the place apart had gone to great pains to find whatever he was looking for.

It didn't seem possible for that someone to have been Simon Eberle. And yet, if not Simon, then who? And what was he looking for? I wondered what Jorie Flowers would think when she got home and found the mess. It also struck me odd that with all the mess left behind, nobody had apparently heard anything unusual taking place. It would take days to clean up, and who knew how much time and money to replace what had been damaged. Which made me wonder all over again: Where the hell was Jorie Flowers?

The answer to that wasn't long in coming. She was in the bedroom. She had been there the whole time I was looking around, and quite a lot longer than that. And she was far beyond the point of caring about what had happened to her apartment.

She was sitting on the floor. Her back was propped against the wall, her legs extended straight out in front of her. Her arms hung at oddly unnatural angles at her sides. The palms of her hands were upturned in a ghastly parody of the lotus position. Her fingers were bloated and discolored where the blood had settled. Her mouth hung slackly open, and her dark, dull eyes stared resolutely at nothing, or maybe at me. To Jorie Flowers, now, and in this place, it would be all the same.

She was wearing a short blue terrycloth robe and a pair of bikini underpants. Just at the point where the swell of her left breast began, there was an ugly purple wound, the size and kind made by a small caliber bullet. There were no signs of a struggle and practically no blood. She had almost certainly been dead before she hit the floor, shot through the heart.

I stood there for a long time, just looking at her. I don't know why. In life, she had been extraordinarily beautiful, a woman who could have aroused any man and who, to a near-recluse like Simon Eberle, must have seemed like nothing short of a walking miracle. Now, in death, she would never be anything except a memory to anybody, ever again.

There was nothing left to do, no point in spending any more time looking around. Whatever the killer had been searching for was almost certainly long gone by now. And even if it had still been there, I wouldn't have had the slightest idea what it was or how to recognize it.

I shivered involuntarily, and then I remembered that the air conditioner had been running full blast the entire time I had been standing there. I started to walk over and turn it off and then decided not to bother. I would be leaving directly, and I knew Jorie wouldn't mind whether it kept running or not.

Chapter Eighteen

An hour later, I was sitting in Richard Eberle's study in the same chair I had occupied the night we'd first met. He had been waiting for me. When I walked in, he was drumming his fingers impatiently on the arms of his chair. A glass of Jack, straight up, and an open decanter sat on the desk in front of him. He wasn't happy.

"Have a good flight?" I asked.

"I expected to hear from you first thing," he said, ignoring the question.

"First thing, I didn't have anything to tell you. Now I do."

"You've found Simon?"

"No."

"But you know where he is?"

I made a show of looking at my watch. "As of one o'clock this afternoon, I don't have the faintest idea where to even start looking."

He compressed his lips angrily. "Please don't play games with me, Mr. Gamble. That's not what I'm paying you for. Do you have something to tell me, or don't you?"

"Yes, sir, I've got something to tell you. Jorie Flowers is dead. She was shot through the heart, up close, with a small caliber bullet, most likely a .22, or maybe a .25. If I had to guess, I'd say it happened a couple of days ago."

He looked at me. "I'm sorry to hear that." He said it so smoothly that I was sure he already knew it. "If you haven't already guessed, I wasn't fond of her. I didn't think she was right for Simon. But, like her or not, life is too precious to lose prematurely."

"Good of you to say so. I'm sure she'd take comfort."

"However," he continued in a tone intended to convey that the matter was closed as far as he was concerned, "I'm afraid I don't see what her death has to do with finding my son."

"No? Really? Are you sure?" When all that got was a blank stare, I continued. "Then let me draw it out for you," I said, fighting an overpowering urge to jump on top of his desk and squeeze his head until it cracked like a walnut.

"Simon was seeing Jorie—has been seeing Jorie—apparently as recently as last Saturday night. Now Jorie is dead, and Simon is in the wind. Simon has a history of unstable, occasionally even violent behavior. Jorie has been shot dead, and Simon is in the wind. Is it beginning to make sense yet? Can you see where there might be a connection in all of this?"

He shook his head doggedly. "You're mistaken. Simon doesn't even own a gun."

"There's nothing that says a person has to own a gun in order to use one, Mr. Eberle."

He sat, thinking. "Have you told anyone else about this?"

"Not yet."

"Good man." He reached into his desk drawer and took out a plain white business envelope. With exaggerated casualness, he tossed it over to me.

"There's five thousand dollars says it stays that way."

I picked up the envelope and looked inside. There was a thick stack of bills, twenties and fifties, all used. I removed the money from the envelope and held it in my hand. It felt warm, heavy, and moist, as money like that always does.

"All I have to do is forget about Jorie Flowers, is that it?"

"That's it. And keep on looking for Simon, of course. When you find him, there'll be another envelope for you just like that one. What do you say?"

I looked at the money again. I riffled the edges of the bills with my thumb. I put them back into the envelope. I sighed. Then I tossed the money back on his desk.

"I think we're done here," I said.

He gave me a pained look, as if I were a slow student struggling to solve a simple equation. "Oh, come on, Mr. Gamble. I admit my proposition wasn't any too subtle, but I hope you aren't going to try to make me believe I've hurt your feelings."

"Not at all. I just don't like being played for a sucker."

"I'm sorry, Mr. Gamble. I don't know what you're talking about."

"Sure, you do. You know what I'm talking about even better than I do. I think you already knew Jorie Flowers was dead. You knew it even before you had Clarence Darrow call me. Otherwise, why call? And why have an envelope full of cash, all ready to go?"

"Since you already seem to know, I expect you're getting ready to tell me."

"It's like this. You wanted to be sure Jorie's apartment was one of the first places I'd go. That's why, of all the pictures of Simon you could have given me, you gave me one that showed the two of them together. Then, to make sure I'd take the bait, you gave me a song and dance about how she was just somebody Simon used to go out with, and not at all relevant to the case." I leaned back in my chair. "Come to think about it, it must have frustrated you no end that Jorie's apartment wasn't the first place I started looking."

"Interesting, if a bit farfetched. What makes you believe I'd want you to do that?"

"It's like this. You knew Simon and Jorie were still seeing one another. Close as you keep tabs on that boy, you could hardly have helped knowing it. That's why, when Simon disappeared, the first place you checked or had somebody else check, was Jorie's apartment."

He stared at me, expressionless.

"Was she dead when you got there, Mr. Eberle? Or was she killed because she wouldn't agree to stay away from Simon?" A sudden bit of enlightenment came to me.

"No, I'm wrong. I'll bet you didn't go there at all. You sent Walter to see if he could squeeze her. You thought either Simon had moved in with Jorie or else she knew where he was, didn't you? That's what all the theatrics the other night were about."

"If I'd done that, why would I need to hire you?"

"Good question. You needed me because you don't trust Walter to follow instructions. You never have, not since the time he cost you all that money on the land deal he torpedoed. You needed somebody to take another look at Jorie's apartment. First, because for all you knew, Walter might have killed her himself. Certainly, that's possible, although a small caliber handgun seems a little out of character for him.

"Second, you sent me because you needed to know whether there was any evidence to connect Simon to the killing. I just have one question. How could you be sure I wouldn't go straight to the cops after I found the body? Or did your Clarence Darrow tell you for five grand I'd roll over and let you scratch my belly any time you wanted?"

The barest smile tugged at the corners of his mouth. "As a matter of fact, he assured me your dealings could be relied upon to be completely above board. And discreet." He spread his hands as if to embrace the inevitable. "And here we are. What else can I say?"

"I'm here, all right, and I'm the soul of discretion. Only I'm not your problem. Walter is."

"Come again?"

It was my turn to smile. "When I went to the apartment, I found the back door practically torn out of the wall. That's not exactly subtle, wouldn't you say? When I got inside, I found Jorie dressed in a rather revealing bathrobe. Now you tell me, what woman is going to wait around half-naked for somebody to break down her door so he could get inside to shoot her?"

"I'm sorry, but this time you really have lost me, Mr. Gamble."

"The sequence of events is all wrong. Whoever broke into that apartment had to have done it after she was already dead. Otherwise, she would have heard the noise and simply run out into the hallway screaming her lungs out. But since she was already dead, and Walter couldn't be sure Simon hadn't killed her, he tore the place apart to make it look as if her death had resulted from a home invasion gone wrong. You do see that, don't you?"

He nodded, but he didn't appear convinced.

I said, "It had to be that way. Simon may or may not have killed her, but he had no reason to toss her apartment. If he needed to remove evidence of a crime, he'd have known what it was and where to look for it. He wouldn't have had to cut up the furniture to find it. That means somebody other than Simon was in that apartment.

"You know, if Walter had been a better burglar, you might have pulled this off. I probably would have come back here and told you that Jorie was dead, killed by a person or persons unknown. I might have suspected Simon, but again, what reason did he have to turn her place on end? Somebody else did that."

I shook my head. "You're supposed to be a smart man, Mr. Eberle, but I'm beginning to wonder. This is about the dumbest thing I've ever seen anybody do. You not only tightened the noose around Simon's neck, you also put one around your own, and Walter's, as well. You should have told him to leave things the way he found them and called the police right away. Now, they're going to see that everything is all wrong, and they're going to ask themselves the same questions I asked myself."

"In my experience, the police aren't that clever."

"They don't have to be clever. It isn't going to take them more than a couple of hours to connect Simon with this. They won't have the same head start I did, but there's at least one witness who can put Simon outside Jorie's door last Saturday evening. That, plus Simon's past history, will be enough for them to get a warrant. Then they'll be at your door, and after that they'll find Simon and lock him up so far back, he'll have to eat his meals with a slingshot."

Eberle was unmoved. "That assumes the police find him before you do. It also assumes they find out about Jorie at all. My understanding is that she has no family and very few acquaintances. She's just the sort of person who would up and leave town without anyone missing her."

He finished off the last of his drink and poured another two fingers from the decanter.

"Let me make you another offer, Mr. Gamble. One that I think you'll find more to your liking. Find some way to tidy this up, and I'll pay you fifty thousand dollars, plus you can keep the five here," he pushed the envelope on his desk toward me with a neatly manicured finger, "as a gesture of goodwill. Find my son before the police do, and I'll pay you another fifty thousand.

That's a hundred and five thousand dollars cash, unreported income, in addition to the retainer I've already sent you. You couldn't duplicate that in three years, working for it."

"Forget it," I said disgustedly. "This is murder, not a parking ticket. Nobody can fix this for you."

"What do you suggest I do, then? Turn my son in for a crime he didn't commit?"

I said, "The police will have to be notified there's been a killing. I'll take care of that. For the time being, we can let them draw their own conclusions. Think of it as a parting gift, because after that, I'm finished. I'm dropping the case. I'll mail your retainer back to you in the morning."

"What? No!" He looked suddenly stricken, like a man having a fatal heart attack. "You can't do that. Not after all this. Not after...."

"Not after a murder? Is that where we're going with this?" I said, "Mr. Eberle, you hired me to find your son. Up to now, I have not been able to do so, and to be honest, I'm not really interested in pursuing the investigation any further."

"But why? I don't understand."

"Two reasons. In the first place, you have been lying to me from the get-go. You gave me a song-and-dance about Jorie Flowers not being a part of Simon's life when, in fact, he's been seeing her right along." He started to say something, but I held up my hand to stop him.

"In the second place, I don't like you, sir, and frankly, your indifference not only to the murder of Jorie Flowers, but also your involvement, however indirect, in the death of a man named Peter Willingham offends me. You may never have even met him, but I believe your close personal friend Rebecca Karlson had him killed, and I believe she used the money you helped raise the other night to set up the hit. The only question is, did you know that's what she was planning to do before you so generously threw that get-together the other night?"

"All she told me was that he was blackmailing her, and that she needed money. I swear to you, I didn't know anything more than that. I certainly didn't know anyone was going to wind up dead."

"I said, "The hundred thousand she said she was going to give to Willing-ham? Where is it now? Did she give it back to you?"

All at once, he seemed smaller, as if he was being swallowed up by his big chair. "I didn't know anyone would be killed. Rebecca said she needed money to pay off an extortionist. We thought the fundraiser the other night would be a good way to take care of her problem. That way, nobody ever had to know the money would be used for anything other than campaign expenses."

"You mean it was a way to launder the money."

He sighed heavily. "What do you want, Mr. Gamble?"

I said, "Willingham was killed at the bus station. There's an old guy—a homeless guy named Hamburger—who lives at the station part of the time. Among other things, he's a CI for the cops, and he knows who I am. Eventually, whoever is investigating the Willingham killing will get around to talking to him. Hamburger saw me with Willingham right before he was shot, and it's very likely he'll point them in my direction. Once that happens, they'll lean on me, hard, and I might let something slip."

"About Jorie and Simon, you mean." It wasn't a question. "I'll ask you again, Mr. Gamble. What do you want?"

"I want to feed Rebecca Karlson to the cops for her part in the murder of Peter Willingham. I want you to help me do that."

He shook his head. "They'll be making right turns at NASCAR before I go up against that woman. You have no idea the power she wields."

"Then we're done here, Mr. Eberle." I got up to leave. "I'll return your check in tomorrow's mail.

I got about halfway to the door before Eberle said, "Mr. Gamble, wait. Please."

Chapter Nineteen

"Very well, Mr. Gamble. You win. I'll help you get what you want. But I must have your absolute assurance that you will do your best to find my son and that you will see to it that no harm comes to him."

I sat back down in my chair. "As long as we're clear. When I go after Rebecca Karlson and her idiot son for the killing of Peter Willingham, I want your absolute assurance that you will not interfere. You need to understand this. I am not going to allow those two to get away with murder."

When he didn't say anything, I said, "Do we have an agreement?"

He nodded reluctantly. "We do."

"Okay, then let's get back to cases. For the time being, the best thing we can do is find Simon and get him to surrender himself to the police for questioning. That way, at least he'll have a lawyer with him before he has a chance to say anything stupid."

His face fell. "Then does that mean you think Simon is guilty of murder?"

"I don't know. I'm as frustrated as you are. On the surface, all the evidence points that way, although I can't figure what his motive might have been."

"But this evidence. It's all circumstantial. You said yourself, Walter could just as easily have done it."

"Yeah, but why? If Walter killed Jorie Flowers, then she had to be alive when Walter went looking for Simon. Also, she would have had to be physically in her apartment for him to get at her."

"So?"

"So then, why would he have had to break in? It seems to me all he would have to do is just ring the doorbell. Since Simon had been seeing her for a while, then she must have been to your home at least a few times. That means she would have met Walter and Elaine on at least one of those occasions. If he knocked on her door, she would have opened it, and that would have been that. There was no reason for him to break in through her back door."

"Maybe she didn't want to talk to him. As you said, she knows who he is, and she probably knew why he was there."

"But that doesn't make any sense either. It's pretty clear that whoever killed Jorie Flowers was already in her apartment for some time before the shooting. And from the way she was dressed, I'd say she didn't think that person posed any threat to her."

Eberle licked his lips. "You admit, though, this is all just speculation. Nothing you've said changes the fact that he could have done it." He was intrigued with the idea, as if it was sounding better all the time. I could see the wheels turning as he mentally measured Walter for a nice, snug frame.

"There's another possibility we haven't considered," he went on. "What if Walter and Jorie were seeing one another on the side? They could have had a falling out. You see what a hothead he is. Maybe he just lost his temper and killed her."

"No. I saw the way Walter went after you. If Walter had killed her, he would have strangled her or broken her neck. No way Walter would kill somebody with a shitty little popgun like a .22. There isn't a shred of evidence to support anything like that."

"I'll bet you could find some if you tried."

"Sure, I could. Give me a couple of days, and I could find enough evidence to prove damn near anybody killed her. Including you."

"Is that a threat, Mr. Gamble?"

"No, I just wanted you to see where that line of thinking can lead. Look, we're wasting time here. Let's get back to Simon. Without saying he used it to kill Jorie, would it be possible for him to get a gun?"

"Not unless someone gave it to him or bought it for him. He has two suicide attempts and that one assault charge on his record. I don't think he could get past even a cursory background check."

"Okay, then, what about friends? Could he have gotten a gun from a friend? I'm thinking of a guy named Ray. Kind of a rat-faced hippie type, tends bar over at the Million Seller."

He looked at me as though he hadn't heard me right. "The Million Seller is not the kind of place I regularly go to expand my horizons, Mr. Gamble."

"That's not what I mean. Ray apparently knows who Simon is, so it's reasonable to assume Simon knows Ray." I omitted mentioning my own meeting with Ray the bartender the night before, as well as the plans I had for settling that score. "Under the circumstances, I thought you might have met him. Maybe he's been here at the house at one time or another?"

"I have to confess, I haven't met very many of my son's friends," he said. There was a note of sadness in his voice, as if he wished he could have been one of those friends. But the look in his eyes was eloquent testimony that he didn't have the slightest idea how to begin.

* * *

We sat quietly for a few minutes, each of us lost in his own thoughts. From the faraway look on Eberle's face, I couldn't tell where his were leading him. Perhaps to a time and place where things like murder didn't happen to the better families.

I broke the silence. "Maybe you could tell me about Jorie. How did Simon meet her?"

He stirred uneasily, like a man waking from a nightmare.

"Jorie worked for Simon's doctor. At the time, Simon was a regular patient."

"His doctor. We're talking about Doctor Frank Tabor?"

"Why, yes. How did you know that?"

I let the question pass. "How often was Simon seeing Doctor Tabor?"

"Twice a week. Sometimes oftener."

"And the pills upstairs, did Doctor Tabor prescribe those?"

"Yes."

"Do you know what they're for?"

"Some kind of tranquilizer. Clonidine, I believe. I try not to involve myself in that sort of thing."

"What sort of thing is that, Mr. Eberle?"

"The pills, Mr. Gamble, the pills." A note of evangelical fervor crept into his voice. "A person cannot go through life relying upon pills as a crutch to deal with every misfortune that comes his way. Look around, and everywhere you see life's harsh realities. Ignorance, poverty, failure, disappointment, you name it. It's out there. It always has been, and it always will be."

I waited.

"Don't you see?" he went on. "No number of pills, or alcohol, or meditation will make things better, and those who believe otherwise are fools. At some point, a person has got to face up to his problems and recognize them for what they are."

"Which are what?"

"Minor obstacles, nothing more. Minor obstacles to be faced and overcome. That takes clear vision and strength of character. That's why I never held with the pills. Pills can't solve anyone's problems."

"No. But sometimes, they can make the pain more bearable. I would think a man in your situation would know that."

"Elaine," he said darkly. "She shouldn't have told you."

"She wouldn't have if I hadn't asked. As it is, I don't know whether she's more worried about Simon or you."

He took another drink of his bourbon and sighed. "The doctors tell me I have three months to live, six at the outside. I don't want to spend that time defending my son from a murder charge or visiting him in some hellhole for the criminally insane."

"Then let's make sure we get this all out. Tell me about Jorie Flowers. What did she do for Doctor Tabor? Was she a clinician, or what?"

"Not that," he said, searching for the right descriptive term. "More like—like an office manager. She kept the appointment books, did the billing, handled the insurance forms, things like that. As far as I know, beyond basic CPR, she had no medical training at all."

"When did she and Simon begin seeing one another?"

"About a year ago. Maybe a little longer. As you surmised, Simon brought her home on a few occasions." He frowned at the recollection, as if the events had not been happy ones.

"So, they had been seeing one another right along. They didn't break up like you told me."

"No, although I didn't know that for a fact until a week or so ago."

"What happened then?"

"Simon started spending a lot of nights away from home. When I questioned him about it, he became evasive. I wasn't at all satisfied with his explanation, so I had him followed."

"Who did the following?"

"One of your competitors. He wasn't particularly smooth, but I expect Simon didn't pay much attention."

"Love is blind. Where did your man follow them?"

"Back to her apartment, mostly. The important thing is that they were together, not where they went."

I wondered whether the point was worth pressing. "What made you think Simon had stopped seeing Jorie in the first place?"

He brushed at an invisible spot of lint on his sleeve. Because I asked him to."

"Just like that?"

"Just like that," he said flatly.

"And that was because you weren't, what was it? You weren't fond of her?"

"That's right."

"You mind telling me why?"

He looked as if he minded very much. "It's hard to explain."

"Try anyway. Nothing else seems to be getting us anywhere."

"Well, when Simon first started seeing Jorie, I wasn't concerned. After all, we've been hoping that Simon would eventually be able to function like anyone else. As a matter of fact, it occurred to me at the time that she might be a good companion for him, since she was familiar with his problems and might be more understanding of his needs."

"His needs?"

"For a relationship free of undue stress. Simon does not respond well to any kind of pressure. I thought, since she worked with his doctor, she might understand that."

"Didn't she?"

"Oh, I suppose she did. They got along well enough, and even I would have to admit that she had a certain physical charm."

"Then what was the problem?"

"Mr. Gamble, do you have any idea how much money a person earns working in a doctor's office?"

I didn't, but I tossed out a figure anyway.

"That's generous, but let's accept what you say for the sake of discussion. The fact is, the amount you've suggested wouldn't even pay for the clothes that young woman wore. I'm no expert on women's clothing, but I can tell you, Elaine is. She noticed the same thing I did, although she probably didn't attach the same significance to it."

"Her clothes were too expensive," I said.

"That's right. Here we have a woman working in a low-paying occupation who is nevertheless able to dress very well. From what your predecessor was able to find out, she had a pretty nice car, too. Now I ask you, Mr. Gamble, as any reasonable person would, exactly where was her money coming from?"

"Maybe she was just frugal," I suggested, without really believing it myself. "Maybe she was willing to give up other things to have nice clothes and a new car. I've known people to go without eating lunch for weeks at a time to pay for something they wanted badly enough." I threw up my hands in frustration.

"Hell, I don't know where her money came from. Maybe the good doctor was knocking a little off on the side and slipping her something extra for that."

"Well, I did a little checking."

"And why doesn't that surprise me?"

He plowed straight ahead, as if he hadn't heard me at all.

"I've got a few friends in the banking business, friends I asked to make an inquiry or two. Turned out, Jorie had only one checking account, which never had more than a few hundred dollars in it at any one time. She had no charge cards except for a single Visa, which she rarely used. Her car was paid for. In fact, she paid cash for almost everything she did. And yet, as far as anyone can determine, except for sources such as you have already suggested, there was no way she could have gotten her hands on any cash at all. Now, what do you make of that, Mr. Gamble?"

I had to admit there wasn't too much I could make of it, except that it didn't look very good. "And that's why you told Simon to quit seeing her?"

"Asked him," he corrected.

"Asked him, then. Is that the reason?"

"That, yes. And other things. Jorie had been married and divorced once, and she hadn't mentioned it to anybody. Simon didn't know it, I'm sure. But if she'd try to cover up something like that, who knows what else she was covering up? I just didn't like the looks of things."

"Then Flowers was her married name?"

"No, it was Raymond. She was married to a fellow named Jeremiah, or Gerald, or Jerome. Something or other like that. I forget. We never did quite turn him up, though. Word had it he'd left Nashville some months earlier."

"Just out of curiosity, did you get that on your own, or did you have somebody check it for you?"

"Somebody checked. The detective I mentioned earlier. A fellow named Opperman. Do you know him?"

I did, well enough to make me wonder whether anything Eberle had been telling me was even close to being right. "So, you got this information and decided that Simon shouldn't be seeing any more of Jorie. What did he say when you told him that?"

"Not what you'd expect. Not what I expected, anyway. I thought he would give me an argument, but instead, he heard me out and agreed to do as I'd asked. I reckoned that was the end of it. I can see now all he did was get a little more circumspect about his comings and goings."

"Did you ever confront Jorie directly with any of this?"

He shook his head. "There was no reason to."

I was beginning to wonder whether I was ever going to get a straight answer. "Mr. Eberle, what was the purpose of Simon's visits to Doctor

Tabor?"

"He was using regression therapy—hypnosis—to get at the root of these fits of depression Simon keeps having."

"You said Tabor was also prescribing Clonidine. Clonidine is used to treat PTSD. Why would Simon need that?"

I noticed his hands beginning to shake. "It's hard to explain. You have to understand, the problem is a very complicated one."

"Elaine doesn't think so. She says it's got to do with your second wife's suicide."

He stiffened. "She had no right telling you that."

"Elaine told me Simon was in the room when your wife shot herself. She thinks the shock of that is the cause of his condition. I mean, seeing someone, let alone your own stepmother, commit suicide, that's pretty traumatic, wouldn't you say?"

"It's not what Elaine thinks, it's what Doctor Tabor thinks. His opinion is that Simon believes he's responsible not only for Alicia's suicide, but also for the death of his birth mother. That somehow the two are linked." He let his eyes drift toward a spot on the ceiling. "Are these questions absolutely necessary? This is all very painful for me."

"I don't know what's necessary. What's your take on Dr. Tabor's theory?"

"I'm not sure I have one. Obviously, Simon didn't kill his mother or his stepmother. On the other hand, what he made of them in his own mind is anybody's guess." He sighed. "I didn't want to get into this, but I expect it's best now you hear the whole story from me.

"Elaine may have already told you this, but my first wife died as a result of complications with Simon's delivery. I loved her very much, and for the longest time, I didn't even want to think about getting married again. When I finally did, it was out of concern for the well-being of my children. You need to understand that."

"Does it really matter anymore?"

"To me, it does. I did what I did for Simon and Elaine."

"You mean you had to do it because Elaine was getting ready to leave for college, and you were about to lose your babysitter."

"She didn't leave. I practically had to throw her out. As I already explained, it was sometime after my wife's death before I remarried. During that time, I didn't do much except work. Maybe I needed an outlet. I just don't know anymore. It wasn't a very happy time for any of us.

"In any case, I neglected Elaine and Simon badly. That's why Elaine claims she was the one who raised her brother. In a way, she did, but that's not to say she didn't have help. There was Odell, of course, and what seemed like a whole succession of nurses and housekeepers. But Elaine felt responsible for being the woman of the house, and I expect I just let her do it.

"Now, please don't misconstrue my meaning. I'm not talking about anything improper. I'm only saying that I leaned on Elaine pretty heavily to run the household, especially when she got a little older. I just didn't realize that for a young girl, there are limits. She had very few friends and participated in almost no school activities.

"Eventually, she became embittered. She saw others at school doing things she should have been doing, except that, in her own mind, she felt she couldn't. Finally, I saw what was happening, but not before it became clear that Elaine was one desperate little girl. So much so that she began to take her anger out on Simon."

"Take it out how?"

He twisted his face into a look of disgust. "I don't see where graphic descriptions are necessary. She abused him physically and psychologically. I won't say anything more than that."

"Well, then tell me this. Is it possible Elaine gave Simon the idea that he was the cause of his mother's death? Or the death of his stepmother?"

"That's a nasty notion, Mr. Gamble."

"But is it possible?"

"Maybe, but what's the point? Eventually, I realized that the anger Elaine was projecting at Simon was actually meant for me. That's when I knew I no longer had any choice in the matter."

"So, you went to town and came home with a wife."

"Yes, and as it often happens, bad luck was followed by worse. The marriage was a disaster. Alicia loved the children, and they took to her,

139

right away. But she needed a husband, too, and thought she was getting one. The Good Lord knows I tried, but I never was able to develop any real feelings for her.

"Alicia always had trouble sleeping and so relied heavily on medication to get her rest. But then she started drinking, especially nights I was on the road. One night, nobody knows why she took her own life. The sheriff telephoned me in Memphis with the news. I can tell you, sir, it was an awful shock. I didn't even know she owned a gun."

"Lots of people seem to have guns you don't know about. What happened to this one?"

"I have it here."

On a hunch, I said, "May I see it?"

"I don't see why not." He spun around in his chair and opened a drawer in the wall unit behind him. There was a moment of silence, and then he said faintly, "It's not here."

"Are you sure?"

"Look for yourself. It's been in that same drawer for the past twenty years. Nobody has ever touched it."

I was pretty sure I already knew the answer, but I asked anyway. "What kind of a gun was it?"

"A .22 revolver, a small one with an ivory handle." A stricken look crossed his face. "You said that you thought Jorie Flowers might have been shot with a .22. Do you think whoever killed her used this one?"

"You tell me. Is the drawer kept locked?"

"Never any reason to. No one went in there."

"It didn't walk away by itself," I said. "Who else knew you had it?"

"I don't know. Up until now, I would have said no one." He sagged in his seat like a punch-drunk fighter.

"What are we going to do now, Mr. Gamble?"

I was damned if I had an answer and said so.

Chapter Twenty

I left Eberle alone with his thoughts and drove into town to get something to eat and make a telephone call. Springdale was too small and likely too particular about its image to have something as pedestrian as a McDonald's, so I ended up settling for a diner on East Church Street. It was past normal lunchtime for working folks, so the place was devoid of customers except for a tired-looking housewife and her brood of hyperactive kids. She was thumbing through a *True Romance* magazine and trying her best to pretend that her kids belonged to somebody else as they crawled around the unoccupied booths playing hide and seek.

I got a dollar's worth of quarters from the cashier and fed three of them into the pay phone. I thought that might be a better choice than using my cell, since I knew the cops kept a record of incoming calls. I dialed the Metro Police Department's Central District and waited four rings for an officer named Wheeler to answer.

"I want to report a burglary," I told him.

"Where at?"

"Castle Gate Apartments, second unit on the left as you drive in. I think the apartment number is 107."

"Is this your residence, sir?"

"No."

"Is the intruder there now?"

"I don't think so."

"Well, did you actually see or hear anyone break in?"

"No."

"Then what makes you think there's been a burglary?"

"Because," I said, my reservoir of community spirit spent, "the goddamn door in the back is standing wide open, and when I looked inside, the place was all torn up. You interested in any of this, or should I try the fire department instead?"

"No, sir, we'll send a car over to check it out. Can I have your name, please?"

"Nah, I don't want to get involved," I said and hung up.

I ate a quick early supper and then walked back to my car. I was settled in behind the wheel with my seat belt buckled before it hit me that I didn't have the haziest idea what I should be doing next. The only real lead I had was Ray, the friendly bartender, and I couldn't do anything about him for another couple of hours, until the Million Seller opened. Other than that, zip. It was like looking for a white rabbit in a snowstorm. Simon was out there somewhere, but until he did something to call attention to himself, there wasn't much way other than dumb luck anybody was going to find him.

Worse, talking to the Eberle family was like pushing a string. In half a dozen separate conversations, I had gotten lots of facts—some of them contradictory—and almost no useful information. It was as if after living together for thirty-some-odd years, none of them had managed to learn anything of substance about any of the others. Either they were all going around lost in their own private fogbanks, or they were conspiring in a slick bit of theatre designed to keep me running in circles until I dropped from exhaustion. For the life of me, though, I couldn't see the point in that. Simon was gone, that was sure. And I was convinced more than ever that unless we got a quick break, he wasn't going to be coming through the front door any time soon.

I was pulling away from the curb when I caught sight in the mirror of a car coming up behind me that I had last seen parked at the Eberle home the first night I was there. I waited until the dove-gray Mercedes-Benz SUV rolled past, and glimpsed Walter Murdock at the wheel. He was alone. He kept his eyes dead ahead as he drove by. He gave no indication that he had seen me.

I let a few more cars go by before pulling into traffic behind him. For all I knew, he was going to the hardware store to pick up a pound of nails, but I figured following him was better than doing nothing. Up to now, the only thing I'd done to earn my fee was get the hell beaten out of me. I hated to think it was the best I could do.

Murdock drove south along Route 231 until he was nearly out of town. Then he made a left on Route 62 and headed east toward the Interstate. I followed, about a quarter mile back. The idea was to keep him in sight while remaining as inconspicuous as possible—a tall order considering I was driving a half-century-old car that was about as inconspicuous as a Jefferson Davis Day parade float.

The sun was beaming down warmly, making for a nice afternoon to be driving through the country. I was beginning not to care where Murdock was going. He did, though, because once we got clear of Springdale, he began to accelerate until he was rolling along at better than eighty. On the curving secondary highway, he was a lot better outfitted than I was for high-speed touring, and I had to flog the Thunderbird hard to keep from losing him altogether.

We flew along like that for nearly twenty miles, as horse farms and stands selling Georgia peaches and shelled pecans receded into the distance at a frightening rate in the rear-view mirror. Finally, just outside a tank town called Manchester, I saw Murdock's brake lights flash, and the amber turn indicator signal a right turn. I kept going as Walter pulled into the unpaved parking lot of a hole-in-the-wall roadside tavern. The weather-beaten sign outside announced to the world that this was the Kountry Kuzzin Bar and Grill.

I drove down the highway another half mile or so until I found a driveway entrance where I could turn around. Then I headed back to the Kountry Kuzzin. By the time I got there, Murdock had already disappeared inside.

There were three other cars in the lot besides Murdock's and my own: a battered, two-decade-old Mercury Mariner, a four-door Toyota pickup, and a Chevrolet Impala of late-1990s vintage that was tricked out like a hot rod with chrome wheels, side exhausts, and eye-popping red metal-flake paint. I found a spot in the corner of the lot where I could see the other cars, shut off my engine, and sat back to wait for something to happen.

Maybe I sat there fifteen minutes, maybe longer. During that time, two guys in mud-streaked softball uniforms rolled up in a Dodge pickup the size of a locomotive. As they went in, the guy with the hot rod Chevy came out. He was dressed as though he'd just stepped off the set of *Grease*, in tight-fitting blue jeans, dirty T-shirt, and long blond hair that was slicked into an outrageous conk. He fired up the Chevy and blasted off with an impressive display of automotive acrobatics that scattered dust and pea gravel in its wake. I could hear him for a mile down the highway, burning rubber on his way back to Springdale.

I checked my watch. It was after five, starting to feel like a long day. The aches and pains, I'd been holding at bay with extra-strength Tylenol since my beat-down behind the Million Seller were coming back with a vengeance, and I shifted uncomfortably in my seat. Another five minutes, I told myself. After that, Murdock would have to get drunk all by himself. I still wasn't sure why I'd followed him, except that I hadn't had anything else to do.

And then everything changed.

At the moment I finally decided that enough was enough, that it was time to get back to work, my work got back to me. The two softball players came back out, carrying a six-pack each, and right behind them came a guy wearing a face I had last seen behind the Million Seller Lounge eighteen hours before. It was my old friend Ray, the bartender. Ray, the tough guy. Ray, the terror of day-rate detectives.

Ray, the guy who spent his afternoons in flytrap taverns where Walter Murdock hung out. Conclusions clicked into place inside my head like wheels in a slot machine. Except the cherries didn't line up quite the way they should have.

If they had, I wouldn't have sat there and watched Ray climb into his crapwagon Mercury. I wouldn't have played a hunch and let him drive off. If I hadn't done that, I could have followed him and prevented one more death, maybe two. But that's not what I did. Instead, I reached into the glove compartment, got out a sixteen-ounce leather sap, and dropped it into my coat pocket. Then I got out of my car and went to look for Walter Murdock.

Chapter Twenty-One

T he Kountry Kuzzin was pretty much what you might expect. There was a bar fronted by bar stools and a pass-through section for customers, or maybe a waitress, to pick up food orders. Behind the bar was a metal rack where cellophane bags of potato chips, pretzels, and "cracklins" were hanging in neat columns. There was also a dark-tinted mirror framed with colored lights that alternately blinked and then chased back and forth around the perimeter of the mirror. There were booths and tables, a jukebox, a dartboard and a couple of pinball machines. There was a pool table covered in orange, rather than green, felt. A flat-screen television tuned to some ESPN sports talkshow hung on one wall. A collection of stuffed and mounted fish and deer heads hung on another. I stepped inside and waited for a moment while my eyes adjusted to the semi-darkness. Then I spotted Walter. He wasn't hard to find. A guy like Walter Murdock never is, no matter where he goes. In a redneck dump like the Kountry Kuzzin, he stuck out like a rabbi in an Alabama whorehouse.

He was hunkered in a booth, all the way in back, with his back to the door. His big hands were wrapped around a half-empty highball glass. His head was bowed, like a man absorbed in thought, or maybe in prayer. I walked over and slid into the seat across from him.

He looked up and stared at me blankly. Then recognition came to him, and his face twisted into its accustomed scowl.

"What the hell do you want?"

"Strange as it may seem, I want to help you."

He made a sound like a harsh bark. "It'll be a cold day in hell before I want any help from you, Gamble."

"You may not want it, Walter, but before the day is over, you're going to need it. Unless I miss my guess, you're also going to need a lawyer. And an alibi."

While we were talking, the bartender appeared next to the booth. He had an order pad in his hand and an expectant look on his face. I smiled and said, "Bring me a bottle of whatever beer you've got that's coldest and a menu, if you've got one. My friend here will have a Dr. Pepper."

"I'm not having anything," Murdock growled. "I'm leaving."

"You're staying," I contradicted.

Murdock leaned across the table. "I guess you're gonna make me stay? I thought we already talked about what would happen the next time I saw you."

I gathered the looped end of the sap around my wrist and banged the business end on the table, hard. The impact made Murdock's glass jump like a startled bullfrog, spilling what was left of his whiskey in the process.

"I brought a friend," I said.

His body shifted slightly, as if he were getting ready to make a move. I said softly, "Walter, you're a big guy, and probably pretty tough, but so help me, if you even twitch, I will rap you so hard, by the time you come around, your clothes will be out of style."

The bartender's eyes got bigger than my missing hubcaps. He stayed glued to the spot where he was standing and kept his hands in plain sight. I couldn't blame him. In a place like this, he likely would have seen enough Saturday night bar fights to figure the next thing to make an appearance would be somebody's Smith & Wesson.

"Hey, now, y'all, we don't want no rough stuff in here. Y'all want to mix it up, take it on outside."

"There isn't going to be any rough stuff," I said. "You just run along and fetch that order I gave you, and don't worry about a thing. My friend and I are going to sit here and have a quiet talk."

He moved back toward the bar but didn't turn his back until he was a good three steps out of my reach.

Murdock curled his lip. "You know, you talk real brave. You should use that act on my wife. She likes when you get rough. Or maybe you already know that."

I skipped past the answer I wanted to give him. "You and Ray have a nice visit?"

"Who's Ray?"

"I figured you could tell me."

"I don't have anything to say to you. You've brought nothing but trouble from the minute you walked into our lives."

"Yeah, but I was invited, remember?"

The bartender brought over the drinks and the menu. While I looked it over, he kept a wary eye on Murdock and me, trying to decide how close it was safe to stand. I ordered a short slab of ribs with fries on the side. He took the order and the menu and hot-footed it back to his post.

"You're about to find out what real trouble is, Walter," I said, picking up the conversation where we'd left off. "The likelihood is, you're going to be talking to homicide detectives before the day is over, and I can tell you, they aren't nearly as easy to get along with as I am."

"What would they want to talk to me about?" I almost laughed out loud at that. It was a half-assed bluff, and we both knew it.

I said, "You know what about. Jorie Flowers. She's dead, but then, you don't need me to tell you that do you?"

"That's got nothing to do with me."

"So, then you do know."

"What if I do? That's still got nothing to do with me."

"It's got everything to do with you, Walter, and unfortunately, Richard Eberle thinks so, too. As a matter of fact," I added blandly, taking a drink of my beer, "he's sitting home right now cooking up a story that's going to make it look like it was you that killed her."

"That's not true!" he said hotly. She was already—"

He caught himself as the bartender looked nervously up from the pitcher he was wiping.

"Easy now, Walter," I said gently. "You'd do well to get hold of that temper of yours, and I'd suggest you do it quickly. I'm telling you the truth now, and the truth is, you are up to your eyeballs in Jorie's murder. Don't make things any worse by doing something stupid."

"Richard can't make a story like that stick. Where would he get the idea that I killed anybody?"

"I gave it to him."

"You gave—what did you do that for?"

"I wanted to see how he'd react."

"You sure found out, all right," he said sourly.

"As a matter of fact, I did. He acted just like a man who hadn't thought of it on his own. That means you probably didn't do it, and he knows it."

"Then why would he say I did?"

"He wants to throw suspicion away from Simon. Put yourself in his place, Walter. What would you do? Simon is his son. You're . . . well, he's already made it clear how he feels about you." I said, "Look, maybe I can help you, maybe I can't. But if you want help, you're going to have to give me some straight answers right now. Otherwise, I'm out the door, and you're on your own."

He thought about that. "I guess you figure you've got me," he said slowly.

"I'm not interested in getting anybody, Walter. I know you didn't kill Jorie, and I also know when you went into her apartment, you were just trying to make it look like a home invasion gone wrong. My only goal right now is to keep you and Simon both as far away from this as I can, but for me to do that, I'm going to need your help."

He wiped his mouth with the back of his hand and took an unhappy swallow of his soft drink. "All right, what do you want to know?"

"Well, for starters, who's this guy Ray? And what's your connection with him?"

"His name isn't Ray. That's just what he calls himself. His name is Raymond. Jerry Raymond."

"Raymond?" The connection hit me like a slap in the face. "So, did he say his name was Jerry or Jeremiah?"

"He said Jerry, but I guess it could be Jeremiah," Murdock answered, picking up on the sudden uptick in my interest. "Why, what's the matter?"

"Maybe everything," I said, trying to fit this new piece of information into the picture that was suddenly starting to take shape. "How much do you know about this guy?"

"Not a damn thing. I never even heard of him until yesterday afternoon. He called the house after you left. He said he had some information for me."

"He asked for you by name?"

"He didn't have to. I answered the phone. He wanted to talk to Elaine, but she was—she couldn't come to the phone." He looked at me with embarrassment. "He told me, well, then, he'd just have to deal with me. He said I needed to meet him here this afternoon, and he'd let me know what he wanted."

"Let me guess. He knows something, and he wants money, or he tells the police what he knows about Simon and Jorie."

"That's right. He wants a hundred thousand dollars." He stared dumbly at his hands, as if he had just let an easy interception slip through them.

"He said that he had evidence that could tie Simon to Jorie's death. If I didn't pay him, he'd turn it over to the police. He said it would land Simon on death row."

"And you figured if you could pay him off and get the heat off Simon, it would make you a hero to Elaine and her father."

He nodded miserably. "Something like that."

"Did he tell you what kind of proof he had?"

"No."

"But you did ask him?"

"Of course, I asked. What do you think, I'm stupid?"

"If you're planning to pay him any money, then yeah, I think you are. No matter what Raymond told you, once the cops find Jorie's body, they're going to be all over the Eberle family like crows on roadkill."

His expression was one of pure misery. "I couldn't pay him that much if I wanted to. I haven't got a hundred thousand in cash. I told him I'd need some time to raise it."

"What did he say to that?"

"He laughed. He called me small-time." The memory of that made his face screw up all over again.

"Come on, Walter, he must have said more than that. Don't make me drag every word out of you."

"He told me he'd give me until noon day after tomorrow. After that, he was going to the police. I should have torn him apart while I had him here, that cheap little bastard."

"Now, you're thinking. That would have gotten Simon home and brought Jorie back to life, all at the same time." I took a swallow of my beer. "What are you supposed to do, call him?"

"I gave him my cell. He's going to call me."

I thought about that. "Okay then, here's what I want you to do. And remember, you're not doing this for Richard or even for Simon. You're doing it for you, and for your wife, if that makes any difference to you. By the way, how much have you told Elaine about all this?"

"Nothing at all."

"Well, you'd better tell her now."

"All of it?"

I nodded. "Every word. I want you to go home and stay there. And for God's sake, talk to Elaine. It's important now that she understands what's going on."

"All right."

I looked at him, hard.

"Damn it, I said I'd do it."

"Make sure you do. And stick with the Dr Pepper, will you? I may need you on short notice, and you won't be any use to anybody if we have to dry you out first."

"What are you going to do?"

"What I've been doing right along. Keep on looking for Simon. Raymond thinks he's got things going his way, so he won't be making any more moves until tomorrow morning. Meantime, I've got one or two leads of my own I need to follow up."

"What should I do when he calls?"

151

"Keep it short. Tell him you've got the money, and that you want him to meet with me to make the exchange. Remember that. He meets with me, not you, or there's no deal. After you talk to him, call me right away. If I don't pick up right away, leave a message, and I'll get back to you within half an hour."

"Yeah, well, there might be a problem before that." He looked at me uncertainly. "What am I going to do about the money? What I told him? I was just stalling for time. It'll take at least three or four days to raise that much cash."

"Then I'll get it," I said, remembering the envelope in Richard Eberle's desk drawer, which was almost certainly part of the same money he had raised for Rebecca Karlson.

"You're going to get it from Richard?"

"Do you have a better idea?"

"No. Only let me talk to him, will you?"

"All right, but whatever you do, don't get into a fight with him before he gives you the money. The main thing is still to find Simon. Until that's done, we don't have a thing."

He sat, thinking. "Did Simon kill her?"

"I don't know. The evidence points that way, but somehow, he just doesn't seem like the type."

"Listen, Gamble," he said with sudden firmness. "Whatever goes down tomorrow, I want to be there."

"I'm not sure that's such a good idea. You're liable to get wound up and kill him before we get what we came for."

He shook his head stubbornly. "If I don't go, nobody goes. I've got to try to put things right. Remember, it's me he's going to call."

"All right, suit yourself," I said, figuring I'd find a way to give him the slip when the time came. "Now, go home and talk to Elaine. And stay cool. If you want to be a hero, this is your chance."

He started to get up. "What if the cops come nosing around?"

"They won't. Not yet, anyway. They don't know Jorie's dead, although they ought to be finding out right about now. But it's going to take them a while to figure out where to start looking for leads. By that time, we should have this wrapped up one way or the other. Besides, Richard still has a fair amount of influence hereabouts. I expect they'll tread easy around him until they're sure they've got a case."

He nodded his head and extracted himself laboriously from the booth. "I hope to hell you know what you're doing."

So do I, I thought. But I kept my mouth shut and watched him walk outside into the gathering darkness of a soft summer evening.

Chapter Twenty-Two

After I got home, I parked myself on the couch with a bag of potato chips and a bottle of Stella and thought about the connection between Jorie Flowers and Jerry Raymond, and what it meant to the Eberle case. It occurred to me that, if Maggie were with me, she might be able to help me put the random facts I had rattling around in my head into some recognizable order. But then, she was five hundred miles away, in Mansfield, Ohio, enjoying a visit with her family. Idly, I wondered whether Stanley was getting along any better with them than he did with me.

Returning to the problem at hand, I considered the possibility that Jorie's death was the result of a quarrel with her ex-husband. But over what? Simon Eberle? If that were the case, then it seemed more likely that Raymond would have also killed Simon. That, at least, would explain why I was having so much trouble developing any leads. It also meant that what had started out as a simple missing person investigation had now turned into a double homicide. But then, where was Simon's body?

On the other hand, it was also possible that Simon's friendship with Jorie and his acquaintance with Ray were two separate things, and nothing more than a coincidence arising from his fondness for bluegrass music and attractive women. For all anybody knew, maybe Jorie had introduced Simon to Ray, just so Simon would have a drinking buddy to hang with at the Million Seller. The problem with that explanation was that it posed more questions than it answered.

For one thing, it still left Simon as the prime suspect in the killing of Jorie Flowers. For another, it didn't explain what Ray was so nervous about that

154

he thought it was necessary to try to scare me off with a beat-down. It seemed likely that he had known at the time that Jorie was dead. He also knew, or at least thought he could convince the Eberle family, that Simon had had something to do with the murder.

The next morning, I was still trying to come up with a plausible theory when I suddenly remembered something else that I had been wondering about since I had first heard it. I had a little time to spare, so before I went back to the office, I drove over to the Nashville *Times* building, at the corner of Eleventh and Broad. Ten minutes later, I was squinting into a computer screen in the newspaper's morgue.

It took about an hour, but I finally found what I was looking for. There were two of them. The more recent was dated July 25, 1999. It read:

EBERLE, Alicia Marie (Martingale), nee Lawler, suddenly July 23. Beloved wife, loving mother, devoted sister, past president of the Springdale Cancer Society, member in good standing of the Daughters of the Confederacy. In lieu of flowers, donations to Cancer Society requested. Graveside service for family members only.

The second one was dated April 14, 1995:

EBERLE, Clara Elaine, nee Bridges, Saturday, after a brief illness. Beloved wife, loving mother and sister, aunt of many nieces and nephews, member of the Order of the Eastern Star. Visitation will be Friday at Springdale Funeral Chapel, interment Saturday at All Saints Mausoleum.

I printed out the information, such as it was, and stuck it into my pocket. Then I went off to track down Jerry Raymond.

* * *

Like a cut-rate hooker the morning after, the Million Seller was considerably less appealing in daylight than it was after the sun went down. Without the band, the noise, the crowd, and the colored lights, the place seemed old and tired. It also looked more than a little past due for a visit from a county health inspector.

I got there about two hours before opening time. I figured that would give me enough time to do what I had to. There was business that needed to be taken care of in private, and I didn't want to have to be stepping around a crowd of music lovers in case things got out of hand.

When I walked through the door, I spotted the petite brunette I had spoken with the night before working behind the bar, up to her elbows in a sink full of soapy water. She smiled in recognition when she saw me coming.

"Kind of a rough night for you the last time you were in, wasn't it?"

"It got a little bumpy toward the end, yeah."

"That's what they tell me." She put the pitcher she had been rinsing into a dish drainer and wiped her hands on a bar towel. "Let me see if I can guess. Today, you're looking for a sexually liberated, brown-eyed divorcee who's working her way through college tending bar and who gets off tonight right after the eleven o'clock set."

"You know anybody who fits that description?"

"One or two, maybe," she said. "So, were you ever able to hook up with that guy you were looking for?"

"Not so far. Have you seen him?"

"Sorry. The brown-eyed bartender is the best I can do."

"It's a tempting idea," I said. "Right now, though, I need to talk to Ray for a few minutes. Is he around?"

She put down the mug she was wiping and looked at me as if she were seeing me for the first time. "Is there a problem?"

"Why would you think that?"

"Because Ray should have been here an hour ago, and now you show up asking questions." Her brow furrowed suspiciously. "You wouldn't be a cop, would you?"

"It's the question on everybody's mind," I said. I took out my wallet and flipped it open on the bar in front of her. She eyeballed my I.D. and license before pushing it back to me.

"I get it. You're working for Earl, right?"

"Who told you that?"

"Nobody has to tell me anything." An errant strand of hair fell across her face. She gave her head a toss to one side to flip it back where it belonged.

"The cash drawer came up a hundred and a half light last night. Earl damn near came unglued when he found out. He accused Ray of taking the money."

"Why Ray?"

"Because Ray emptied the registers after we closed. Earl added up all the tapes, and they didn't match what was in the till." Her hair fell down again, but this time she ignored it.

"It'd be just like Earl to hire a detective over a lousy buck and a half. Most nights, he skims more than that before ten o'clock all by himself."

"Well, I hate to disappoint you, but I'm not working for Earl."

"Then what?"

"It's a simple missing person investigation," I said. "The guy I was asking about last night. I got some information that Ray might be able to help me find him, but now I'm having trouble finding Ray."

"Oh," she said, sounding disappointed. "Well, maybe Donny might know where he is."

"Who's Donny?"

"Donny Loomis. He's the big Kudzu County kid who collected your cover charge last night. Donny used to be Ray's roommate."

"I guess we both know the next question, then."

"He's in the back." She indicated the direction with a jerk of her thumb. "Don't tell him I sent you, though."

I nodded and started toward the back room.

"Hey!" she called to my back. "Are you going to tell me how this comes out?"

"Keep your ears open," I said. "You might just hear it for yourself."

I went through a curtained doorway into a room that had once been a kitchen, but that now was being used as a storeroom. It was crowded with aluminum pony kegs and cardboard beer cases, stacked from floor to ceiling like a funhouse maze, so that it was impossible to see from one end of the room to the other.

I found Donny Loomis in the back. He was working with his back turned toward me, loading cases and kegs into a walk-in refrigerator. He had a music player in his pocket and was wearing earbuds, so he didn't hear me coming up behind him.

Just as he was bending over to pick up another stack of cases, I came up behind him and hit him on the back of his left knee with my sap. The knee buckled, and he fell over backwards with a yelp of pain and surprise. Before he had a chance to react, I stepped quickly around him and sapped him a second time on his right shoulder. It wasn't a damaging blow. I didn't want to injure him, just take a little of the fight out of him and keep him on the floor for a while.

I reached down and lifted the buds out of his ears. "Remember me?"

He gritted his teeth in pain as he rubbed the spot on his arm where I had sapped him. "Ow-w-w, son of a bitch. You broke my damn arm," he moaned.

"No, I didn't. But if you even think about moving your ass from where it is right now, you'll wish that's all I did." I pulled over an empty keg and sat down next to him. "It'll be numb for a while, and then it'll be sore, but it isn't broken." I gave him my sincerest smile. "Trust me."

"Well, it sure feels broke," he whined. "What'd you do that for, anyway?"

"It makes us even for last night, remember?" I slapped the sap against the palm of my hand. "You want to leave it that way or go for two out of three?"

"That was you?" When I nodded, he said, "Oh, well, then, I guess I got it coming. My daddy always told me, don't get mad, get even."

"Your daddy knew what he was talking about. Listen, Donny, I'd love to sit here and visit with you for the rest of the afternoon, but I'm in a hurry, and I can see you're busy, so let me come straight to the point. I need to find Jerry Raymond."

Loomis looked at me blankly. "Who?"

"And I thought we were going to be friends." I leaned over and sapped him on top of his kneecap, not hard. He yelped and scooted back a couple of feet,

158

just in case I might decide to hit him again.

I said, "Don't fuck with me, Donny. You're a big kid, and you take your lumps like a man, but I'm a lot meaner than you are tough. If you make me, I'll crack you open like a piggy bank. Now, where is he?"

"He ain't here. I don't know where he is."

Strike two," I said, slapping my open palm with the sap. "One more, and you're out."

"Honest, I don't know," he said, his voice rising an octave. "He's supposed to be here right now helpin' me ice down all this beer. You think if I knew where I could find him, I'd be doin' this all by myself?"

"Point taken. Where does he live?"

"Madison. He rents a place on North Jackson, over in Madison. I don't know the number."

"I can find it," I said. "Have you talked to him since last night?"

"Not hardly. We got the hell out of here right after—well, you know. It was damn near time to close, anyhow." He propped himself up on one elbow. "Say, mister, you think I can get up off this floor? I'd feel a lot better if I could sit up straight."

"Make yourself comfortable," I said, pointing to a stack of empty cases across from me. "But what I said before still goes. Act up, and I'll make you think a piano fell on you."

"I heard that," he said, gingerly gathering himself up on all fours. He stood up straight, steadying himself against the door of the refrigerator, and limped over to sit down where I had indicated.

"All better now?" I asked.

"Some," he nodded. "You hit me when I wasn't looking."

"Just be glad I wasn't still mad at you. You were starting to tell me about Raymond."

"Oh yeah, right. Well, there ain't too much to tell, like I said. I just met him about a year ago. He started working here right after I did. His old lady had run him off, and he needed a place to stay, so I took him in. He only stayed with me until he could find a place of his own. As it was, he stiffed me out of half a month's rent."

"But he paid you something back last night, didn't he? A hundred and a half, in cash. It was your payment for helping him do a number on me."

His eyes widened in amazement. "How'd you know that?"

"The money was missing from the cash register. Earl noticed it right away, and figured Ray must have taken it. The girl up front thinks I was hired to get it back." I let him chew on that for a few seconds.

"You got a record, Donny?"

"You mean with the law?"

"No, the Billboard Top One Hundred."

He forced the corners of his mouth downward. "I ain't so sure I ought to be telling you anything else. I ain't sure you got the right to make me."

"Well, there are a couple ways to answer you that one. The first is, you already know I'm private, so you're right, you don't have to tell me anything. In that case, I could try to beat it out of you, except we both know I'm not going to do that. But the real answer is that Raymond is up to his ears in what's starting to look like a double murder, or maybe a murder and a kidnapping. So, if you want a piece of that, be my guest. I know any number of homicide detectives who'd love to hear what you have to say."

"You're kidding me, right?"

"Am I?"

He groaned miserably. "I knew this was going to happen. I told Ray I didn't want any part of it."

"Any part of what, Donny?"

"What happened last night. Ray said you were asking questions. He said we'd have to run you off before you started to make trouble." He pressed his hands together prayerfully, like a penitent inside the confessional. "I knew it wasn't going to work. I told him you'd just come back again. He said, then maybe we ought to kill you, but I said no, I wasn't going to do no killing."

"Back up a minute," I said. "What was I asking questions about?"

"Somebody that was in here the other night. I don't know his name."

"Simon Eberle? Blond guy, small, with a moustache?"

"I never heard his name, but yeah, that's the one."

"What night was he in here?"

CHAPTER TWENTY-TWO

"Last Saturday."

"Are you sure?"

"Sure, I'm sure. We had Amos Winslow playing. I wouldn't forget that. He plays a hell of a fiddle."

"Was that the first time you saw him here?"

"No, he plays here a lot."

"Not Amos, goddamn it. Simon."

"Oh. Yeah, I seen him before, too."

"Was he by himself Saturday night?"

"Far as I could tell, he was."

"How come you got nervous when Raymond told you I was asking questions about Simon?"

"Well, it was what happened when he was here. I mean, he got falling down drunk, and Ray had to drive him home."

"You mean they left together? How drunk was he?"

"He passed out right at the bar. It was a funny thing, too. He wasn't here more than a few minutes before he just sorta fell off his stool." Loomis made a humming noise in his throat. "He must've really tied one on before he got here. You figure with that watered-down beer we serve here, you'd have to drink a bucketful of it to get that loaded."

"Where do you fit into all this, Donny?"

"I helped Ray carry him out and put him in his car. Then they took off, and that was it. I never thought no more about it until last night."

"What did you think then?"

"I didn't know. I figured Ray might have robbed him or stole his car or something, and you came down here looking to get it back." He swallowed dryly. "Something happened to that guy, didn't it? That's why you want to find Ray."

I said, "Simon's been missing since the night he left here with Raymond. Sometime after that, Simon's girlfriend was murdered in her apartment. I don't know how it all fits together yet, but Raymond seems to have had a part in that, too."

"Oh, Lord, no," he whispered. "Listen, mister, you got to know something.

When I was sixteen, I got a year's probation for riding around with two of my buddies in a car we hot-wired out of the mall parking lot. Am I going to go to jail on account of this?"

"Not if you're telling the truth. Otherwise…." I let his imagination take over.

"I thought I was just helping that dude get home safe, and that is the truth. I didn't know Ray was going to do anything. He said he knew the guy and he'd carry him on home. What was I supposed to do?"

"Not much you could have done, but there is something you can do now." I handed him my card. "If either Raymond or Simon Eberle shows up here tonight, I want you to call me at this number."

"Oh, I will. You can count on me." He slipped the card into his shirt pocket. Then, to my surprise, he held out his hand for me to shake. Not knowing what else to do, I shook it. Then I walked back outside and got into my car.

Chapter Twenty-Three

My first impulse was to abandon all caution and beat a path on up to Madison, hot on the trail of Jerry Raymond. My second was to use my head for something besides a punching bag for a change and stop by the office to pick up some reinforcements. I had a feeling that whatever happened the rest of the way was going to get very ugly, very fast. In that case, I was going to need more than a sap and a line of snappy dialogue.

Afternoon was dissolving into early evening as I opened the door and stepped into the outer office. There was a single, plain white envelope on the floor under the mail slot. I tore it open and found a check for five thousand dollars, made out to cash, and signed and endorsed by Richard Eberle, and presumably delivered by messenger. I supposed the check was some kind of extra incentive to stay on the job, just in case I'd changed my mind about staying on the case.

I unlocked my desk, dropped the check into the middle drawer, and took out my Colt .380 auto. I loaded it with a full clip and strapped on my shoulder rig. Most law-enforcement types don't care for the .380. For one thing, it's the gangbanger weapon of choice, so the cops don't have a lot of respect for it. For another, it doesn't have the stopping power of a .357 or a .40 caliber, but it's light, has an 8-shot capacity, and it'll punch a big enough hole in most things that the difference probably wouldn't be noticed by anybody not drawing a paycheck from the medical examiner's office.

Before going out again, I called the answering service. There was just one message, from a Mrs. Elaine Murdock. Could I call her back right away?

I dialed the number she'd left with the service. It rang once, and then Elaine picked up.

"Thank heaven I reached you," she said, sounding out of breath. "I've been sitting here going out of my mind."

"What's the problem?"

"Simon. He called here. I spoke to him."

"Wait, what?" I sat up straight in my chair. "When?"

"About an hour ago. He said he was all right and not to worry, that he'd be home soon."

"Did he say where he was?"

"Just that he was staying with some friends. He wouldn't tell me who or where."

I swore under my breath.

"Did I do something wrong?"

"No, you did fine. Did he say anything about Jorie?"

"Jorie? No, why? Do you think that's where he could be staying?"

"I'm pretty sure that's the one place he isn't," I said. "Didn't Walter talk to you?"

"Walter left early this morning, before I was even up. Why, was he supposed to tell me something?"

I heard a buzzing noise inside my head. "Walter's not there now?"

"I told you, no. What's happening here, Gamble? What was Walter supposed to tell me?"

I took a deep breath and let it out slowly. "Jorie Flowers is dead, Elaine. She has been for at least several days."

There was silence on the line. I said, "Did you hear me?"

Her voice sounded flat. "Tell me what happened."

"She was murdered, Elaine. Somebody shot her."

There was a pause. "Anything else?"

"She's dead, Elaine. Isn't that enough?"

"Do you think Simon did it?"

"Somebody went to a lot of trouble to make it look that way," I said. "You're sure he didn't give you any idea where he was when you talked to him?"

"No, he didn't. I already said that."

"What about caller ID? Did you get the number he was calling from?"

"The number was blocked. I'm sure that was on purpose."

"You didn't think that was odd?"

She let the question pass. "Where does Walter fit into all this?"

"Did he say anything at all to you last night?"

"Walter came home late. He had a couple drinks and went to bed. This morning, like I told you, he went out. He didn't say where he was going."

Shit.

I said, "The night after Simon disappeared, your old man sent Walter out looking for him. One way or another, he wound up at Jorie's apartment. When he got there, it looked like nobody was home, so for whatever reason, he broke in through the back door. I can't imagine why he thought that would be a good idea, but that's what he did. Anyway, he found the body and then tore up the apartment to make it look like a burglary."

"Wait a minute," she cut me off. "Are you saying this took place three days ago and nobody's told me about it?"

"Sunday or Monday. I guess I'd have to say that's right."

"You guess!" she echoed furiously. "What else didn't he tell me? And by the way, where did you get all this information, or should I not ask?"

"You can ask," I said, tackling her second question first. "I went to Jorie's apartment myself, this morning. I found things pretty much the way Walter left them."

"And you didn't come back and tell me?"

"I told your father. I thought maybe I'd caused you enough trouble already."

"What did he say?"

"He offered me a hundred thousand dollars to get rid of the body."

"Oh, Jesus. And I suppose you took it?"

"Sure, I did. That's why I'm talking to you now. I want you to run away with me to Las Vegas so we can get married."

"What are you talking about?"

I said angrily, "I didn't take the damn money, Elaine. It would make me an accomplice to murder."

Her voice climbed back down from the ceiling. "I'm sorry, Gamble, I didn't mean what I said. I'm just very upset. Why didn't Walter tell me what happened?"

"I don't know. I talked to him for more than an hour last night. He was supposed to fill you in so you'd know what was going on. Something has come up, you see."

"You mean there's more?"

"I'm afraid so. The night Simon disappeared, he was seen at the Million Seller Lounge. Apparently, he passed out while he was sitting at the bar, and one of the bartenders drove away with him in his car. The story at the time was that he was going to take him home."

"Go on."

"The bartender was a man named Jerry Raymond, although he goes by the name Ray. He's Jorie Flowers's ex-husband. Raymond telephoned Walter yesterday, claiming to have information linking Simon to Jorie's murder. He told Walter he wanted a hundred

thousand dollars, or he was going to the police to tell them what he knew."

"How did you find out about this?"

"Walter told me yesterday afternoon. I followed him out to a redneck beer bar in Triune. That's where he met with Raymond to set up the deal."

"How much of this do the police already know?"

"Not much. I sent them over to Jorie's apartment to check out a burglary. By now, they'll have found her body. How much further they've gotten is anybody's guess." I didn't mention there was a witness who could put Simon literally at Jorie's front door right around the time she was murdered."

I said, "Elaine, does Walter own a gun?"

"He has some kind of a rifle. When we first moved in, he used to use it to shoot at groundhogs and raccoons. I don't think he's touched it in years."

"No. I'm thinking more of a handgun."

"As far as I know, the only gun he has is the one I told you about." There was a pause. "Gamble, do you think the police might already have arrested Walter?"

"No. Jorie's apartment is in the city. The Nashville cops aren't going to come looking for somebody in Springdale until they have better evidence. That's going to take them some time."

"Then where is he?"

"Maybe he went over to talk to your old man. He said he'd have to go to him for the money."

"Should I call there?"

"I think you'd better. I have a bad feeling that Walter has decided to be a hero. It seems likely now that he didn't tell me everything there was to his end of the story. But either way, your father has got to know what's happening, particularly since he's going to have to front the money."

"I'll call him right now."

"Do that. And a couple other things while you're at it."

"Tell me."

"First, if Simon calls again, it's absolutely critical that you get him home again or at least get him to tell you where he is. Do whatever you have to. Tell him your father has had a heart attack and is calling for him with his dying breath. Anything, you understand? We've got to get him rounded up before the cops find him. Otherwise, it's going to be close to impossible to convince them he's innocent, even if he is."

"What's the other thing?"

"Walter. When he shows up, make sure you keep him home. He's got a job of his own to do, and we can't afford to have him running around by himself screwing things up. He stays put, and he stays sober, you got that?"

"What are you going to do?"

"I'm going up to Raymond's house to see what I can find out. He may not actually have Simon with him, but I'd say it's a pretty safe bet he knows where he is. I'll just have to try to convince him to let me in on the secret."

"Can you do that?"

"I can be very persuasive. In the meantime, you just do what I told you. I'd like to think there's at least one person in the family who can follow instructions."

"I will."

"And call me if anything else happens. I especially want to talk to Walter when he gets back. Have him call me right away. I don't want him to do anything or go anywhere without talking to me first, clear?"

"I'll take care of everything," she told me, suddenly sounding very tired. "You can count on me."

Chapter Twenty-Four

They were two of the most mismatched cops I'd ever seen, like before and after, in a Weight Watchers ad. Under other circumstances, I might have found a little humor in the contrast, but just then, laughter was the farthest thing from my mind.

That there were two of them made it a business call. That they were in my office at all made it a certainty that they'd tumbled to the phony burglary I'd reported at Jorie Flowers's apartment and had managed to connect me with the corpse they'd found when they got there. I didn't need a fortune teller with a crystal ball to tell me I was about to be leaving on a journey.

The first cop through the door was a big, barrel-shaped man decked out like a black version of the Big Bopper. He wore a pale blue linen suit, brown and tan wingtip shoes, and a wide-brimmed planter's hat with a gaily colored band. The Bopper's name was Bill Merlin. He was a detective sergeant with Central District homicide. I knew him a little from my time with the district attorney's office. He was an okay cop, not above dropping his buzzer on the counter when he thought it would score him a free meal, but who otherwise could be counted on to give the taxpayers a day's work for a day's pay.

His partner was as different from the Bopper as doo-wop from hip-hop. He was new to me, younger than Merlin, and lean as a bullwhip. He was tall, with close-cropped blond hair and eyes the color of storm clouds. He reminded me of a Parris Island drill instructor, just as cold and just as convinced that, no matter what was the question, he had the answer. A cop like that would take a long time to get to know and forever to get to like. I decided I wasn't even going to try.

Merlin eased his considerable bulk through the doorway and wedged himself into the customer's chair. He lifted his hat and wiped his brow with a sweat-soaked handkerchief. The younger cop moved in behind him and propped himself in the corner next to the file cabinets.

I showed Merlin a tired smile. "Who's your friend, Bill?"

"New man," he grunted. "Name's Gardner. Came over from county sheriffs. We'll be workin' together for the next couple weeks."

"He seems like a nice boy," I allowed. "Have you got him housebroken yet?"

Gardner started to say something, but Merlin cut him off. "Don't pay him no attention," he said to his partner. "Gamble likes to crack wise, but he's okay."

To me, he said, "We're not here just to kill time, Jackson, so before you start askin' about the wife and kids and all, this is official." He mopped his brow again and gave me his best strictly-business look.

"Okay," I said.

"A woman named Jorie Flowers. Know her?"

"I never met her," I said truthfully.

"Nice try," he said. "But that's not what I asked you."

"I said I didn't know her," I told him. "And for some reason, mostly because you're here, I get the feeling I'm not going to get the chance."

Gardner piped up. His voice had an edge that made it sound as if he worked on it every morning while he shaved. "How about if you just answer the questions, okay Gamble? We'll take care of the asking."

"That's very good," I said. "NCIS or Blue Bloods?"

Gardner's eyes narrowed ominously. "Listen, wiseass, we're trying to conduct a homicide investigation here. We have reason to believe you have information that could be relevant. Now you can either cooperate and tell us what you know, or we run you in right now on a charge of withholding evidence."

"Well, thank you very much," I said. "And now that we've got that all straightened out, why doesn't somebody fill me in on the rest of it?"

Merlin made an unhappy face. "About two o'clock this afternoon, we get a call from some concerned citizen. He doesn't give a name; he just says he thinks there's been a B and E over at the Castle Gate apartments. We sent a car over there to check it out. Metzger and Keefe get the squawk. I don't know, maybe you remember them?"

"Sorry."

"Could be they came after your time. Anyway, they drive over to see what's up, and sure enough, it did look like there'd been a break-in. Only nobody seems to be home, so our guys go in. They found the Flowers woman half naked on the floor with a bullet in her chest."

I picked up a pencil and drummed the eraser on the arm of my chair. "And you didn't have anything better to do than come and see me about it?" I asked. "I already told you, I never met her."

"Aw, come on, Jackson, you can do better than that. Right after Metzger and Keefe got done dragging their size thirteens all over the place, messing up the evidence, they finally remembered to call the detectives. It couldn't have taken more than ten minutes to get a positive ID on you from the woman across the hall. The way she tells it, you were there the day before, asking questions about this same Jorie Flowers. Now, we ain't saying you popped her, but you also know the drill. We have to get some kind of statement to explain what you wanted with her."

"I have a client," I said. "This client could be seriously hurt by a lot of premature publicity. I don't think I can say too much more than I have without talking to him first."

"Suit yourself," Merlin sighed, "but if that's the way you want to play it, Captain says we'll have to bring you downtown."

"You got to do what you've got to do," I said and started to get up. I was halfway to my feet when Gardner pulled his service weapon and leveled it at my chest.

"Hold it right there, asshole. Hands behind your head."

I froze where I was but kept my hands at my sides. "I don't believe this character, Bill. Is he for real?"

Merlin said, "Ease off the gangbusters, will you, Gardner? Orders were to bring him in. Nobody said anything about a roust."

"He's got a gun," Gardner protested. "I can see it under his coat."

"I don't give a shit if he's wearing lace panties and a garter belt. I said back off."

Gardner shot him a sideways look, but otherwise kept his pistol pointed squarely at the middle of my chest.

Maybe I was tired, or frustrated, or maybe I just didn't like having guns pointed at me for no reason. I counted to three in my head, and when Gardner didn't lower his weapon, I said, "Next time you point that thing, junior, you want to make sure you take the safety off first. Otherwise, somebody a lot bigger than you is liable to take it away from you and make you eat it." I grabbed his Glock by the barrel and twisted it out of his hand. Then I gave the gun to Merlin, grips first. I took my own gun out of my shoulder rig and handed it over as well.

"Are we leaving now, or do you want to beat me up first? You could always claim I was resisting arrest."

"You know it ain't like that, Jackson," Merlin complained. "There ain't any need to make this any tougher than it has to be. Besides, you ain't under arrest. Captain just wants to ask you a couple questions."

Nobody had anything to ask me on the way downtown. I sat by myself in the back seat of the unmarked detective car. Gardner sat in front with Merlin, who used the driving time to deliver a pep talk on the proper procedure for handling firearms. I was pretty sure it wasn't being received in the spirit it was intended.

When we got to headquarters, they had me wait in the drunk tank. There were no windows and only one door. The tiny opening in its center consisted of heavy wire mesh laminated between two grimy panes of glass. The door locked automatically when the hydraulic closer swung it shut.

There was another person in the tank with me, a shabbily dressed wino stretched out full length on the bench bolted to the opposite wall. He was snoring noisily, dreaming, I guessed, of palmier days and better brands than the stuff he reeked of now.

I sat down on the other end of the bench, tilted my head back against the wall, and closed my eyes. I forced myself to think about nothing. It turned out to be surprisingly easy. I was actually able to doze off for a few minutes.

Three-quarters of an hour passed before Gardner reappeared in the doorway. He wore a serene, almost beatific look on his face, the way a person does when he's finally reached a decision about something that's been bothering him for a while.

"Let's go, Gamble," he said, bathing me in the warmth of his smile. "The captain's ready for you now."

I got up and walked over to the door. I had a pretty good idea what was going to happen next, and I knew there was nothing I could do except take it.

Gardner let me pass by into the hallway before grabbing me by the collar and banging me headfirst into the wall. Then he threw a wicked punch that landed squarely on my right kidney. It was a solid shot, and it left me momentarily seeing stars and planets.

"That's for making me look bad in front of Sergeant Merlin," he hissed between clenched teeth. "And this is for just in case you ever get any ideas about trying it again." He hit me a second time with his left, a little lower than before. It wasn't the hardest I'd ever been hit, but it was hard enough. I had to use both hands to steady myself against the wall until I was able to stand up straight without having the world spin out from under me.

Then we went upstairs to see the captain.

Chapter Twenty-Five

C aptain Harry Roodhouse's office was on the third floor, in the southeast corner of the detective division. To get there, you walk through the bullpen, where the third-grade officers have their desks, and past a half dozen interview rooms. Two of them are larger and relatively non-threatening, with even overhead lighting, comfortable-looking chairs, and tables without the metal bars used to attach one end of a pair of handcuffs. The others, less fancy by a long shot, are exactly what they appear to be: windowless, airless boxes equipped with microphones, video recording systems, and two-way mirrors. where interrogators and suspects sit and sweat in a test of endurance until one or the other cracks, and the mechanism of the law is served. Once in a while, justice is the outcome. More often, a deal is struck, a plea entered, and cop and crook are set free to get back to plying their respective trades.

Harry Roodhouse had been homicide skipper at Central District for going on a dozen years. He was close to sixty, small and wiry, with thinning gray hair and a long, sad face that only a mother, or another cop, could love. When Gardner and I walked in, he was sitting behind his desk, leaning back in his chair and smoking a cigar. He looked cool and comfortable. His feet were propped up on his desk, and his hands were folded in his lap. A big oscillating fan in the corner was running full blast, blowing stale air and cigar smoke into every available space.

Gardner sat me down in a hard, wooden chair and began reading tonelessly from his notebook.

"So far, what we've got is a witness that puts him outside the victim's apartment approximately twenty-four hours before the body was discovered. Acting on that information, Sergeant Merlin and I went to his office to interview him. Just routine. We didn't threaten. We explained our business and requested his cooperation. He became belligerent and abusive and went for his weapon, so we brought him in."

"'Belligerent and abusive,'" Roodhouse said. "That a new one for you, isn't it, Gamble? I thought you were the very soul of cooperation."

Gardner looked up from his notebook. "If you want my opinion, Captain, I say we book him right now as an accessory after the fact."

"If I want your opinion, I'll send you a text," Roodhouse growled around his cigar. "Meantime, go see if you can find something useful to do."

He waited until Gardner was gone and the door was closed. "Sorry to keep you waiting, Jackson. We've had a little bit of a dustup here just now. Seems like a couple of our officers made a traffic stop that went bad. The driver of the vehicle ended up getting shot multiple times and was dead on the scene. He may or may not have been reaching for his identification, but he had a Smith auto inside his jacket, and it looked to the officers like he might be going for it."

"Tough luck," I said. "Both your guys okay?"

"They are, but there's going to be a shitstorm just the same. Turns out the guy they shot was the son of a state senator named Rebecca Karlson. I don't know, maybe you've heard of her."

"I know who she is," I said, hoping he wouldn't follow up.

"Well," he said after a moment, "I guess this isn't your problem."

We sat quietly for a moment, each of us looking at the other. Finally, Roodhouse said, "So, let's get started. What can you tell me about this... what's her name, this Flowers woman? Any ideas about how she got dead?" His tone seemed friendly enough, but the smile behind it could have frozen a fresh pot of coffee.

"Not really. It's like I told your detectives, I never met her."

"Okay, say you didn't, but you were hanging around her apartment building asking her neighbor questions about her. What was that all about?"

"Not much." I shifted my weight in my chair, trying without success to find a comfortable spot to rest my back. "Her name came up as part of a missing person investigation I was hired to take on. I thought she might have some information that would point me in the right direction."

"And did she?"

"I don't know. It's like I said. I never talked to her."

"Okay, then how about you tell me about your missing person. Who are we talking about here, as if I didn't already know?"

"If you already know, then what am I doing here, Harry? You know better than to expect me to roll over on a client."

The muscles in his neck tensed. "That's Captain Roodhouse to you, smartass. Harry is for my friends, which right now we most definitely are not." He swung his feet onto the floor and leaned across his desk until I could smell the onions he'd had with his cheeseburger.

"You don't seem to appreciate the spot you're in, Jackson. We got a young woman in the morgue and a suspect who ought to be in a mental institution, except, of course, nobody seems to know where he is. We also got an ex-cop private star who's the only known connection between the two and who hasn't got enough sense to figure out if he doesn't quit playing dumb, he's about five minutes from having his license suspended."

"On what grounds?" I asked. "We're living in the twenty-first century, Captain, not the nineteen-twenties. You might want to keep that in mind, because it takes a lot more than heavy breathing to pull a private ticket these days. The only thing all this *film noir* dialog will get you is a big horse laugh down at the licensing board."

"Is that so?" His voice rose another ten decibels. "Well, maybe we can turn up the wick a little, then. How about obstruction of justice? How about withholding evidence in a murder investigation? Or if you don't like that, I think we might be able to strap you into a charge of aiding and abetting a felon in a flight from justice. Now, is that enough for you, or would you like me to have Detective Gardner escort you back to your luxury suite while I think of something else?"

When I didn't answer, he went on in a more reasonable tone. "Look, Jackson, we know it was you that called in here today. All those nine-one-

one calls are recorded. Now, maybe I can't prove it, but I think we both know I don't really have to. I can tie you in knots for the next five years without having to prove anything. When I finish passing the word on you, you'll be lucky to find work as a repo man."

He had me there, and this time we really did both know it. Like every private investigator, my ability to function effectively depended on at least the grudging cooperation of the local police. Even if they couldn't revoke my license, they could make it impossible for me to do my job. An innuendo here, a "friendly" warning there, and my sources, official and otherwise, would start to dry up faster than a puddle of rainwater in the August sunshine.

I sighed. "What do you want to know, Captain?"

"For starters, you can tell me why you were nosing around asking questions about a woman who just by coincidence happens to be dead with a bullet in her heart."

"The answer to that is, I didn't know at the time she was dead. I thought she might have some information about the case I'm working on."

He took his cigar out of his mouth and set it on the edge of his desk. "The case being Simon Eberle, right?"

"Do you really have to ask?"

"Just humor me."

"Okay, then, yes, I'm looking for Simon Eberle. His father hired me a couple days ago to try and find him."

"When you talked to him, what did he tell you?"

"Not much. He said his son had been missing for a couple of days, and that he wanted him home again."

"Didn't that seem funny to you? I mean, Simon Eberle is long past the age when he ought to still be living at home."

"The short answer is yes. It did seem odd. The more complete answer is, if I questioned the motivations of everybody who ever hired me to do a job, I'd be working security at a Wal-Mart within a month. And besides, Eberle made it pretty clear the boy doesn't have both oars in the water a lot of the time. He's worried Simon might be a possible suicide case."

"Homicide is more like it, or didn't he tell you that?"

"Not directly," I said, assuming he was referring to the earlier stabbing incident, "but I got the story anyway."

"Then let me tell you another. We're pretty damn sure Simon Eberle killed Jorie Flowers. We don't know why yet. With cuckoos like him, sometimes you never know why. But we know he did it, and we're going to take him down for it."

"Okay, you've got it all worked out, then. What's the problem?"

"The problem," he said sourly, "is that we're still sitting on square one. I should have my officers out on the street right now, tracking this guy down. But we can't, because as it is, we don't have enough evidence to get a warrant. You see what I'm getting at?"

"Then bring him in and hold him as a material witness. You shouldn't have any trouble getting a judge to sign off on that."

He shook his head. "It won't work. If we do that, it'll just put Richard Eberle on high alert. He'll lawyer the kid up, and we won't get a thing. That means right now, the only witness we've got is you."

"Well, this must be my slow night, Captain, because as far as I know, I'm not a witness to anything."

"You say."

"I do say. I don't know anything more than what I've already told you."

Roodhouse brought his fist down on his desk, hard enough to make his ashtray jump about an inch. "You better smarten up, Jackson, and I mean right the hell now. I want this guy bad. I want him fast, and I want him cold, so if you know anything at all that you're not telling me, you better give serious thought to coming across, because if you're holding out, you'll be working at that Walmart a lot sooner than you think."

Satisfied he'd made his point, he leaned back in his chair and re-lighted his cigar. I sat in my chair and considered my options. And all the while, the fan in the corner droned monotonously on, bringing no comfort to either of us.

Chapter Twenty-Six

We must have sat staring across the desk at each other for the better part of a minute before I finally figured out what he was telling me. When it came to me, I let my face split into a grin that stretched from ear to ear.

"You think this is funny?" he growled.

I said, "Tell me something, Captain, and this time I promise not to laugh. How much of this story have you told to the suits upstairs, the Chief of D's maybe, or the D.A.? Or how about Richard Eberle; has anybody gone out to Springdale to see what he thinks about all this?"

When he gave no answer other than to bite down harder on his cigar, I went on. "That's what I thought. You guys not only don't have a case, you don't have any guts, either. That's why you're leaning on me. This investigation is a firecracker with a short fuse. You want to be sure if it blows up, it's in my face and not yours."

That last was too much. Before I had a chance to duck, Roodhouse grabbed a handful of file folders from the pile on his desk and flung them in the general direction of my head. They missed, but not by much. A heartbeat later, he was standing over me with his fist cocked.

"You listen to me, Jackson, and you listen close. You ever say anything like that to me again, and friends or no friends, I swear you'll go out of here feet first."

"Okay, I'll take it back," I said slowly. "But then, you tell me just what the hell you think I ought to say. You roust me out, toss me in the tank, threaten me with my license, and demand that I serve up my client on a platter, just to save you the trouble of doing your own job. Then you've got the nerve to get snotty because I don't thank you for the evening's entertainment. I thought we were working on the same side of the law here, Harry, but after all this, I'm starting to wonder."

"I'm wondering the same thing myself," he said. "I've been around this city too long to be afraid of anybody in it, and that includes Richard Eberle. Anybody that says different doesn't know me at all.

"Anyway," he added, the barest smile tugging corners of his mouth, "it'll be one cold day in hell before I need a third-rate snooper like you to do my job for me, you hear?"

"I hear," I grinned. "So maybe I didn't use the best choice of words. No disrespect intended. But that doesn't change the fact that, from what I can tell, you don't have any evidence. You could maybe—maybe—pull Simon in for questioning, if you could find him, but you can't prove he murdered anybody."

"I wouldn't be so sure of that if I were you."

"Then why don't you just head on down to the courthouse and find some judge to issue a warrant so you can bust the apple of Richard Eberle's eye?"

"Not because I'm afraid to, I can tell you that. They can't touch me at city hall. I've got enough time in here to retire with full benefits any time I want to. I could have done it three years ago, for that matter."

"All right, forget it," I said. "Don't tell me."

"I am telling you, if you'd just listen. Whether I like it or not, Richard Eberle is still a very big dog in this neck of the woods. He's got a lot of friends over at the capitol who are just as big, sitting in powerful positions. If I move on this before I've got everything nailed down tight, he, or somebody he knows, will shut me down cold. I don't imagine it would surprise you to find out that kind of thing has happened before."

"And?"

"It isn't so much a question of being afraid as it is a question of timing. For all I know, Eberle may not even be aware yet there's been a murder."

"He's aware," I said.

"Are you sure?"

"He knew it when he hired me. It's very likely why he hired me."

He licked his lips in anticipation. "Would you swear to that in court?"

"Sure, right after I confess to rigging the last election. You may have your pension all sewed up, but I've still got to make a living in this town. Besides, I'm not so sure you're on the right track with this thing."

"What do you mean?"

"Just this. From what I know about Simon Eberle, a shooting just isn't his style. As far as I've been able to find out, he's never shot anybody, or even tried to shoot anybody. Besides," I added, hoping to draw him off the track, "where would a guy with a history like his be able to get a gun? Aren't the Feds supposed to check up on that kind of thing?"

"That's right, get simple on me now."

"Well, okay, but what about Jorie's ex-husband?"

"You mean Raymond? What about him?"

"This about him. If you talked to the same neighbor that I did, you probably found out he was coming around to see Jorie, maybe as often as Simon Eberle."

"So? Maybe they were hoping to reconcile."

"Sure, they were. Only what you might not know is that last Saturday night Simon and Raymond were seen leaving the Million Seller together. Except Simon didn't leave on his own two feet. The way I get it, he passed out at the bar."

Roodhouse raised his eyebrows a fraction of an inch. "I'm listening."

"I think it's possible Raymond didn't like the idea of Simon getting close to his ex and killed them both. The fact is," I said, letting slide Elaine Murdock's earlier telephone call from Simon, "I haven't been able to turn up any kind of a lead at all to find Simon."

He thought for a moment. "It's too complicated. I don't buy it."

"What's complicated? A jealous ex-husband kills his ex-wife because she's seeing somebody else? And then, just to square things up, he kills her lover? At the very least, it's worth pulling him in to talk about. If nothing else, he may know where Simon is now. After all, Raymond was the last person to have seen him before he disappeared."

"Then why aren't you looking for him?"

"I was, or at least I was about to start before your guys showed up. There's no telling where he could be by now."

"We'll check it out," Roodhouse said, "unless you've got some objection."

"Not me," I said innocently. "That kind of stuff is strictly up to you. I have no police powers. My interest is in finding Simon, not tracking down murderers."

"Sure. And I'm first cousin to the King of Siam."

"I'm serious, Harry. I just want the kid. Besides, how do you know she wasn't simply killed by a burglar? You said the place had been burgled."

"It was supposed to look that way, all right, but it was just a smoke screen and not a very good one at that. There had to be close to thirty grand worth of jewelry in the bedroom. Why wasn't that stolen?"

"Maybe they were just looking for stuff that could be turned into drug money."

"What, you can't sell jewelry? Besides, there was also a TV set, a laptop computer, a microwave, and a lot of other shit that can be easily turned into cash. Now, if a burglar doesn't want to steal that stuff, what does he want?"

"Money? Or drugs, I don't know."

"I don't, either. There weren't any drugs we could find, so I guess it could have been that. If Jorie Flowers was dealing, it would explain how she was able to buy all the other stuff." He paused to light a fresh cigar.

"Problem is, if you were going to steal drugs, you'd have to know they were there to start with. That puts the murder back on somebody who knew her. Money's definitely out, though. There was over six hundred dollars in cash in her purse, and I don't see how anybody could miss that. That's why I say, this whole thing stinks."

An idea began scratching around in the back of my head. "Did your people find a notebook or an address book or anything like that?"

"No, why? You know something we don't?"

"Just a thought I had. Suppose Jorie was blackmailing somebody. Suppose that same somebody got tired of making payments and decided to close his account once and for all. Maybe he went looking for what she had on him and found her home when she wasn't supposed to be. So, he panics, shoots her, and then, realizing what he's done, tears the place apart, looking for the notebook."

"I think you've been watching too much television. It's working on your brain, what there is left of it. Anyway, like I already told you, there wasn't any address book."

"There wouldn't be if somebody took it," I offered lamely. "Look, I'm not saying that's the way it happened. I'm just saying it's a possibility. Why are you so dead set on pinning this thing on Simon Eberle? Is this something personal with you?"

Before he could get mad again, the telephone rang. He picked it up and listened for a moment without speaking. I couldn't make out what the voice at the other end was saying, except that it was being said in highly excited tones.

Roodhouse said, "Yeah," a couple times, then, "Here? Now?" and finally, "I'll be there in five minutes."

He hung up the phone like he thought it might explode in his hand. "I'm afraid we'll have to continue our discussion a little later, Jackson. Much as I've enjoyed it, of course."

"Of course."

"However, I've just been informed the D.A. has gotten wind of the case and is on his way down here right now." He gave me a pained look. "I almost hate to ask whether you've got any ideas how that might have happened."

"That's right, blame me. It's my fault you've got some overachiever in your own department who can't keep his mouth shut."

His eyebrows pinched together a little at that, but he let it pass.

"I don't suppose you want me to stick around, then."

"Are you nuts? I want you out of here right now. Go home, get drunk, crawl into a hollow log, whatever you want to do. Just make yourself scarce. I'll find you when I need you."

I started to say something else to him, but the phone was ringing again, so I just waved him good night. Then I rode the elevator down to the first floor and walked out the door like any other self-respecting taxpayer.

Chapter Twenty-Seven

I got most of the way down the front steps before I remembered that my car was still sitting in a parking lot halfway across town. That left me standing like a tourist without a map outside the cop house, wondering not only where I ought to go next, but also how to get there.

While I was mulling it over, a dark blue unmarked police car rounded the corner and rolled to a stop in front of me. Bill Merlin leaned across the front seat and rolled down the window on the passenger side.

"Need a lift somewhere?"

"Can I sit in front this time?"

"Aw, lighten up," he grumped. "Wasn't any of this my doing, and you know it."

I almost got both feet inside the car before Merlin hit the gas. "You in a hurry?"

"You might say that." He kept one hand on the wheel and reached inside his coat with the other, retrieving my .380. "Here's your piece. Try and find someplace to put it where you won't get into trouble with it."

I took the Colt and secured it back in my shoulder rig. "Where's your little helper?"

"Roodhouse wanted to talk to him. Something about a telephone call from the D.A.'s office." He made a low, chuckling noise in his throat. "I figured it was a good time to get the hell out of there before somebody decided he wanted to talk to me. Where are you headed? Back to the office or what?"

"The office, yeah."

"Do you ever go home?"

"What for?" I asked him.

As we approached the corner of Second and Broad, two stylishly dressed men stood waiting for the light to change. They snuggled together in the warm night air, holding hands like a couple of small-town newlyweds getting their first look at the big, bad Music City.

The light changed, and the pair crossed the street, still holding hands. Merlin watched them disappear into a bar called Jacks or Better and shook his head.

"I remember that joint when a guy named Barefoot Thompson owned it. It was a good place to go and get your ass kicked on a Saturday night. Back then, if those two queens even tried to walk past the door, we'd be scraping 'em off the sidewalk about five seconds later."

Barefoot Thompson acquired his nickname after a hitch in the Army when he'd gotten his feet frostbitten while standing guard duty at Fort Richardson in Fairbanks, Alaska, on a night in January. After that, his feet hurt him so much that he found it painful to wear shoes, so when he worked the bar, he padded around in flip-flops or no shoes at all. After military service, Barefoot bought the bar from some country singer who had released a string of records that flopped and who needed quick money to keep from losing his house. Over the years, the bar, which Barefoot named the Longneck Lounge, became a hangout for bikers and assorted other tough guys who like nothing better than a knock-down, drag-out brawl on a Saturday night.

Barefoot operated the place for a number of years until one night, things got out of hand right before closing time. Punches were thrown, tables were overturned, and shots were fired. One slug caught Barefoot almost directly between the eyes, and that was the end of that. Afterward, the Longneck was sold to a couple of guys who may or may not have been gay, but who went out of their way to make gay patrons feel safe and welcome.

"I remember that place, too," I said. "Times change. Best of my recollection, when Barefoot was running it, it catered to white boys only. First drink was on the house for Klan members if they showed up in a white robe."

"It's a hell of a world, ain't it?" He looked over at me with sad brown eyes. "I understand Gardner stepped on you a little back there."

"I had it coming." I squirmed on the sticky vinyl seat, trying to find a spot where the springs hadn't broken down past the point of no return. "Somebody makes a cop look bad, he has to do something about it. Otherwise, he gets no respect."

"Some do," he said. "Some know how to earn it."

We drove another block in silence. "Why do you figure Roodhouse is so anxious to burn Simon Eberle?"

"Because he did a murder, Jackson. Roodhouse is a homicide cop. How many more reasons does he need?"

"I don't know, it's just that there's something here that's not quite adding up. Even granting the Eberle family is politically connected, it still seems like Harry's going at this all wrong. Like he wants to make his case so badly, he's trying to make the facts fit the theory."

He glanced in my direction. "You never done that, I guess."

"Sooner or later, when you get to be a captain, you also become a politician. I don't know, I guess I always figured Harry Roodhouse might end up being better than that."

"Don't sell him short. If he thinks he's got his man, he probably does. He just needs a little time to make his case."

"Yeah, I guess. Listen," I said, changing subjects, "you know anything about a doctor named Frank Tabor?"

"Never heard of him. Why? You sick?"

"Not me. This guy is a psychiatrist. He's got a clinic in Franklin."

"So, what does that make him to you?"

"Maybe it makes him the key to the Eberle case. Tabor has been treating Simon off and on for clinical depression for the past several years."

"The name don't ring any bells, but I can ask around if you want. You looking for anything in particular?"

"I'd be especially interested in whether there's ever been any funny stuff with drugs. Also, if there's anything not quite kosher with his finances. Like for example, where did he get the money that he used to build his clinic?"

"You don't want much."

"Not to ask is not to receive," I said.

CHAPTER TWENTY-SEVEN

"I guess not. You say he's a head doctor?"

I nodded. "He believes Simon's problems stem from his childhood. He had some pretty rotten things happen to him when he was a kid."

Merlin snorted. "That don't give him leave to do murder. I had a rotten childhood too, and I never murdered nobody."

"Maybe, but you never had the experience of waking up and finding your mother dead from a .22 caliber migraine."

"Well, now, the way I heard it," he said slowly, "that's something that could have stood a little looking into. I don't know that I would have said a psychiatrist is the guy I'd pick for the job, though."

"Can I have that again, in plain English?"

"Aw, I don't know all of it. I heard some of the old heads talking in the day room. You know how it is. When somebody like Eberle gets his name mixed up in a murder, all of a sudden everybody's an expert."

"So?"

"So, this. Somebody, I don't remember who it was, was saying that suicide you were mentioning just now didn't look like no suicide he ever saw. According to the coroner's report, the vic was so full of Demerol there was no way she could have shot herself besides."

"What else?"

"Nothing else. At the time, some people thought old man Eberle might have done her himself. But, hell, there was no proof. And besides, he was two hundred miles away at the time, and nobody could think of a motive, so that was that."

"You mean nobody followed up on it?"

"Followed up how? It was a long time ago, and even at the time, there was no real evidence. It just didn't look right, that's all. You can't make a case out of that. You know how cops like to talk. They'll say anything to sound like they know more than they do. If the name Eberle hadn't come up, nobody would have remembered any of this."

"You're probably right," I agreed.

"And anyhow," he continued, "couldn't you have seen us ramrodding an investigation like that the way things worked around here back then? Eberle would have had his lawyers all over us like ham fat on collard greens."

"That's what Roodhouse said, too."

"Well, he was right. Listen, Jackson, let me give you some advice. I don't know what you and Roodhouse talked about in there. I don't think I even want to know. But you been gone from the force for quite a while now, and things aren't like they used to be. If you're thinking about jacking him around or holding out on him, think about it some more. Friends are friends, and that's all fine, but he's different now. He's a captain now, and he's pretty damn serious about how he does his job."

"I tried to answer all his questions."

"That's what I'm talking about. You keep heaping that kind of double-talk on his plate, and you'll be sitting there until your ass comes to a point. The only reason you got out of there tonight is because he didn't want you anywhere the D.A. could get his hands on you."

He pulled over and stopped the car in the parking lot behind my building. "I don't know what you got planned for the rest of tonight, but if I was you, I'd give some serious thought to going home and going to bed. Roodhouse is going to want to ask you some more questions in the morning, and you don't want to have to tell him any more lies than you already have."

I got out of the car and leaned over to face him through the window. He said, "You hearing me on this?"

"I'm hearing." I gave him a wink and a big grin. "And since you were willing to give me a ride plus all that good advice, let me give you a little something in return."

"I can't wait," he said.

"Okay, here it is. Earlier tonight, there was an officer-involved shooting. A guy named Scott Karlson spooked a couple of uniforms during a traffic stop and got himself shot to pieces. They thought he was going for his gun, and maybe he was. But either way, it's going to be very ugly, because his mother is a state senator. Those two cops are in for a bumpy ride."

"So?"

"So have the ballistics techs in your lab test the slugs from the gun Karlson was carrying and compare them against the ones they took from another

188

shooting victim named Peter Willingham. In case you forgot, he took three in the chest in the parking lot behind the bus station a couple of nights ago. I'm pretty sure they're going to find the slugs they took out of Willingham are going to match the bullets in Scott Karlson's gun. If I'm right, it'll clear the Willingham shoot and get your guys off the hook for what happened tonight."

He looked at me. "And you know this how?"

"Just a guess," I said. "It'll probably get you a promotion. But if you don't want it, I'll give it to Gardner. I owe him one."

He stared at me, open-mouthed, for a moment. Then he said, "Aw, why don't you just...," and drove off.

* * *

For the next week or so, the shooting of Scott Karlson by the two Metro cops was all over the local television and print news. At first, the senator was outraged and tearful, fuming at the "trigger-happy" cops who killed her son for no apparent reason, and hinting that maybe de-funding the police, whatever that means, might not be such a bad idea. But then, as the story began to further unfold, it became known that the gun Scott Karlson was carrying at the time of his death was the same gun used in the shooting of a man named Peter Willingham in the parking lot of the downtown bus station. That prompted a second investigation, this time into the connection between Willingham and Scott Karlson. After two more days, out of the clear blue, Rebecca Karlson announced that she was suspending her re-election campaign and would resign from the state senate in order to spend time with her grieving family. Almost immediately thereafter, the story fell from the headlines, and the investigation was concluded. At least for a while.

At the end of August, Rebecca Karlson was found dead in her expansive home outside Murfreesboro. A medical examiner's report indicated that the cause of death was a mixture of barbiturates and 151-proof Bacardi rum. There was a funeral where no less than the governor and both of Tennessee's United States senators gave stirring eulogies praising Mrs.

Karlson's dedication to public service.

At no time during any of the investigations related to Peter Willingham, Scott Karlson, or Rebecca Karlson did my name come up.

Chapter Twenty-Eight

After Bill Merlin dropped me off, I walked into my building and through the lobby, where a uniformed security guard was snoozing peacefully next to the elevators. I got into an open car and pressed seven. I rode up to my office feeling tired, dirty, disgusted, mean, and ready to finish any fight that might be headed my way.

I unlocked my office, went inside, and sat down behind my desk. It had been very nearly a four-hour merry-go-round ride from desk to police car to police station to police car and back to desk again, and it hadn't gotten me anywhere except one-sixth of a day closer to collecting my social security.

I picked up the phone and dialed the answering service. No messages from Mr. Murdock, no messages from Mrs. Murdock, no messages from anybody at all. That wasn't good, or maybe it was terrific. It was getting so I couldn't tell any more.

I tried Elaine Murdock's number and heard the phone at the other end start to ring. Once, twice, no answer. Five, six, no answer. Eight, nine, ten, still nothing. I hung up, waited five minutes, and tried again. Same routine, same results. Nobody home.

After I hung up the phone, I leaned back in my chair and tried to make sense of the way the case was proceeding. For the life of me, nothing seemed to be taking any discernable shape, and the more I thought about it, the more confused I was getting. After about ten minutes, I decided it had been a long day, too long, and it was time to go home and try to get some sleep. Tomorrow, I thought, would be soon enough to take another run at it. But before I could close up shop, the telephone rang. Since I knew Maggie would call on my cell rather than the office line, I considered not answering, then decided, what the hell, what's a few more minutes?

"Mister Gamble, this is Clarence Darrow," the voice on the other end said. "I was hoping to catch you before you left for the day."

I sighed. "It's nearly nine o'clock at night, Mr. Darrow. What can I do for you?"

"Did you talk to Walter Murdock earlier today?"

I was immediately on my guard. "I did," I said. "Is something wrong?"

"You could say that, yes. I just got off the phone with Mr. Murdock. He called me from the sheriff's department in Rutherford County. Apparently, he just walked in there and confessed to shooting a woman named Jorie Flowers. Can you meet me there in an hour?"

* * *

The sheriff's department office in Rutherford County is located on New Salem Highway in Murfreesboro, a fair-sized university town about 35 miles southeast of Nashville. On a weekday night, it took me about forty-five minutes to get from my office to the county jail. Clarence Darrow was already there, waiting for me. He was in the parking lot, standing next to his car, smoking a cigarette. I guessed that wherever he was when he got the summons, it was someplace other than the office, as he was dressed in cotton wash pants, a golf shirt, and topsiders.

"You ready for this?" He dropped his cigarette on the ground and crushed it with his right foot. Then he turned and led the way inside. There was a desk sergeant, who asked us our business, then handed us a clipboard with some papers attached that we had to sign. "Wait here," he said and left us standing in the lobby while he disappeared through a doorway behind the reception counter.

"What the hell happened?" I asked.

Darrow shrugged. "Murdock wandered in here about two hours ago. Said he shot some woman in her apartment back in Nashville. The cops recognized him and right off called Richard Eberle. Eberle called me, I called you, and now here we all are."

After a few minutes, the desk sergeant returned. "Right this way," he said. We followed him back through the door through which he had just emerged and walked down a short corridor. There were steel doors with small, wire-mesh windows on both sides of the hallway. The sergeant stopped in front of one of the doors, knocked on the glass, and then opened it so Darrow and I could enter. Inside was a table with four chairs. Walter Murdock was sitting in one of the chairs with a plastic bottle of water in front of him. His eyes were downcast, and he didn't look up at either Darrow or me when we entered. A Rutherford County Sherriff's detective, who introduced himself as Dwight Farrell, was seated across from Murdock. He had a pad and pencil in front of him and had evidently been taking notes.

Darrow shook hands with the detective. "I'm Clarence Darrow, Mr. Murdock's attorney." He jerked his thumb in my direction. "This is my associate, Mr. Gamble. Has my client made a formal statement, detective?"

"Not to me. This shooting he's been talking about, if there was one, we still don't know anything about that.

"Did you read him his rights?"

"We did. He says the shooting took place in Davidson County. That's not our jurisdiction. We're just keeping Mr. Murdock comfortable until somebody from the city comes down to scoop him up. Until then, he's all yours. He's not under arrest, but he is being detained, so just make sure he stays put until Nashville PD gets here."

"Okay, thanks, detective. We'll take good care of him." Farrell nodded, then got up and left the room. Darrow and I sat down in the two chairs across from Walter Murdock.

"Well, Walter," Darrow said. "I guess I don't need to ask you what you've been up to. And before you say anything, I'm not going to ask you whether you actually committed a murder, so don't tell me."

I raised my hand. "I can answer that," I said. "He didn't. He is guilty of breaking and entering and failure to report finding a dead body, but that's it. He didn't kill anybody."

Darrow looked at me. "You're sure of that?"

"Absolutely sure, yes. Either he's about to be framed, and he's trying to get out ahead of it, or else he's covering up for somebody else. I'm betting on door number two. Off the top of my head, I can think of at least three other people, and maybe four, who would have had a motive to kill Jorie Flowers. Mr. Murdock, however, is not one of them."

"So then, you think Simon Eberle did it." It wasn't a question.

"Let's hold off on that for a bit." I turned to Murdock. "Walter, after we talked earlier, we agreed you were going to go home and talk to your wife, remember? The deal was you were going to stay put until you heard from me. Why couldn't you just follow instructions?"

He didn't look up. "I have my reasons."

"I'm sure you do," I said. "And I think I'm beginning to understand what they are."

Darrow said, "Are you ready to share with the class?"

"Not yet," I said. "I still have a little more digging to do."

Murdock said, "So, what happens now?"

Darrow looked at me and raised his eyebrows. I said, "Tell him."

"Walter, as I understand it, you made some sort of a confession to the sheriff's detective before we arrived here. Now, as you know, I deal in corporate law—civil cases, mostly. Some acquisitions. I'm not a criminal attorney, but based on my limited experience in that area, here's almost certainly what is going to happen next. In a very short time, a couple of homicide detectives from Metro are going to walk through that door. They're going to read you your rights—again—and ask you to repeat your confession. On my advice, you are going to remain silent. They may ask you a few more questions, which you will decline to answer unless I tell you to do so. They will then cuff you and take you back to the city. After that, they will sit you down in an interrogation room. I will be at your side the entire time. I will instruct you not to answer any questions, and if you know what's good for you, you will do as I tell you and keep your mouth shut.

"At that point, since they won't be able to do anything else, based on the statement you made to Deputy Farrell, the Metro detectives will place you under arrest and charge you with suspicion of murder. You'll be searched, fingerprinted, and placed in a holding cell overnight. In the morning, you'll be arraigned. At that time, I will enter a not guilty plea on your behalf. Then, we'll arrange for you to post bond and be home in time for supper."

He looked at me. "That sound about right to you?"

"I think you've got this covered," I said. "You don't need me anymore tonight."

"What, you're leaving?"

"I've still got a killer to catch. I'll see you in court."

Chapter Twenty-Nine

I t was a good exit line, but the fact of the matter was, I didn't have the first idea how I was going to catch a killer, or for that matter, who the killer even was. I was all but certain that it wasn't Walter Murdock, but after that, all I had were "what ifs" and "yes, buts." The more evidence that piled up, the more it seemed like the only logical choice was Simon Eberle. And yet, for reasons I couldn't quite figure out, Walter Murdock had decided to take the fall in his place. What I should have done at that point was to just head for home, get a good night's sleep and then reconnect with Murdock and Clarence Darrow in arraignment court in the morning. But I was much too buzzed from all that had happened during the day to even think about sleep.

Instead of heading straight home, the first thing I did was to try calling Elaine Murdock. I hoped by now that somebody would have gotten in touch with her to let her know what was going on with Walter. In particular, I didn't want to be the one to break the news that he was likely to be charged with murder. But I did want to make sure she absolutely understood the seriousness of the situation and that she stayed put and didn't do anything foolish before tomorrow morning's arraignment. Not that there was much she would be able to do. By the time the Nashville cops got through in-processing Walter, it would be well into the small hours of the morning, and nobody would be permitted to see him until regular visiting hours the next day.

As it turned out, I didn't get a chance to tell her anything at all, as I got no answer when I called. I left a message on her voice mail, outlining in general terms what had taken place, and telling her to try to stay calm and sit tight until morning. I let her know that Walter was probably in the custody of the Nashville police and that she shouldn't bother trying to go and see him until after tomorrow's arraignment. The best thing she could do, if she wanted to help, would be to call Clarence Darrow or her father to see about arranging bail money. And since there was nothing more I could do, I decided that I might as well take my own advice and call it a day. Maybe I could find something on late-night television to keep me company until I could fall asleep.

And then I had another idea. I stopped for gas at a late-night service station, and while the tank was filling, went into the restroom, where I washed my face, straightened my tie, and tried to make myself generally presentable. Then I got back into my car and drove back to the city, downtown to the G-Spot.

The G-Spot was located on Second Avenue, about a block off Broadway, in an area popularly known as "Lower Broad." In days long past, that part of the city was a warehouse district, served by freight railroads and riverboats alike. But that time is long gone, and the stretch of Broadway between First and Seventh Avenues is today the epicenter of Nashville nightlife. The G-Spot was, first and foremost, a bar that could accommodate maybe a hundred or so customers and had a postage-stamp-sized dance floor for customers who felt like busting a tricky move or two. Some nights, usually on the weekends, Grand Ole Opry headliners would drop by to pose for selfies with the customers and maybe sit in with the house band for a set. Those nights, the place would be SRO, with a hefty cover charge and a line out the door. Tonight, there wasn't a celebrity in sight, and the G-Spot was sparsely patronized.

I took a seat at the bar opposite where the bartender was stationed. He glanced disinterestedly in my direction, then let me sit while he finished his conversation with another customer. At last, his point having been made, or maybe lost, he shuffled over and took my order for a Stella.

A woman who looked vaguely familiar got up from a table near the dance floor and took her place at the piano. She was dressed in a black evening gown that was slit to mid-thigh and cut in front in a wide "V" that covered just enough of her breasts to keep her out of jail. She wore a rhinestone choker, a matching pair of bracelets, and enough eyeliner to qualify as first runner-up in a Cleopatra look-alike contest. I had to do a double take to recognize that this was the same Serena Robbins I had spoken with the day before. In the getup she had on now, she would have looked right at home stripping at one of the tuck-a-buck clubs over on Printers Alley.

About the time she started playing, the bartender showed up with my beer. "Be anything else?"

"No, but hang on a minute." I took the cardboard coaster he'd set under my glass and wrote a short note on the back. I passed it across to him with five dollars from my change.

"Could you see to it the lady at the piano gets this?"

He picked up the note without reading it but left the bill on the counter. "You a tourist here in town, or what?"

"Why, is there a discount?"

"I was just wondering if you might, you know. I thought you might be looking for a little action."

He smiled knowingly at me. I smiled back. Instant connection. We were friends already. We understood each another, and why shouldn't we? It was basic supply and demand. I was buying, he was selling.

"Because the thing is, if you are, and this isn't a request for 'Moon River,' you're wasting your time with that one. She's strictly eye candy." He lowered his voice, as if to take me into his confidence. "I wouldn't want to swear to it in court, but I don't think she goes for men, if you take my meaning."

"I take it," I said.

"So, how's about you let me fix you up with somebody I know? She's a lot more your type, and she just lives a couple minutes from here. Let me give her a call for you. What do you say?"

I shook my head but left my smile in place. "Some other time. But thanks just the same."

"Sure?"

"I'm sure. Just give her the note, okay? Then bring me another beer and buy something for yourself."

He shrugged. "Whatever you say. But you're wasting your time."

He waited until Serena finished her number, then took my note over and set it on the piano where she could see it. She glanced at it without expression before looking quickly around the room. I raised my glass in salutation. She gave me a tight smile and went back to work. She played competently and sang well enough in a voice that was clear and musical. I sat back to nurse my beer and just listen. It felt good, for a change, to be doing a normal thing among normal people. That is, if drinking alone in a downtown bar at eleven o'clock at night is normal.

She played and sang a few more songs, some that I recognized and some that I didn't. To wrap up her set, she sang a Carole King rocker, "Jazzman." But without backing vocals and full orchestration, she sang it softly, with only simple chords from her piano, and without the powerful instrumental finish of the original. The difference was not lost on the remaining patrons, who were no doubt disappointed not to hear an ending crescendo and gave her only halfhearted applause. She thanked them just the same, then came over and sat down on the stool next to me.

"I didn't think I'd see you," she said, sounding strained. "Not after yesterday."

"Why, what happened yesterday?"

"Don't you know?"

"You mean because you talked to the police? You did the right thing. If you had told them anything other than the truth, you'd have been making a big mistake."

"I trusted you, and now Jorie's dead."

I didn't quite get the connection. "I didn't have anything to do with that, Serena. When I talked to you the other day, I was looking for her, yes, but the fact is, she was already—well, there wasn't anything I could do. I know it isn't much, but I'm sorry. I wish there were something else I could say."

I tried putting my hand over hers, but she drew it back. "The police asked me to go over and look at her," she said dully. "Jorie didn't have any family here, and they needed somebody to identify her body. She was—it was horrible. She was just—staring."

"I know."

"But you said—"

"I went back to her apartment the day after I talked to you. I had to. I wasn't getting anywhere with the other leads I had. The back door had already been broken open, so I just walked in."

"Then it was you that called the police?"

"Yes, but they don't know that. Or rather, they do know it, but they don't care anymore."

Her eyes grew wide as if she had just remembered something vitally important. "Gamble, the police are looking for you. I'm supposed to call them if I see you."

"Save your minutes. They already found me. We had a long talk earlier, and all is forgiven."

"I couldn't help it," she said apologetically. "I left your card on the table in the front room. When the officers came in, they saw it right away. I had to tell them you'd been there. I couldn't think of anything else."

"Be glad you couldn't." I reached for her hand again, and this time she let me take it. "It's not a problem, Serena. They just wanted to ask me some questions. There wasn't any reason for you to lie to them."

"What happens now? Are they going to arrest Simon?"

"Yes, they probably will, but not right away. For one thing, they don't know where he is. For another, they have a suspect in custody, but it's not the right guy. If they don't know that already, they'll figure it out pretty soon and kick him loose. By tomorrow afternoon at the latest, they'll get back to looking for Simon."

"And then what?"

"They'll probably find him, and when they do, they'll do their best to pin Jorie's murder on him. They're convinced he's the man they want."

She looked at me quizzically. "You say that as though you don't think he is."

"I don't know what he is. I do think we'd have a lot better chance of finding out if he'd give himself up. As it is, he's making it harder for everybody."

"The police seemed to think you might know where he is."

"No, they don't. They were just fishing. They thought if they told you that, you might confirm it for them. Right now, they haven't got a thing."

"Gamble, if Simon didn't kill Jorie, who did?"

"I wish I knew. I had an idea or two, but so far, they don't seem to be panning out. Listen, would you like something to drink? Some brandy, maybe, or a glass of wine?"

She shook her head. "I think what I'd like to do is just go home. This has been a horrible day for me, and the sooner I can get it over with, the better. Is that all right with you? I know you just got here and all."

"Not a problem," I said. "Do you have your car here, or can I give you a ride?"

"I'd like that, if it's not out of your way." She slid down from her stool. "Give me five minutes to get my things, and I'll meet you out front."

She was already waiting when I brought the car around. A couple of tourists were standing on the sidewalk near the door, getting a breath of air the way people do when they're not tired enough to go to bed and too tired to do anything else. They watched as Serena walked out and got into the Thunderbird. One elbowed the other animatedly in the ribs and said something I didn't need to hear to understand.

I said, "That Queen of the Nile getup really changes your image all around. I almost didn't recognize you tonight."

"Why doesn't that sound like a compliment?"

"It wasn't meant as one. Or a criticism, either."

"Well, to tell you the truth, I feel a little ridiculous myself, getting all tarted up like this. But I guess I'd stand on my head in a birdbath if I thought it would get somebody to take a look at my songs."

"That's an odd way to put it."

"What's an odd way to put what?"

I said, "If I were a singer, I'd want people to listen to my songs, not look at them."

She laughed. "If I were a singer, I probably would, too, but I'm not. You should know that. You listened to me for twenty-five minutes."

"I don't know. You sounded pretty good to me."

"Pretty good isn't nearly enough, not in the music business. I don't have the voice or the stage presence to do anything more than what I'm already doing, and there's no future in that."

"Then why do it at all?" I asked, aware that what she had given me was a fairly succinct description of my own career prospects.

"Because what I want to be is a songwriter, not a singer. A lot of what I play while I'm working is material that I've written myself. I keep hoping a producer or an established artist will walk in one night and hear something he likes. So far, none of them has. Meantime, I just keep plugging away." She turned and stared out the window into the darkness.

"You know, I think if I could just get somebody to look over my songs and really give me an honest opinion one way or the other, I'd be satisfied. If he'd say, hey, kid, your songs suck, well, that would hurt, but at least I'd know. But up to this point, I've never been able to get past the receptionists and the office boys."

"What do they tell you?"

"That I write good music, but it's not commercial. Do you have any idea what that means?"

I shook my head. "No."

She sighed. "Neither do I. That's why I need somebody to give me an honest appraisal of my work."

I said carefully, "I might be able to help you with that."

"Don't tell me that among your many other talents, you're a music critic?"

"Not me. I can't tell a fugue from a fandango. But I do know somebody who's in the business. He could give you a no-shit evaluation, if you're sure that's what you really want."

"Do you think he'd do it?"

"I can ask. He still owes me a favor or two."

She leaned over and kissed me excitedly on the cheek. "Oh, Gamble, that would be just great. You can't imagine how much it would mean to me if—but wait a minute," she broke off. "Does this mean that I'm going to owe you a favor, too?"

I said, "Yeah, but tell you what. This has been a hell of a day for me, too, and I haven't had a thing to eat since five o'clock this afternoon. If you can see your way clear to whip us up some breakfast, we'll call the whole thing even. Deal?"

"Deal."

She settled back into her seat and folded her arms around herself, like a kid trying to keep the happiness she feels inside from getting away.

It was a perfect night, warm and just a little muggy. Tiny patches of ground fog were beginning to form in the low areas along the road, like the promise of dreams waiting to be dreamed. There were few other cars, and the only sounds were crickets and locusts and the soft hum of the tires against the pavement. I was dead tired, and yet, at that moment, just knowing I had made someone happy, I felt as if I could have driven another ten thousand miles.

Chapter Thirty

I woke up the next morning smelling fresh coffee and tasting stale bile. The room was quiet, with soft light filtering through the drapes. It took me a moment to realize I wasn't at home but on the couch in Serena Robbins's living room. She was already up, sitting at the dinette table, shuffling through a stack of paper. She was wearing a pink terrycloth robe and humming contentedly to herself.

"Good morning." She smiled when she saw I was awake. "How are you feeling?"

I yawned and tried to stretch some of the kinks out of my back. "Like I slept on a railroad track. What happened?"

"That's a question I should be asking you. You dozed off right in the middle of one of my best compositions. If you weren't so heavy, I'd have pitched you out in the hallway. As it was, it was all I could do to lay you out lengthways so I could throw a blanket over you." She glanced in the direction of the kitchen.

"I made coffee, if you want some. Clean cups are in the dishwasher."

"Thanks anyway. What time is it?"

"It's nearly seven. Why? Do you have to be someplace?"

"Pretty soon," I said, remembering I needed to be in arraignment court at nine to hook up with Walter Murdock and Clarence Darrow. That, in turn, reminded me that Walter had a noon deadline to deliver a hundred-thousand-dollar payoff to Jerry Raymond.

"What are you working on there?"

"I'm just looking over some of my sheet music. As long as there's somebody

204

who might be willing to look at it, I want to make sure I'm giving him my best." She looked at me earnestly.

"You weren't just making that up last night, were you? I mean, do you really know somebody in the business?"

I nodded. "This is pretty important to you."

She straightened her papers into a neat pile and squared it up on the table in front of her.

"Right now, it's just about everything to me. I don't think I've ever wanted anything in my life as badly as I want to succeed at this. I just hope—who is this friend of yours, anyway? I don't remember that you ever said."

"I didn't," I said and told her my friend's name. "Do you know him?"

Her eyes widened. "Know him? Well, no, I don't actually know him, but I know who he is. I mean, who doesn't? I don't think there's been one hit song that's come out of Nashville in the last five years he didn't have something to do with."

I smiled. "I think even he'd tell you that might be overstating it just a bit."

"Not by much. How does somebody like you—I mean somebody in your line of work—oh, damn it," she blushed. "I haven't gotten used to being friends with a private detective yet. Help me out, will you?"

"Famous people have problems the same as everybody else. Theirs just cost more money to straighten out. That's how people in my line of work get to meet anybody. They have a problem, and they can't go to the police. In this case, my friend had a singer under contract who was being shaken down over some videos that were shot before she'd made a name in the music business. You can imagine what they were. He asked me for help, and I was able to get the original video and the copies back for her. It saved them both a lot of money and embarrassment. My friend was grateful, so he does me a favor now and then."

She grinned at me. "You're amazing, Gamble. Absolutely amazing."

I doubted whether Kady Standley would agree with that.

* * *

Arraignments for criminal cases are usually held at the Davidson County Circuit Court, located at the Public Square in downtown Nashville. I left Serena Robbins's apartment a little before eight, which just gave me enough time to go home for a quick shower and to change into a clean shirt before heading back into the city. I arrived at the courthouse around nine and located the courtroom where criminal arraignments were already underway. There were a dozen or more defendants, a few wearing jailhouse orange jumpsuits, the rest street clothes, all seated in the spectators' gallery, awaiting their all-too-brief appearance before the judge. Over to one side, a couple of lawyers, an assistant prosecutor, and a public defender, I supposed, were conferring in low tones, perhaps working out an early plea agreement. I sat and watched as, one after another, they pleaded not guilty to charges ranging from possession with intent, to prostitution, to aggravated assault, to breaking and entering. What I didn't see was Walter Murdock, who, like Clarence Darrow, was nowhere to be found. I wanted a few more minutes to see whether they might have been delayed, and when they didn't show up, I stepped back into the corridor to make a telephone call.

Clarence Darrow was in his office and seemed to be waiting for my call.

"I left a message with your service early this morning." His voice was flat. "Guess you haven't made it into your office yet."

"No, I'm at the courthouse," I said. "Where's Murdock?" I had a bad feeling he was about to tell me Walter had hanged himself in his cell or had been shivved in the breakfast line at the jailhouse mess hall.

"Home, I expect," Darrow told me. "Already ROR'ed out, with a mandatory psych evaluation to follow. By the time we got to the detention facility here in town, he had gone ahead and changed his mind and recanted his confession. So, right away, I called Richard Eberle, who called some judge he knows, and next thing you know, Murdock is out the door. He never set foot inside a courtroom."

"I guess who you know really does make a difference."

"I guess it does," he said. "Of course, he's still looking at a charge of filing a false police report back in Rutherford County, but I expect that'll go away before too much longer. I doubt we'll ever hear another word about it."

"So now what?"

"Well, the last time we talked, you were on your way to find a killer. Don't let me keep you from it."

Chapter Thirty-One

Before I left the courthouse, I had one more person I needed to talk to and two more phone calls to make. My first call was to Walter Murdock. But it was Elaine, not Walter, who answered on the third ring.

When I realized who I was talking to, I said, "I missed you last night."

"Who is this?"

"Inspector Clouseau."

"Oh, Gamble, it's you. What do you mean you missed me? Was there someplace I was supposed to be?"

Her voice sounded thick. Sleepy, maybe, or hung over. Or something worse.

"I tried to call you last night, around ten-thirty. I thought I asked you to stay close to home."

"I did. I went to bed early, as a matter of fact. I must not have heard the phone ringing." Then she added, "I took a sleeping pill. I guess it hit me harder than I thought."

I had to think about what I was going to say next. "Have you talked to Walter since yesterday?"

"Walter?"

"Walter, yes. Your husband. The man with whom you share your meals and a marital bed. That Walter."

"Oh. No, I haven't." I heard her stifle a yawn. "What about Walter?"

"So then, he didn't talk to you when he got home?"

"No, I already told you. I took a sleeping pill, so I guess I didn't hear him

208

when he came in. He was asleep in the guest room this morning when I got up. Sometimes, when he comes in late or when he's in a bad mood, he doesn't come to bed with me."

I tried to remember whether I'd ever seen him in a good mood. "Okay, I need to talk to him now. Is he there?"

"No, I don't think so. I mean, no, he's not."

"Do you know where he went?"

"Back over to see my father, I suppose. More than an hour ago. For the money. He couldn't last night." She was talking in fragments of sentences, as if the effects of the sleeping potion hadn't quite worn off yet. "Is something wrong?"

"Nothing you don't already know," I lied. "Has Simon checked back in yet?"

"I...no."

I swore softly. "All right, I'm going to try to get hold of Walter if he hasn't already left your father's place. In case I miss him, make sure he stays put when he gets back."

I hung up feeling unsettled, as if something had passed between us that didn't quite make sense. Rather than waste time worrying about it, I called the Eberle place. When Odell answered, I asked for Walter and got the old man. He didn't sound as if he was having a good morning, so I didn't wish him one.

"It's about time you called," he rasped. "Where the hell have you been?"

"Did you have a particular time in mind, or are we speaking generally?"

"I mean last night. Where did you go after you talked to Walter yesterday afternoon?"

"I got picked up by the police. I went to jail."

"I expect you think that's funny," he said sourly. "Maybe I ought to warn you, I'm not in the mood for jokes this morning."

"That's what the cops said when I told them I didn't know anything about the body in Jorie Flowers's apartment."

"You're serious, then. What did you tell them?"

"Forget it. You aren't in the mood to hear that, either."

"Well, I hope you had enough sense to leave Simon out of it."

"Now, how do you suppose I would have managed that after I've been running all over town asking questions about him? Even the police aren't dumb enough to swallow that."

"So much for your supposed discretion," he grumped.

"Look," I said, wishing there was a way to reach through the telephone and throttle him by the neck, "I did the best I could without telling any out-and-out lies. Unless something else happens, I don't think they'll be bothering you for a while. But all the same, if I were you, I'd hurry up and find a good lawyer. Simon is going to need one."

"I've been working on that. Despite what you might think, I am no fool."

"I'm relieved to hear it. Did you give Walter the money?"

"No. He hasn't been here. I told him I didn't want him doing anything on his own, so I assumed he was stopping on his way to meet up with you before coming here."

There was a silence, then he went on. "Let me remind you. Wherever he goes with that money, I want you to go with him."

"I'll be with him every step of the way," I said. "But right now, I don't know where he is. I spoke with Elaine just a few minutes ago. She said he left over an hour ago and that he was on his way to see you."

"She must be mistaken, then. Either that, or he's gone off and gotten himself into trouble again. You can never count on him to do anything right."

"All right," I said. I've got one more person I need to talk to this morning, and then I'll come by and pick up the money myself. If Walter shows up in the meantime, keep him with you until I get there."

"Just a minute, please." His voice was softer now. "With all that's been going on, I hope that you don't lose sight of why I hired you in the first place. My primary concern is the safe return of my son. Whether he is guilty of killing Jorie Flowers, or whatever else he might have done is of secondary importance until I know he is safe. After that, he will turn himself in to the police, and we will cooperate fully in their investigation."

"I understand. I'll do my best." And that left me with one last thing I needed to do.

$$* * *$$

It was nearly eleven o'clock when I pulled up to the locked gate outside the Tabor Clinic. If there was anything more to the place than a guard shack, a high chain-link fence, and a driveway that wound into the trees beyond, I never got close enough to see it. An armed security man who looked like he meant business stopped me right there.

He leaned in the open window on the passenger side and looked at me through yellow-tinted sunglasses. "Visiting hours aren't until this afternoon, sir."

"I didn't know," I told him. "I'm here to see Dr. Tabor."

"Your name?"

I gave it to him. He backtracked into the shack, picked up a telephone, and spoke for a few moments to somebody at the other end. Then he held the line for a minute or two before nodding his head and hanging up.

"There isn't any record of your appointment at the office," he said in a voice at least twenty degrees colder than before. "I can't admit you to the grounds without an appointment unless you're visiting family members."

"I understand." I took my ID out of my wallet and showed it to him. "Could I use your phone to speak with the doctor? I didn't expect to need an appointment, but I do need to talk to him right away."

"You've got yourself a problem then 'cause Doc ain't expected for least another two hours."

I took a deep breath and counted to five as I let it out. "Is there someplace I can reach him quickly? It concerns one of his patients. It's very important."

"Don't it always seem to be?" he asked. "Maybe you could try the phone book."

"His home number is unlisted," I said, sure that I was telling him something he already knew. "Doesn't he have an emergency number?"

He rubbed his thumb and index finger together in a circular motion. "Sorry, but I can't let you have that without proper authorization."

"Right," I said, reaching for my wallet a second time, "got it. Old Hickory speak with enough authority for you?"

"I could hear him a lot better if he was U. S. Grant."

"For that much, I'll take the address, too." I held out two twenties and a ten. President Grant was nowhere in sight, but the security man didn't seem to mind.

"I shouldn't be doing this," he grumbled. "They find out in the office, it's my job."

He handed me a piece of paper with Tabor's address and telephone number written on it. The address was on Park Street, no more than a ten-minute drive from the clinic. I turned the car around in the driveway and headed back the way I'd come.

Park Street was in an older, meticulously maintained part of Franklin. The houses were big, with wide, breezy porches and broad, shady lawns. The streets still had a few places where the original granite paving stones hadn't been asphalted over, or where they'd been dug up and replaced, and the sidewalks were still made of brick. It was a timeless kind of neighborhood where even the Thunderbird didn't look too badly out of place. I parked at the curb and walked up the path to Dr. Frank Tabor's front porch.

My knock was answered by a slender, attractive woman in her late thirties. She was dressed in blue jeans, sneakers, and a man's flannel shirt.

I asked, "Mrs. Tabor?"

"I'm Delores Tabor."

"Mrs. Tabor, my name is Jackson Gamble. I'm a private investigator from Nashville."

She looked at me curiously but without any particular surprise. Given the nature of her husband's work, I realized she had probably grown accustomed to having all sorts of people turn up at her door, claiming to be everything from Jimmy Hoffa to Vincent Van Gogh. I showed her my identification.

"I'm sorry to be interrupting you like this," I continued, "but I was hoping to speak with Dr. Tabor for a few minutes if it's convenient."

"Can I tell him what it's about?"

"Yes, ma'am. One of his former patients has disappeared from home. I've been retained by his family to find him. I thought the doctor might be able to help."

She nodded. "Frank's around back with the boys, unloading the camper. We just got back this morning. If you'd like to come in, I'll call him for you."

"No trouble," I said. "I can walk around."

I found Tabor hefting an outboard motor from the back of a Toyota pickup that had been fitted with a camper shell. Two boys, aged about six and twelve, were helping him, or maybe just getting in his way. With kids that age, it's not easy to tell.

"Hello, there," he called out and waved when he saw me. He was a tall, lanky man, a few years older than his wife. He had dark brown eyes, a head of thick, sandy-colored hair, and a beard to match. He was dressed in the same kind of mountain-man outfit his wife had been wearing. It made him look like a guy who used to pitch pork and beans on television.

"Dr. Tabor?"

"That's me. Something I can do for you?"

Before I could tell him what, the smaller of the two boys ran over and stood next to his father. He looked up at me with a gap-toothed smile.

"Are you here to see my dad?"

"Yes, I am," I said. "Would it be all right if I borrowed him for a few minutes?"

He stuck his hands in his pockets. "I guess so. Are you a crazy person?"

Tabor's face showed a mixture of amusement and embarrassment. "Andrew, what did I tell you about that?" He called to the other boy. "Jason, take Andrew with you and air out the sleeping bags, will you?"

To me, he said, "As you can see, we've just returned from an outing. I like to get away with the family whenever I can, Mister...."

"Gamble," I finished for him. I opened my wallet and showed him my ID and license.

"Pleased to meet you," he said finally, handing the wallet back to me. "What can I do for you?"

"I need some information about a former patient of yours named Simon Eberle, and also an employee named Jorie Flowers."

"Former employee," he corrected me. "Jorie left the clinic several months ago."

I did some fast arithmetic. "That would have been about the time you stopped treating Simon Eberle?"

"It could have been. I never connected the two."

"When Jorie left, was it voluntary, or was she discharged?"

"She quit. She didn't say why. I assumed she must have gotten a better offer from somebody else."

"Could you tell me, what was the nature of her job?"

"She was my office manager. She kept the books, scheduled appointments, did the insurance billing, things like that."

"Did she have direct contact with your patients?"

"Not in a therapeutic capacity." He stroked his beard distractedly, as if he had only recently discovered it growing there. "What's this about, anyway?"

"I'm trying to understand her relationship with Simon Eberle. I assume you know they were seeing each other socially on a regular basis."

"Mr. Gamble, I don't know how things are done where you work. As far as I'm concerned, what my employees—past or present—do on their own time is their own

business."

"Even when it affects the welfare of your patients?"

"I think," he said deliberately, "before I answer any more of your questions, you'd better tell me what's going on here and who you're working for."

"That's a reasonable question," I said. "I'm working for the Eberle family. Simon's been missing from home since last Saturday. I'm trying to find him."

"So that's it," he said, not sounding surprised. "I should have guessed."

"There's more. Jorie Flowers is dead. She was murdered the same night Simon disappeared."

"Jorie murdered?" This time he really was surprised. "Are you sure?"

"I discovered her body, Doctor. She was shot through the heart."

"And you think Simon killed her?"

"A lot of people do, although I'm not convinced myself," I told him. "I was hoping you might be able to give an expert opinion."

CHAPTER THIRTY-ONE

"Me? How in the world would I know?"

"You're his doctor. You've been crawling around inside his head for who knows how long. You must have some idea what's rattling around in there."

He shifted uneasily from one foot to the other. "You're right, I should. And to a certain extent, I suppose I do. But the fact is, I never made the progress with Simon I would have liked. For a variety of reasons."

"Such as?"

"Well, for one thing, his is an extremely complicated case. Simon's problems are deeply rooted in the sense that they go a long way back to his childhood. For another thing, his recovery has been hampered by an almost total lack of support from his family."

"I'm afraid I don't understand."

"It's like this, Mr. Gamble. The process of psychological rehabilitation is a slow and difficult one. In simple terms, it's based on being able to take a series of small steps forward. We look at the problem a little bit at a time, in other words, until we can finally look at it all at once."

"Go on."

"How long this takes depends not only upon the patient, but also upon the patient's immediate circle of family and friends. Their support for the therapy is frequently the one element that can make or break the entire process."

"You're saying there was a problem?"

"In Simon's case, that support was not there. For every step he was able to take forward, someone would drag him backward before I saw him again."

"Didn't you speak to anyone about it?"

"Absolutely, I did. I recommended to the family on several occasions that they consider placing him in the care of the clinic as an in-patient for a while, so that he could be removed from what I felt were negative influences."

"What was the family's response to that?"

"They turned me down flat. I didn't want to force the issue for fear I'd lose him altogether."

"It was that important to you?"

He looked at me levelly. "All my patients are important to me."

"Doctor, what was the protocol you followed with Simon?"

"Well, without getting overly technical, he was placed under hypnosis and then asked to recall the experiences he'd had that seemed to be contributing to his problem."

"Would these experiences include the deaths of his mother and step-mother?"

"In part, yes."

"I'm just guessing here, but would they also include abusive, even violent treatment at the hands of his sister?"

"I'm sorry, but I don't think I can discuss that with you."

"Well, tell me this, then. Have you ever treated Elaine Murdock for any kind of psychological disorder?"

"I'm afraid I can't discuss that with you, either. I'm sorry." He made a show of looking at his watch. "Mr. Gamble, I don't mean to be rude, but I'm due back at the clinic in a little over an hour, and I've still got a good bit of unpacking to do."

"I understand. I've just got a couple more things, and then I'll get out of your hair."

He said, with obvious reluctance, "Go ahead."

"Thank you. I promise I'll be brief. Apart from the professional fees you received for Simon's treatment, do you have any other financial ties to the Eberle family?"

He stiffened. "May I know the purpose of that question?"

"Just curious. You don't have to answer."

"I will. The answer is no. What else?"

"Would it be reasonable to assume you made recordings of the sessions you had with Simon?"

"Naturally."

"Video or audio?"

"Both. And before you ask, I will not allow you to access them."

"Did you prepare transcripts?"

"That's not the usual procedure unless our plans call for writing a case study. In Simon's case, we weren't doing that. But even if we had...."

"Doctor, excuse me," I interrupted. "Through this whole conversation, you keep saying 'we.' Is another professional consulting with you, or is it just a figure of speech?"

"Sorry, a figure of speech."

"All right. So, you didn't make transcripts. What did you do with the recordings?"

"We—I stored them. There are special computer files for them."

"Would Jorie Flowers have had access to those files?"

"Yes, of course. All our patient files, whether transcribed or not, are kept in the same location."

"So. Since she and Simon were seeing one another on a regular basis, if she wanted to find out more about him, she could have easily accessed your files."

He frowned. "I suppose so. I hadn't really considered that."

"Right. Okay, one more thing. When Jorie quit, you said you assumed she was leaving for a better offer. Can I take it you were paying her the prevailing wage for a clerical job?"

"I tried to be competitive. I even offered her a raise if she'd stay on."

"But she turned you down?"

"Yes, she did. Obviously."

"And yet, she seemed to have plenty of money." I had a thought. "Doctor Tabor, did you ever visit Jorie at her apartment?"

His face reddened. "It sounds very much as if you're asking me if I was having an affair with my secretary." He wrinkled his forehead in thought. "Or are you asking me whether I killed her?"

"I wasn't, but I probably would have gotten around to it before long."

"I'll save you the trouble. The answer to your first question is no. The answer to your second question is also no. The answer to any other questions you may have is you've used up your nickel. Now before either of us does or says something he might regret, I think it would be best if you were on your way."

I stood there for a moment, wondering whether it was worth pushing my luck to ask him the one question we'd managed to talk completely around.

Then I figured, what the hell? What did I have to lose?

"I understand," I said, "and I apologize if my questions were offensive. But I've been at this long enough that I can't help thinking that there is one very big secret the Eberle family, and that includes every one of them, wants desperately to protect. And Doctor, I believe you know what that secret is."

"I'm sorry, Mr. Gamble," he said in a tone that told me we were finished talking. "I can't help you with that."

I left the doctor to his unpacking and walked slowly back to my car.

Chapter Thirty-Two

I was running out of time and out of gas when I pulled into the Amoco station outside Springdale. I got out of the car and got the pump started when the phone in my pocket started buzzing. It was Bill Merlin from Metro Central District homicide.

"Thought I should give you a call, Jackson. Strictly off the record, of course, but I wanted to let you know."

"Know what?"

"Two things. First, I ran a check on that doctor friend of yours."

"And?"

"He's on the level, Jackson. Degrees from some fancy college out east, residency at Johns Hopkins. Otherwise, no record, no scandals, no rumors, no nothing. Not even a hint of any funny business."

"Okay, thanks. What else?"

"Like they say, good news and bad news."

"You found Simon Eberle?"

"Sorry, don't have a clue. Want to try again?"

"Raymond?"

"You got it."

"When?"

"This morning. Couple hours ago. I tried to call your office."

"Where was he?"

"Out by the boat ramp off Bell Road, close to Priest Lake Park. Couple fishermen found him right after they put their boat in the water."

"Is he dead, or otherwise?"

"He was floating face down. They don't come no deader."

I felt my heart sink. "Any idea what happened, or is that a foregone conclusion?"

"What do you want me to tell you? His neck was broken. It looked like somebody tried to twist his head clean off his shoulders. Came damn close to doing it, too." He hesitated just for a second. "Looks like that Eberle kid is on his way to running up a big score."

"Anything else?"

"Ain't that enough?"

"Well…a witness would help."

"Sorry, not today."

"In other words, you really don't have anything except a body. I don't know if you've ever seen Simon Eberle, but I can pretty well guarantee he's not in any kind of shape to break somebody's neck. At least not without a couple more guys to help him."

Or maybe just one more, I thought. Just one would do it.

"I wouldn't know," he said. "Right now, we only got one person of interest."

"Has the time of death been determined?"

"M.E. thinks sometime late last night, or maybe early this morning. It's hard to tell, because he was in the water when the fishermen found him."

"Was he carrying anything when you found him?"

"Car keys, some change, pack of smokes, maybe a few bucks in his wallet. Why?"

"No reason, just a thought I had."

"Okay, so what happens now?"

"What do you think? Soon as we can track down a Rutherford County judge to get a warrant signed, we'll be on our way to Springdale. Roodhouse wants to tear his old man's house apart, see what he can find."

I heard several voices talking at once in the background at his end of the line. Merlin said, "Yeah. Yeah," and then, "Okay, I'll be right there."

To me, he said, "Listen, Jackson, I gotta get going here. Anything else I can do for you right quick?"

"Not right now, Bill. Thanks anyway."

I hung up the phone and just sat there for a moment, wishing there was a way to avoid what I knew was coming next. I paid for the gas and got the key to the men's room. I used all the soap they had, trying to wash away the dirty feel of another needless, violent death. It didn't help. Nobody had ever made soap that strong, and nobody ever would.

I leaned over the sink and looked into the mirror. The face staring back at me looked old, and tired, and sad. It was a face I didn't like very much.

Walking back to the car, I took another shot at calling the Murdocks. This time Walter answered right away.

I said, "This is Gamble."

"I was just getting ready to call you," he said, sounding as amped up as a jackrabbit on speed. "It's past noon, and Raymond hasn't called yet. What do you think we should do?"

"Save it for your next arraignment, Walter. It's over. I'm coming for the boy." When he didn't answer me, I said, "Are you listening to me?"

"Yes."

"Then, for once, I need you to do what I'm about to tell you. I want you to stay where you are. Do not go anywhere, and do not talk to anybody except your lawyer. And make absolutely sure Elaine stays there with you. You're going to need each other now."

"I understand."

"Nobody does anything until I get there. Is that clear?"

"Yes."

"All right. I'll be there in half an hour."

Chapter Thirty-Three

In fact, it was twenty minutes later when I skidded to a stop in the Murdocks' driveway, right next to Walter's gray SUV. I made a quick check of the vehicle. There was nothing inside except the key fob, lying on the console between the front seats. I retrieved the key and dropped it into my pocket. Not that it would have been much of a problem for him, but if he had ideas about making a run for it, he'd have to get past me.

I mounted the porch steps carefully, not sure what kind of reception to expect. I pressed the doorbell and stood to one side, just in case somebody started shooting.

Nothing.

I rang again and called out to both Walter and Elaine.

No answer.

I tried the door. Locked. I thought about kicking it in, then remembered there was an easier way. It only took a moment to get my screwdriver out of the car and another few seconds to run around to the swimming pool enclosure alongside the house. I pried the lock on the sliding door leading to the pool. Then I pulled my weapon, racked a round into the chamber, and eased inside.

The house was quiet as a mausoleum. The pool apron was deserted, except for the little table Elaine had used to serve lunch the other day. Only one chair was there now, along with a single white rose in a bud vase and the remainder of a morning coffee service for one. There was lipstick on the rim of the cup. The coffee in the pot was still warm enough to drink.

A low, moaning sound coming from inside the house froze me where I stood. I aimed the Colt at the middle of the doorway, ready to pour a full clip into anything that acted even remotely unfriendly. Then I saw the blood on the floor outside the den and on the carpet just inside the doorway. I let the hammer down on the Colt and went into the house to look for the damage.

I found Walter Murdock, lying on his back on the floor next to his big television. He had been shot once in the head, just below the hairline, and one more time in the stomach. Both wounds were bleeding profusely, soaking his clothes and the rug where he fell. He was alive, but that was about all I could tell for sure. I got down on my knees to take a closer look.

The head wound wasn't as bad as it had first appeared. The bullet had struck his forehead at an angle and, as it happens more often than one might think, had deflected to the side instead of penetrating the skull. The slug had tunneled under the scalp and ripped its way back out at a point just behind the right ear. Apart from all the blood, and very likely a monumental concussion, the bullet didn't appear to have done much harm.

The other wound I had no way of knowing about. Small caliber bullets almost never travel in a straight line once they hit soft tissue. Depending on where this one went, it might or might not have hit a vital organ, a kidney, or the liver, perhaps, or perforated the stomach. A worse fear was that it might have lodged in his spine, leaving him paralyzed for the rest of his life.

I put my ear lightly against his chest. His breathing was shallow and raspy, but there were no bubbling sounds that would have meant blood in the lungs. His pulse was rapid, but regular. If he could hang on for a few more minutes, I thought he had a chance to make it. In the meantime, there wasn't much I could do for him except leave him right where he was. I found a quilt folded up on the couch and covered him with it.

I used the telephone on the desk to call the sheriff's office. As quickly as I could, I identified myself, outlined the situation, and requested medical assistance and an ambulance for Murdock. I stayed on the line until I was sure the deputy at the other end had gotten the address right, but not long enough for her to start asking me a lot of questions.

I looked over at Murdock, to be sure he was still breathing. His eyes were open and staring at me. He was trying to say something, but the words were too soft for me to make out. I got down on the floor next to him.

"I told her…I told her it was time to give him up. Let things take their course."

"You mean Simon?"

"Simon, yeah." He coughed once. "I told Elaine everything would be okay. But she said…."

He tried to finish his thought, but I cut him off. "I called the police, Walter. They should be here any minute. When they show up, don't admit anything, you understand? Especially don't say anything about Simon. I think we can keep everybody in the clear, but not if you start running your mouth."

"He…he called me small time. I showed him small time."

"You sure as hell did, Walter."

He looked at me, and his lips moved a little, but this time, no sound came out.

I said it for him. "Elaine?"

His eyes blinked once.

"She's with Simon, isn't she? By the river?"

Another blink.

"Okay, Walter," I said, trying to sound more confident than I felt, "help is on the way. I'm going after Elaine. I'll bring her back for you." Then, idiotically, I added, "Don't try to move."

I ran through the house to the front door. I unlocked it and threw it open wide, so the cops wouldn't have to waste time breaking in. Then I went back to the stables where the horses and—I hoped—the jeep was kept.

The horses were there, all three of them. The biggest looked at me indifferently and kept on chewing a mouthful of hay. The other two snorted and stamped nervously, the way horses sometimes do when they catch a scent of somebody they don't recognize. I took a look outside and found a fresh set of tire tracks leading out of the stable yard toward the river road. That narrowed my options to the Thunderbird, the big Benz, or one of the horses. For a second, I flashed on a vision of mounting up and riding to the rescue, like the hero in a second-feature western. Instead, I took the Benz.

Luck, for once, was with me, as the SUV had all-wheel drive.

The road leading to the river wasn't much more than parallel ruts through the pasture, but it provided fairly easy going for the first few hundred yards. Then it twisted sharply to the right and dipped gradually down about twenty feet, where it forded a narrow creek. I knew I could make it down the bank without any problem if the water wasn't any deeper than it looked. It was getting up the other side that had me worried. It was steeper than the side I was on, and just as muddy. I could see from the tracks how the jeep had started up the bank, then stopped, then started again after dropping into four-wheel drive. Even with both axles pulling, it looked as if it hadn't been an easy climb.

I yanked the Mercedes' shift lever into low and stomped on the gas. The big ride rocked and bounced down the bank before it belly-flopped into the creek. The water wasn't much more than hubcap deep, but it was enough to scrub off most of the momentum I had gathered going down.

I had enough of a roll left to carry me about halfway back up to high ground. Then I heard the rear wheels start to sling mud as they clawed for traction and felt the Benz slip sideways. I eased off the accelerator, hoping to get a better grip on the muddy slope. Gradually, the wheels found purchase, and with a judicious application of power, I was able to coax the big beast the remaining way up the bank and back onto level ground. From there, I could see the tree line Elaine had mentioned and the rectangular outlines of the construction company buildings behind them, rusting remnants of Richard Eberle's grand plan for an upscale housing development. I put them at most a quarter of a mile away. I thought it would be better to abandon the vehicle and cover the remainder of the distance to the construction site on foot. I shut off the ignition, bailed out of the Benz, and began running through the wet, knee-high grass, keeping my head low as I went along. By the time I reached the trees, my pants were soaked to the pockets, and my shoes were covered with mud. I stopped in the shadow of a big sweet gum to catch my breath.

From my vantage point in the trees, I could see the buildings clearly. There were four altogether, three in near-total ruin. It was hard to tell what had

225

been their original purpose. Perhaps a place to park construction equipment out of the weather, or maybe to store building materials. The fourth looked as if it might have been a tool shed. It was about ten feet square and built of corrugated metal, now rusted to a reddish shade of brown. It had a single door with a padlock hanging from it and a high window that had been painted over from the inside.

The door was open. The jeep was parked near the doorway.

I moved cautiously through the trees until I was as close to the crib as I could get without breaking cover. I measured the distance across open ground at about twenty-five yards, but for all the protection I would have while crossing over, it might as well have been a mile.

Before I had a chance to talk myself out of it, I grabbed a lungful of air and took off running for the open space between the tool crib and the building next to it. Nobody saw me, or if he did, didn't try to stop me. I reached the opening and flattened myself against the wall. Above my own panting, I heard sirens wailing faintly in the distance. The sheriff, I supposed, and the EMTs for Walter. I didn't expect much help from either of them, though. Unless they were coming in a helicopter or some kind of an all-terrain vehicle, whatever was about to happen would have played out long before they got to me.

I edged around the side of the building until I was next to the doorway. Into the opening, not loud, I called, "Simon?"

When nobody answered, I tried again. "Elaine?"

A woman's voice said, "Go away."

"Elaine, it's Gamble. I want to talk to you. To both of you."

"Leave us alone."

I swallowed hard. "I'm going to come in."

Her voice was barely audible. "Please don't."

I said, "Elaine, I'm alone. I'm not going to hurt either of you. I just want to talk. I'm going to come into the open where you can see me. I'll keep my hands in front of me. Please don't shoot." And before anybody could say anything else, I stepped through the open doorway.

It took a moment for my eyes to adjust to the low light inside the shed. As they did, the shadows gradually gained substance, like the picture tube on an old-style television set that's just been switched on. I blinked once and took my first look at Simon Eberle in the flesh. He was curled up like a fetus on an iron bed that was the only piece of furniture in the place. He lay partly covered with a dirty blanket. There was half a week's growth of blond beard on his face and a wild, disoriented look in his eyes. A chain, about six feet long, was padlocked to his right ankle. The other end was bolted to the wall.

Elaine was sitting on the bed, cradling Simon's head in her lap. With one hand, she was stroking his hair. With the other, she was holding the gun that had killed Alicia Eberle, Jorie Flowers, and maybe before it was over, Walter Murdock and Jackson Gamble. She was dangling it carelessly, not pointing it at anything in particular.

I said, "Elaine, he has to go back."

She shook her head determinedly. "He doesn't! He's not! I won't allow it."

"Elaine, there's no other way. Look at him." She didn't. I did. If Simon heard or understood any part of what was being said, he gave no indication. He just kept staring at nothing.

"Elaine?"

She raised the little gun and cocked the hammer back. Then she aimed it at the middle of my chest. I felt my throat constrict to the size of a cocktail straw.

"You're not taking him away from me," she said evenly. "Nobody is ever going to take him away from me again. Not that horrible woman, not my father, and certainly not you."

A thought came to me. I said, "When I came to your home the other day to have lunch, you knew Walter wouldn't be gone all afternoon, didn't you? You wanted him to find us together."

"I thought he'd kill you, or else you would have had to kill him to save yourself. Either way, after the police came, I would have been rid of both of you."

"It was a good plan," I said. "Sorry it didn't work out."

I took a quick look around. I thought that if I did it just right, I might be able to dive to my left and roll back through the open doorway before she could get off a shot. More likely, though, I wouldn't make it, which put me one mistake away from being dead or seriously wounded. I had nothing to lose. I made a sweeping motion with my arms that I hoped would distract her and took a small step in the direction of the bed.

"Why would anyone want to take him away from you, Elaine?"

"Because they think he's a murderer. They'll put him into prison."

I was fascinated by the gun. I kept my eyes on it the way a cobra follows a snake charmer's reed.

"No, they won't, Elaine. We won't let them. You and I will tell them the truth, and then they won't hurt Simon."

Her eyes seemed to go out of focus. "The truth?"

"Yes. We'll tell them Simon didn't kill anybody."

"He didn't?"

"You know he didn't, Elaine. It was you. You took the gun from your father's study. You killed Jorie because she was using Simon to extort money from you. We'll tell them how she was shaking you down and how you had to put an end to it before anybody else found out the reason why."

She stared at me uncomprehendingly.

"That had to be the way it was. She knew Simon's secret, and she was using that knowledge to squeeze money out of you. The night she was killed, I'm guessing you were coming to see her. She was expecting you, so you had no trouble getting into her apartment. Since you're a woman, she wouldn't have been concerned about how she was dressed when you came. Maybe she thought you were bringing her some more money, I don't know. Maybe you argued. Or maybe she threatened you, and you had to defend yourself. But either way, before it was over, you shot her.

"You'd already gotten Simon temporarily out of the way by paying Jerry Raymond to dose a bottle of beer that Simon was drinking when he visited the Million Seller last week. Raymond told the other bartenders he was taking Simon home, but in fact, he delivered Simon to you, and unless I miss my guess, you've been keeping him out here drugged up ever since. What have you been giving him, Halcion? Or did you mix it with something else, like haloperidol?"

When she didn't answer, I said, "You know, in a way, this is my fault. I should have put it all together sooner. The night I crossed paths with Raymond, he said something about knowing who I was working for. It didn't make any sense at the time, and I was thrown too far off my game by getting the hell beaten out of me to put the two of you together. But I should have realized. He thought I was working for you.

"Ray was trouble for you, wasn't he? He used to be married to Jorie, and he would have seen her with Simon down at the Million Seller. You knew Simon liked to hang around there, and when you came around to enlist Raymond's help, it was easy for him to connect the three of you. Then, when he somehow learned that Jorie had been murdered, he knew it had to be you who killed her.

"After that, he decided there was even more money in it for him. So, he called you, but got Walter by mistake and ended up trying to put the squeeze on him instead. Walter told me Ray's evidence had to do with Simon, but he was lying. It had to do with you. That explains why Walter agreed to pay the money. He didn't care about Simon one way or the other. He was just trying to protect you.

"That's also why he wanted to take the money to Ray himself. He was afraid I might hear something I shouldn't. Only your father wouldn't let him have it, not unless I went with him. But Walter had already made up his mind about what he was going to do about Raymond, so he went to the meeting place by himself, and he killed him. The cops don't know that. They think Simon did it, but Simon isn't strong enough to break a chicken's neck. My guess is we can get both Simon and Walter off the hook, but this has to end now. You have to put down the gun, and we need to take Simon to a hospital."

I let her think about that for a minute. The sun was high in the sky now, and the temperature inside the cramped metal building was rising rapidly. I took another short step. Only a little more to go, and I'd be able to reach her gun arm.

Tears filled her eyes. "I had to do something, Gamble, don't you see? I couldn't let her go on using Simon, and I didn't have any more money to give her."

"I know, Elaine. I believe you. I just don't understand why you had to shoot Walter. He wasn't going to hand you over to the police. He would have done whatever you asked him to do. He loves you more than you know."

"Even if that's true, he wanted me to give Simon up. I couldn't let him make me do that, can't you understand?"

"Yes, I can, but that's just what you're going to have to do now. There isn't any other way." I pointed to Simon. "Look at him, Elaine. He's sick. For all we know, he may be dying. He needs medical attention. So do you."

"No!" she said fiercely. "I'm not going to let anyone take him away. We're going to go someplace where we can be together, like when he was little."

"Oh, Elaine," I said with real sadness. "Listen to me. And please try to hear what I'm telling you. You need help. Simon needs help."

"We could have helped each other. But now, they'll never let me stay with him. They'll put me in prison."

"No. They won't. No court of law will send you to prison for what you did, not after they hear the whole story. They'll make you go to a hospital for a little while, and then you'll walk away from all this. I promise you that's the way it'll be. You'll walk."

She shook her head doggedly. "Walter."

"Walter's not dead. He's hurt, but he isn't dead. He's going to make it. You can make it together."

"Walter?" she said again.

"He loves you very much, Elaine. He was willing to go to prison for you."

She nodded her head sorrowfully. And then, so quickly that I had no chance to stop her, she put the barrel of the gun under her chin and pulled the trigger. At the same moment, as if to exorcise all the demons he had held inside for so long, Simon Eberle opened his mouth and screamed an endless, soul-wrenching scream.

And the word that came out was "MOTHER!"

Chapter Thirty-Four

I spent the rest of the afternoon with cops. I talked to state cops. I talked to Rutherford County cops. I talked to deputies from the sheriff's office in Springdale, and Metro cops, like Roodhouse, from Nashville. And everybody I talked to had one thing in common. They were very, very unhappy with me.

I sat in an airless room at the sheriff's office and told them my story, or at least the part of it I wanted them to hear. I went over it five or maybe it was six times. After a while, I lost track. I don't know yet whether they were able to keep it straight in the end. Probably not, I thought. Like Dr. Tabor told me, sometimes you have to look at things a little bit at a time before you can look at them all at once.

They handed me a lot of the usual cop talk about hearings and inquiries and taking my license away. The state boys even wanted to lock me up as a material witness, but Roodhouse, bless his flinty heart, talked them out of that. In the end, they all agreed to let me go. They had no choice. Nobody could think of a charge they could make stick.

The first thing I did after I was back on the street was make a call to Baptist Hospital. I spoke to a very nice volunteer who worked in patient information. She told me that Mr. Murdock had come out of surgery about an hour ago. He was in the ICU, and his condition was listed as critical, but stable. That meant he was going to make it.

Simon Eberle was being treated for malnutrition, dehydration, and nervous exhaustion, as well as toxic shock from an overdose of the tranquilizer cocktail Elaine had been pumping into him. He was scheduled to be released into the care of his personal physician, probably Doctor Tabor, as soon as his condition would permit him to be moved. That meant he'd make it physically. Psychologically, nobody was talking.

Elaine Murdock had been dead on arrival.

Just before my phone battery died, I made the call I'd been putting off, the one to Richard Eberle. I had done all he'd asked. I had gotten Simon back for him, alive and in one piece. Somewhere along the line, though, things had gone disastrously wrong. I had saved the son but lost the daughter. Now I had to face the father.

I ended up talking with Odell, the houseman. He advised me that Mr. Eberle was resting under doctor's orders and could not come to the telephone. Mr. Eberle had left word, however, that he would receive me at his residence at nine o'clock that evening. I said I'd be there.

That left me with a dead battery and no more people to call. I talked a sheriff's deputy into running me back out to the Murdock place so I could retrieve my car. An hour later, I was home, stretched out on the bed. I lay there thinking, staring up at the ceiling fan. I stayed there like that until the sun was down, and it was finally time to go.

Chapter Thirty-Five

At nine o'clock sharp, I rang the doorbell at the Eberle house. In short order, and for the third time in four days, I found myself in the study, sitting across the desk from Richard Eberle.

He looked more tired than he had during my other visits, but otherwise, not much worse for wear. His shirt was crisp, his tie neatly knotted, his collar pin and pocket square in place. Elaine had underestimated him. He might only have months to live, but he was a tough old bird, maybe as tough as they came. I was about to find out.

"Well, Mr. Gamble," he said, without a trace of irony, "It's been a difficult day."

"Yes, sir, it has," I agreed. "I'm sorry."

He shook his head slowly. "You have nothing to apologize for. Sometimes, despite our best efforts, things go wrong. That's something I hope now, and with help, Simon will come to understand. What I want to know is why."

I said, "How much did the police tell you?"

"They told me that my daughter killed Jorie Flowers and very nearly her husband as well. They said she had my son locked in a tool shed on her property while all this was taking place. And finally, they told me my daughter took her own life. My impression was that they got most of their information from you."

"That would be right."

"Well, then, I think you should tell me now, if you would, please. Why did all this have to happen?"

"I think you know the answer to that." I took a deep breath. "But just to be

233

clear, it happened for two reasons, both of which stem from related events that took place a very long time ago.

"You were right about Jorie Flowers, Mr. Eberle, righter than even you knew. She was an opportunist and, as you guessed, not one to worry over the moral or ethical niceties of the things in which she involved herself. Her relationship with your son proved that.

"Jorie worked for Dr. Tabor. You knew that. And you also knew that Tabor was using hypnosis as a means of inducing his patients to talk more freely about their problems. What you may not have known is that Tabor made recordings of all his sessions with his patients and that Jorie had access to those recordings.

"In essence, she was using those recordings to compile a file of her own, but it was a very special file on very special patients. These were people with problems that needed to stay buried. Patients who could be made to pay if you knew how to apply the pressure. I'm talking about a husband cheating on a wealthy wife he couldn't afford to have divorce him, or a Gospel singer with a cocaine habit, or a TV evangelist with a taste for choir boys. In a big-money town like this, the possibilities are endless.

"For somebody in a situation like that, it wouldn't even take disclosure to be ruinous. A word or a hint whispered in the right ear would do it. And so, Jorie's pigeons paid to make sure things were kept quiet. It worked well enough, in fact, she couldn't risk keeping the money in a bank, for fear of having to account for where all the money was coming from."

"You're talking about blackmail, Mr. Gamble."

"That's correct."

He shook his head. "That's preposterous. Even if what you suggest is true, all anybody would have to do is tell the doctor. That would have put her out of business immediately."

"No, sir, it would not. Telling Tabor would carry the same risk as refusing to pay. Besides, there's no end of people whose careers, or even lives, could suffer irreparable harm from the mere fact that they were getting psychiatric help. Again, the trick to making it work was to select the right victims.

"Your son was one of those people with something to hide. Something very ugly, and for Jorie Flowers, potentially very profitable. Enough so that she felt safe quitting her job, probably with the idea of making one big score before moving on to someplace else.

"But unfortunately for her, there was a complication she hadn't counted on. Simon didn't have any money of his own. And besides, everybody already figured he was a little bit off-kilter, so the opportunity to squeeze him directly was limited. After all, who the hell ever got rich blackmailing a crazy man?"

I took a breath. "As it so happened, however, there was another person involved in Simon's secret. Someone who also had something to hide, and more importantly, someone who also had access to money. That person was your daughter, Elaine."

"What are you talking about?"

"I'm talking about a night twenty years ago when Elaine went into her stepmother's bedroom and found her unconscious from too much liquor and too many sleeping pills. Then she took a gun out of her stepmother's nightstand and shot her with it, making it look like a suicide."

"What, no, you're insane! What reason would she do that?"

"Because she couldn't abide the idea of anybody coming between her and Simon."

"No. Nothing like that ever happened. And even if such a thing were possible, there's no proof."

"Isn't there? I think the recordings Dr. Tabor made of his sessions with your son will prove it, because Simon has known the truth right along. That's what the cause of his problem really is. He knows, and may actually have seen, Elaine murder your second wife. The recordings might not be admissible in court, but as sure as we're sitting here, that's what happened.

"It's also why Tabor couldn't get any cooperation from the family. Except, it wasn't the family at all. It was Elaine. The whole time Simon was in therapy, she was pushing him back every time Tabor helped him take a step forward. She would have known better than anyone how to do that. But the truth is still there, in Tabor's files. Jorie found them and used them to blackmail Elaine. That's why Elaine killed her. I think you knew that, too.

That's why you were so eager to frame Walter. You loved Elaine, no matter what she did. Walter was just some dumb jock who married your daughter and then later fucked up a real estate deal for you.

"Everything else that's happened pretty much follows from that."

"Damn you." He slumped forward in his chair and covered his face with his hands. "God damn you, how dare you tell me these things? What right do you have?"

"Because, Mr. Eberle, you asked. And because you already know it. The cops told me your wife's suicide didn't look quite right, but that the investigation was stopped before it ever got started. Who else but you could have done that? And why else?"

He started to say something else, but I cut him off. "Do you want me to tell you the rest of it?"

"Might as well," he said, sounding resigned to what was coming. "Let's have it all."

"It took me a while to figure it out, and until this morning, I still wasn't sure. But the one common thread that ran through every conversation I had about this case was the unusually close relationship Simon had with Elaine. Even granting the circumstances of your first wife's death, something just didn't feel right.

"I looked up your wife's obituary. Actually, the obituaries for both your wives. I didn't have any particular reason. I was just curious. It didn't register at first. I guess I was thinking about something else. And then, today, it hit me. Clara Eberle, your first wife, died in April 1995. Simon was born in April 1996."

I looked at him. "You see the problem?"

"Yes."

"I don't know what the cause of your first wife's death might have been, but I know it didn't have anything to do with childbirth. That means Simon wasn't her child. He had to be someone else's. And that someone else was Elaine. And I'm betting he was yours. You committed incest with your own daughter when she was just a little girl, and you impregnated her. That's how you got the son you wanted so badly."

There was real sadness in his eyes. "I never meant for any of this to happen. You need to believe that. What took place with Elaine, it was—well, it just happened, that's all. Clara had lymphoma, and she was dying a slow, painful death. Elaine knew her mother was dying, and she was frightened.

"One night, after Clara died, Elaine came into the study. She'd had a bad dream. She was crying, and I took her into my arms to try to comfort her. After that, what else do I need to tell you? It only happened that one time."

"I believe you, sir. I truly do, but that was enough. After Simon was born, you compounded the problem by pressuring Elaine to assume the role of the woman of the family, even if it wasn't in a sexual way. Given the situation, it's no wonder that she would eventually kill her stepmother rather than let her assume the role of Simon's mother.

I said, "I've been trying to decide all day what I wanted to say to you about this, and the only thing I can think of is that you are a morally bankrupt son of a bitch. You have systematically and intentionally destroyed the lives of everyone close to you."

"My Clara died," he said. "I couldn't save her."

"No, and that was a tragedy, and I'm sorry for your loss. But nothing that happened up to that point excuses what you did afterward."

He folded his hands on his desk and looked at me as if he hadn't heard a word I'd said. "What happens now?"

"Now?" I shrugged. "Nothing happens. I didn't discuss any of this with the police, and I don't plan to. As far as the law is concerned, Elaine did what she did to protect her brother from a shakedown artist who was taking advantage of him."

"You think they'll accept that?"

"Why wouldn't they? It's pretty close to the truth. The police are too busy to go looking for complicated explanations when they've got a simple one that fits all the facts. They may not like everything about it, but they'll go along, if only because they know you have enough friends and lawyers and connections to put up a fight that they know they won't be able to win. As far as Walter is concerned, there's nothing I know of to connect him to Raymond's death, as long as he keeps his mouth shut."

"Then we have nothing left to talk about."

"No, sir, we don't. Except that now that this is finally over, I hope you'll use whatever time you have left to square things with Simon and Walter. They're better men than you credit, and they've been through hell on your account." I got up to leave.

"Good night, Mr. Eberle. I won't be sending you a bill. You've paid me more than enough already."

Chapter Thirty-Six

The day after I finished my business with Richard Eberle, I got a telephone call from Wanda Beaudry. "I found your man," she said, without preliminaries.

"McGraw? Where is he?"

"Well, I hate to disappoint you, but he's in a cemetery in El Reno, Oklahoma. The story I got was he sold some bad drugs to a guy who knew a guy who carved up Mr. McGraw pretty good before he slit his throat. It wasn't fast, and it didn't sound painless."

That was all I needed to hear. Kady Standley's account was paid in full. I thanked Wanda for her troubles and promised to take her to dinner at the restaurant of her choice to repay the favor.

The prognosis Richard Eberle's doctors had given him proved to be optimistic, as he died of pancreatic cancer a little more than two months after I last saw him. His funeral was a major event, attended by a great many prominent figures from the Middle Tennessee business community, as well as local and state government officials. It got a big write-up in all the newspapers. The coverage included stories about his success in the real estate business as well as his support for a number of local charities and foundations. Not mentioned was his involvement in the deaths of Jorie Flowers, Jeremiah Raymond, or indeed, his own daughter, Elaine Murdock, whom the written account noted, had died "suddenly and unexpectedly." Months later, I learned from Clarence Darrow that Eberle had left the bulk of his fortune to Rutherford County, with the understanding that his Springdale home and estate would be turned into a county historical museum and a city park. The rest went to his son, Simon, and his son-in-law, Walter Murdock, plus a handsome award to his long-serving houseman, Odell.

Walter Murdock recovered from his gunshot wounds fairly quickly and returned home in good health. The last I heard, he was dating one of the surgical nurses who had looked after him while he was in recovery and that the couple had recently announced their engagement. In the accompanying photo, which appeared in the newspaper, they looked giddily happy. If the cops suspected him of killing Jeremiah Raymond, they never made a case for it, and no charges were ever filed.

After he was rescued from his confinement on the Murdock property and his subsequent treatment at Baptist Hospital, Simon Eberle was voluntarily transferred to the Tabor Clinic, where he remained as an in-patient for a couple of months before leaving Tennessee altogether and moving to some beach community in Central America. After that, I never heard anything more about him, but I hoped he was happy and at peace.

It took a couple of telephone calls, but I was finally able to connect with my record producer friend, who agreed to meet with Serena Robbins to look over the songs she had written. The next afternoon, I stopped by her apartment to give her the news and the number she needed to call to arrange the appointment. She thanked me profusely, jumped around like a kid at Christmas, and then invited me to stick around and share a bottle of wine while she cooked us a dinner for two that she called "her special dish." I was pretty sure I knew where that was going to take us, and it wasn't somewhere I wanted to go. So, after we shared a half-bottle of her wine, I told her I'd take a rain check on the dinner and wished her luck with her music.

It was nearly dark when I turned down my street. The first thing I noticed as I approached my house was that all the lights were on. The next thing I saw was Maggie's silver Volvo station wagon parked in my driveway. She hadn't called, she hadn't texted, and she hadn't sent an email, but it didn't matter one bit.

She was home.

Acknowledgements

As was the case with my earlier Level Best novel, Lost Little Girl, my thanks must first go to Verena Rose, my primary editor, as well as Harriette Sackler and Shawn Reilly Simmons, who, collectively, are the Dames of Detection, the heart and soul of Level Best Books. Absent their faith in *Lost Little Girl* and this volume, *The Gone Man*, private investigator Jackson Gamble would still be just a collection of bits and bytes hidden away in my computer. It goes without saying (but it won't) that I am grateful beyond words for their support and encouragement.

Thanks must also go to the many "Besties" I have met through Level Best, including Libi Siporin, Lori Duffy Foster, Virginia Welker (Lo Monaco), Wendy Eckel, Skye Alexander, Kevin Kluesner, Mark Levenson, Kerry Peresta, Lori Robbins and Cathi Stoler. You are all terrific writers and honest critics, and I'm grateful for our association. I also appreciate the efforts of my "civilian" friends who, although they are not associated with Level Best, have nevertheless taken the time to read my books and offer their suggestions for improvement. These good friends include Barbara Barbre, David Kwinn, Barry Pfanstiel, Nona Nan Chapman, Bill Wade and Tom Neumeyer. I'm also appreciative for the support and encouragement offered to me by the Southeast Missouri Writers Guild and the Heartland Writers Guild. Kudos also to my publicity team at Blue Rooster Company, Robert Price and Gaëlle Byrne Freer, for kicking me out of my comfort zone. I didn't always like it, but I did always understand why. Lastly, thanks as always to my wife, Carol, who tolerates my long hours buried in the basement knocking out what I hope are deathless words of prose.

About the Author

Greg Stout is the author of *Gideon's Ghost* and *Connor's War*, both young adult novels set in small-town America in the mid-1960s, and *Lost Little Girl*, a detective novel set in Nashville, Tennessee, and which has been announced as the winner of the 2022 Shamus Award for best first novel. A complete listing of Greg Stout's published works can be found at www.gregorystoutauthor.com. Greg resides with his wife and two cats, Wallace and Gromit, in Cape Girardeau, Missouri, where he is a member of the Heartland Writers Guild, the Southeast Missouri Writers Guild, and is a member of the board of directors for the Missouri Writers Guild.

SOCIAL MEDIA HANDLES:
  Twitter: @GregStout16
  Facebook: https://www.facebook.com/greg.stout.5602
  Facebook author page: https://www.facebook.com/gregstout48

AUTHOR WEBSITE:

www.gregorystoutauthor.com

Also by Gregory Stout

Connor's War (Beacon Publishing Group, 2022)

Lost Little Girl (Level Best Books, 2021)

Gideon's Ghost (Beacon Publishing Group, 2019)

Route of the Chiefs: The Santa Fe in the Streamlined Era (White River Productions, 2017)

Route of the Rockets: Rock Island in the Streamlined Era (White River Productions, 1997)

Route of the Eagles: Missouri Pacific in the Streamlined Era (White River Productions, 1995)

19 additional titles related to American railroad history (Morning Sun Books, 2004-2021)

www.ingramcontent.com/pod-product-compliance
Lightning Source LLC
Chambersburg PA
CBHW050200120726
47903CB00002B/696